BLITZKRIEG

BRIAN FALKNER

SCHOLASTIC INC.

Library of Congress Cataloging-in-Publication Data
Names: Falkner, Brian, author.
Title: Blitzkrieg / Brian Falkner.
Description: [First US edition]. | New York : Scholastic Inc., 2023. | Originally published: Auckland, New Zealand : Scholastic New Zealand Limited, 2020. | Audience: Ages 12 and up. | Audience: Grades 10–12. | Summary: In Nazi-ruled Germany, twelve-year-old Joe flees to England after his father is arrested by the Gestapo and he is separated from his mother, but when he arrives in London, Joe is recruited by MI5 and given a deadly mission that will put him in the very center of Hitler's ruthless reign.
Identifiers: LCCN 2022021636 | ISBN 9781338857825 (paperback) | ISBN 9781338857832 (ebook)
Subjects: LCSH: Teenagers—Juvenile fiction. | World War, 1939–1945—Juvenile fiction. | Intelligence service—Great Britain—Juvenile fiction. | Survival—Juvenile fiction. | Germany—History—1933–1945—Juvenile fiction. | Spy stories. | Young adult fiction. | Adventure stories. | CYAC: Intelligence service—Fiction. | Survival—Fiction. | Spies—Fiction. | World War, 1939-1945—Fiction. | Germany—History—1933–1945—Fiction. | Adventure and adventurers—Fiction. | BISAC: YOUNG ADULT FICTION / Historical / Military & Wars | YOUNG ADULT FICTION / War & Military | LCGFT: Historical fiction. | Spy fiction. | War fiction. | Novels.
Classification: LCC PZ7.F1947 Bl 2023 | DDC 823.92 [Fic]—dc23/eng/20220517

10 9 8 7 6 5 4 3 2 1 23 24 25 26 27

Printed in the U.S.A. 40

First U.S. printing 2023

Book design by Smartwork Creative and Christopher Stengel

For Cliff and Val,

Todd and Tiffani, Grace, Wil, and Ava.

And, of course, Leigh.

Wonderful people. Great friends.

Thanks to Lynn Wild for her knowledge
and attention to detail.

BOOK ONE

BERLIN

I heard a documentary about me on the wireless,
after the war. They described me as a hero.
I felt more than a little ashamed. I was no hero.
Far from it. I was a villain. One of the worst.
I was just lucky that my side won.

—from the memoirs of Joseph "Katipo" St. George

PROLOGUE

SS *HAMPTON CLAIRE*

North Atlantic Ocean, February 22, 1941

The ocean reaches once more for the boy, sweeping over the starboard railing and raking his face with needle claws of the most bitter cold.

Instinctively the boy turns aft and flings up one of his gloved hands to shield his face. It does little good, and even the fur-lined hood of his oilskin coat can't protect him from the ocean's frigid breath.

He keeps his face aft for longer than he should, knowing that the sea will attack again the moment he turns back. Another gust of wind and frozen sea-spray talons rattle and batter him before he risks another glance forward. Around him the North Atlantic growls and gnashes in eruptions of white-frothed blue.

The early morning watch is the most hated by all the crew; it is the time when the water is the darkest and angriest, the cold the most chilling, and the wind the most piercing. But it is also the time the U-boats love best. They can creep up on the convoy, silhouetting the ships against the glow of the dawn while they attack out of the western gloom.

Already the convoy has lost two ships. One, a cargo ship

carrying iron ore, went to the bottom in just a few seconds, the spine torn out of her by what the Germans call their eels—their sleek, deadly torpedoes.

The other was a Canadian troopship. That sank more slowly, giving most of the troops time to escape, to get picked up by other ships in the convoy or by the escorting destroyers. Even so, over a hundred men were not recovered from the belly of the beast.

The SS *Hampton Claire* carries food—a hold full of corned beef and salted pork—desperately needed rations for Britain. Food isn't Joe's concern however. Nor are the starving children of London. He has his own reasons for being on board the vessel. Secret reasons.

The boy's name is Joseph St. George, although that is too elaborate a name for a boy and everybody just calls him Joe.

Joe had stowed away in New York, sneaking onto the ship at night and hiding in a maintenance area until they were well at sea. Only then did he reveal himself to the crew and, after a chewing out by the captain, was given duties to earn his passage.

He probably would have been locked in a cabin for the duration of the voyage if he hadn't lied and claimed that he had only stowed away so he could join the British army to fight against the Germans. Even then he might still have been locked up belowdecks if it wasn't for the threat of German submarines. Over three hundred ships have already been sunk since the start of the war. All eyes are needed on deck.

He forces himself to turn forward again, into the chilling blast of the wind. His face is already red and raw from the ocean's claws, and each flurry is rubbing salt into a wound.

He scans the dark blue troughs of the ocean, straining his eyes through the gloom and the spray for the slightest sign of anything that doesn't belong. The roiling sea is good cover for U-boats, he knows that, but it also makes them raise their periscopes higher to see over the wave crests, which makes them easier to spot.

He hates the morning watch. But he has little choice. As a stowaway, he has no rights on board the vessel at all. The crew could throw him over the side if they wanted, and nobody would know. So they give him the dirtiest and worst jobs, and Joe takes them without complaint.

Wait . . . there! What is that? He fixes his eyes on one spot, trying to give himself bearings from one of the other vessels of the convoy. A few hundred meters from the stern of one of the ships, he thinks he has seen a gray tubular shape. That would put it inside the convoy. They do that sometimes, sneaking in through the protective screen of destroyers and attacking a convoy from within.

Another flurry of ice and a buffeting blow from the wind has him looking aft once again; then, when he forces his eyes back to the same spot, there is no sign of the periscope. If it was there at all.

He scans the ocean desperately. What has he seen? A periscope . . . or a trick of the mind? The ship lurches into a trough, and he crouches down as he had been taught, lowering his center of gravity and clenching his hands on the railing at the same time.

The ship heaves up out of the trough, leaving Joe's stomach behind. Not that there is much to leave. He emptied its contents over the side in the first few moments on watch, and now the dried spatter of vomit on his "Mae West" inflatable lifejacket is the only reminder of last night's dinner.

From the starboard railing he can see only six other ships; the rest of the thirty-ship convoy are spread to aft, or portside, or just lost in the gritty North Atlantic gloom. Like the SS *Hampton Claire,* they heave and wallow through the jagged hills of the sea; great, lumbering cattle of the ocean, easy prey for the sleek gray wolves of Admiral Doenitz's U-boat fleet.

He has a feeling of unease now. A sense that around the convoy, the flock, the wolves are circling, gathering, waiting for the feast. Only the shepherding destroyers give them pause, and the protection they offer is limited.

Another glimpse of something that does not belong in the icy water . . . Something too perfect, too straight to be part of the turmoil of the ocean waters. Just a quick flash, but it is enough.

There is a wolf among the sheep.

Joe cracks his hands off the railing, where they have already frozen tight, and runs for the alarm bell. The rope is iced over, but he grabs it with two hands and hurls the clanger against the side of the bell. The breath of the beast roars over the side of the ship as he does so, swallowing the sound and whirling it away out into the darkness of the early morning sky.

Two, three times Joe works the bell, but each time the wind and the sky eat the sound. He drops the rope and runs for the metal staircase that leads to the bridge, staggering on the bucking deck. One step . . . two steps . . . three . . .

The staircase, little more than a ladder, seems to be trying to throw him off at every step.

The young boatswain meets him at top, grasping the back of Joe's oilskin to steady him. Wilfred is standing unaided, not even holding on to the railing, somehow sturdy and solid on the pitching deck. Behind him the door to the bridge calls out to Joe, offering shelter, respite from the cold and the storm. But there are more important things now than shelter.

"Where?" Wilfred shouts into the hood of Joe's oilskin. There can be only one reason Joe has made the climb to the bridge.

Joe aims a hand and Wilfred follows his fingers, gazing out across the water with eyes that surely can pierce the ocean and see the evil gray shapes of the U-boats lurking beneath.

Wilfred shakes his head. "Are you sure?"

Joe stares back out at the water for a moment, before shaking his own head. "No, but I thought . . ."

"I'm coming down with you," Wilfred shouts, and makes some kind of hand signal to the officers inside the darkened bridge.

Going down the staircase is worse than going up. The iced metal grill of each stair provides no grip for Joe's boots. Twice the metal edges cut into his shins as he struggles to keep from slipping.

He is glad Wilfred is there. Although not much older than Joe, the boatswain is the kind of solid, dependable man you are glad to be standing next to in a spot of bother.

Wilfred braces himself with a knee against the railing and raises his binoculars.

They both see it at the same time—a dull pinpoint of light, as a momentary ray of early morning sunshine, sneaking through the heavy cloud, reflects off something in the middle of nothing. There is *something* in the valley of waves out there, and that *something* can only be one thing.

Wilfred swears violently but is already running for the staircase and his words just whip out into the sky.

What Joe sees next chills him more than the sea spray or wind could ever. A growing streak of white phosphorescence reaching out across the ocean toward the *Hampton Claire.* He has seen that streak once before, when the troopship went down. It is the track of a German eel.

A white flare goes up from the bridge, the signal for "U-boat sighted." A siren sounds from one of the destroyers, brought to Joe in short snatches by the gusting wind.

He watches the long finger reach out toward him, closer now. Will the captain do nothing? The ship lurches into a huge wave, and when it comes up, it is on a different bearing. The captain *is* doing something; he is spinning the ship around in an emergency turn. But a great lumbering beast like a cargo ship takes a long time to turn and the torpedo is approaching quickly. Far too quickly.

The ship leans as it turns, lowering Joe toward the darkness of the water, and still he can see the track of the torpedo, heading right for him he realizes with a stifled cry. The eel is arrowing in exactly where he is standing. He turns to run, but his gloves have frozen to the handrail and it takes a moment of twisting to crack them free. Then run he does, as best as he can down the sharply sloping deck; the slightest slip would be enough to hurl him against the guardrail, the only thing between him and the ocean.

Joe runs, a stumbling drunken lurch forward, away from where he knows the torpedo will strike. The wind slices at him with razor-sharp claws, but he scarcely notices.

He glances behind just once, to see the track of the torpedo just meters away from the ship. Then suddenly the cold wind of the Atlantic is gone, replaced by a huge balloon of hot air that lifts him off the deck, his hair and clothes on fire, and hurls him over the side and into the mouth of the beast itself, the cold, blue, bottomless darkness of the ocean.

The boy never even hears the explosion.

The Gestapo came for my father on Kristallnacht—
the Night of Broken Glass—November 9, 1938.
It was a bloody awful night. All across Germany, gangs of Nazi thugs roamed through Jewish neighborhoods, smashing and looting shops and synagogues, bashing anyone they found.
A lot of people died that night.

We weren't Jewish, and my parents were diplomats, so I thought we would be safe, immune from the Nazi disease.
But we weren't, and even now I can remember everything vividly, like looking at a photograph.

There were three of them, dressed in those dreadful black uniforms. More of them waiting outside. I was twelve years old, standing in the hallway of our house, desperately clinging to the nightgown of my mother, and they looked like devils to me.

I remember crying—huge sobs that seemed like they would burst through the walls of my chest—shouting at my mother to stop them. She did nothing, and I know now that there was nothing she could have done. In Berlin, in 1938, there was nothing anyone could have done for my father.

—from the memoirs of Joseph "Katipo" St. George

1

THE STRANGER

Thursday, October 13, 1938

The stranger arrived well after midnight. The boy was awake instantly, alerted by the tiniest sound of the scullery door being gently closed. A glance at his cuckoo clock told him the time.

His parents must have been expecting the stranger because they had waited up, and Joe could hear the soft murmurings of their voices. The stranger had come in by the back door, which was odd. Visitors usually entered through the front door. But then again, visitors did not usually call after midnight. Something out of the ordinary was happening this night.

Joe lay still for a moment, breathing in an awareness of the immediate universe that surrounded him. That's what the hero always did, like Lieutenant Urquhart in *Detective Yarns,* or Secret Agent Troy in *Hutchinson's Adventure-Story Magazine,* the most recent issue of which he had received for his twelfth birthday. He used all his senses, like the hero always did. Feeling, tasting, smelling, listening, looking.

The bed he lay in *felt* warm and soft, the big goose-down quilt a warm cloud enveloping him. The pillow was thin and a little hard, but he preferred it like that. Big, soft pillows always seemed to be trying to smother him.

He *tasted* a lingering aftertaste of Doramad, the toothpaste that his mother made him use twice a day. She liked it because it was slightly radioactive and killed germs. Joe didn't like it. He was afraid it would make his teeth glow in the dark.

He *smelled* the tang of pipe smoke in the air. His father only smoked when he was upset and almost never this late at night.

From a small wicker basket in the corner, he *heard* a soft snuffle from Blondie, his new German shepherd puppy. She was a gift from the ambassador himself for Joe's birthday and was the center of Joe's life. He had wanted to call her Betty, after Betty Grable, the beautiful American actress, but his mother hadn't approved of "that temptress," so he had compromised and called her Blondie instead.

He *saw* the drapes were open, letting in the clear night sky. The lower three stars of the Orion constellation were visible just below the top of the window. The sword of Orion. The telescope (actually a big, old brass ship's telescope that his father had borrowed from the embassy) stood proudly on its wooden tripod by the window, staring endlessly out the window at the sky and stars beyond. Keeping watch over the night skies . . . for what, Joe didn't know.

His soccer ball sat on the dresser at the end of the bed. The brown leather showed shiny edges from years of battering but commanded pride of place in the room. That ball had helped his team win the school age-group championship. It was a great ball. On the far wall was pinned a poster of Fritz Szepan, captain of the German national team through the last two World Cups.

A sliver of light from the slightly open bedroom door lay across the face of the cuckoo clock on the wall. The small hand was nearly at the one, but the big hand was camouflaged by the gloom. The cuckoo, half in and half out of its little home, looked back at him, its eyes twinkling with amusement. The cuckoo never went home any more, nor did it fully emerge to announce the hours in its mechanical cuckoo voice. Not since Joe had decided to take the clock apart to find out how it had worked.

Joe lay still for a moment longer, his eyes on the bird, but his mind occupied listening to all the clues that the quiet of the night brought him. The low, but urgent, murmur of voices. The soft footsteps in the passageway downstairs. The quiet clunk of the hallway door closing and a small click as it was latched.

Finally happy that he was fully aware of the world that surrounded him, the complete master of this little piece of the universe, he rolled out from under the thick quilt and stood up . . . putting his right foot smack in the center of his chamber pot. He was relieved to find it was empty.

He padded silently in his thick bed socks to the door of his room. On a hook on the back of the door was his bathrobe, which he quickly donned against the cold night air.

He drew the door open with a sharp jerk that he knew would prevent it from creaking, then paused to assemble his team. This was not a mission he wanted to undertake by himself. Four of his favorite tin soldiers immediately volunteered and, secreting them in the pocket of his gown, he moved stealthily into the hall.

Down the staircase, missing the third step because it creaked . . . so did the seventh . . . and the last. Around the corner to the hallway. Listening at the door for any noise in the passageway beyond. A quick glance through the crack between the door and the jamb to confirm. Then carefully sliding the door latch upward with a slip of thick cardboard that he kept in the pocket of his dressing gown for just that purpose. Pushing the door open wide enough to slip through and easing the latch silently back into place. Leaving the door open a tiny fraction so that it looked closed but would allow him a quick exit. You must always have an escape route. That's what Agent Troy said.

The voices from the scullery were louder now, but still muffled. Joe slid his bed-socked feet across the polished floorboards into the kitchen, which adjoined the scullery. The room was warm. The coal stove had been kept stoked up; no doubt in anticipation of the stranger's arrival. It was dark and he moved carefully so as not to trip over a pot or other utensil that the maid might have left on the floor.

From the next door room he heard his mother's voice. Reassuring, calming. Then his father's more urgent, querying tone. "Why do you think Michaelson didn't show?"

Joe's mother replied quietly, "Perhaps he was delayed, or it just wasn't safe to travel."

"Perhaps," his father agreed, "but these days . . ."

Joe sat, stretching out his legs on the hard wooden floor. He slipped a hand into the pocket of his bathrobe and pulled out the four toy soldiers, placing them on the floor in front of him.

Three were British grenadiers, resplendent in their bright red uniforms. The fourth was a French musketeer. The French one was a little worse for wear, the blue paint having worn off in a number of places, exposing the tin beneath. The French never did very well in Joe's battles.

"If the Gestapo have him . . ." This was a voice Joe didn't recognize. A stranger. There was a tone to it that was unsettling. Joe identified it as desperation, or terror, or both.

The night was getting interesting.

"He wouldn't talk," his mother said quietly. "And in any case, he doesn't know anything about you but your code name."

Joe's musketeer became Michaelson, suddenly trapped in a dark, lonely alley by the three grenadiers, now evil agents of the much-feared Gestapo.

Bam! Michaelson kicked away the gun of the first agent and head-butted the next one in the stomach. The third took a shot at him with his Luger, but Michaelson was too fast and dived to the ground, picking up the first agent's gun and killing the third Gestapo man with a single shot, before escaping down the alleyway that was actually Joe's legs.

He dropped one of the Gestapo agents, and there was a light clunk as it hit the hard wooden floor of the kitchen.

"What was that?" the stranger asked nervously from the other room.

Joe held absolutely still.

"Nothing," his mother said. "Nothing at all. No, no, I don't think that was anything to worry about. This house often makes odd noises like that . . ."

She was talking too much. And his father was silent. She was obviously covering, while his father moved around to deal with the threat. At least that's what Agent Troy would do.

There it was. The faintest click from the scullery door to the hall. His mother was still going on about the old house and the strange creaks and groans it made.

Joe knew he was going to have to move, and move now. But silently. And to where? He urgently scanned the kitchen. There was a small pile of towels in the laundry basket waiting to be washed the next day. It would have to do. He slid across the floor to the basket, climbed over the edge, and curled inside, scooping the towels up and spreading them on top of himself. They were damp and cold, and he gave an involuntary shiver as they touched his face, before commanding his body to absolute stillness. He shut his mouth tightly, in case his teeth really did glow in the dark.

There was a bang, and a glare all around him as the light in the kitchen flicked on. Through a tiny crack in the weave of the basket he saw his father enter the room, poised, alert, and dangerous. In his hand he held a dark metal object and it took Joe several moments to realize what it was. He didn't even know his father owned a pistol!

He knew he was not completely hidden but hoped that the wool of his bathrobe would look like another towel to his father's searching eyes. There would be severe punishment if he got caught. He knew that for sure.

A piece of coal coughed and shifted in the coal range, and after a moment, the lights snapped off again. Joe remained motionless until he heard the scullery door close and his father's voice in the other room.

"Must have been the coal range. Nobody there."

Joe eased himself out of the basket and slid back to his position by the wall.

"You have the documents?" his mother was asking.

"Yes. They were in the dead-letter box as planned," the stranger said.

"No chance of a trap?"

"No. I was very careful."

There was a long silence, broken only by the rustle of paper. Joe staged a few more battles between tattered blue Michaelson and the bright red Gestapo agents to fill in the time.

"Okay," his father said at last. "We'll microfilm these and get them to London."

"I hope to God we're not too late." That was his mother speaking.

"Do I go back?" the stranger wanted to know.

"No, we can't risk it. If Michaelson has been taken . . ." His father trailed off.

"Here's the address of the safe house." His mother's voice, and the scratch of a fountain pen. "They'll ask you for a password, it's *Violet*—don't forget it."

His father said, "Good luck, Dusko."

Joe sensed the meeting was over. Quickly and quietly he relatched the hallway door and tiptoed back upstairs, pushing his bedroom door to the same angle it had been before.

He was in bed by the time he heard the back scullery door

open and the man named Dusko stumble out into the cold and dark of the night.

Joe lay facing away from the door, in case his parents should check on him, and stared out of the window. If he moved his head forward just a little, to get a better angle, he could see the rest of the constellation.

Orion, the hunter, was in the night sky.

And Joe's father owned a gun.

Klaus Bormann was my best friend in those early days in Berlin. He was two years older than me, so he wore trousers while I was still stuck in short pants. Being tall for my age, I was about the same height as Klaus and it seemed unfair to me that he could wear long pants and I couldn't.

What was worse, he was a member of the Deutsches Jungvolk—the junior section of the Hitler Youth—and got to take part in a lot of exciting activities that I couldn't, because my parents wouldn't let me join.

But he also had to shave, about once a week I think, which seemed like a pointless and rather frightening activity to me, so I wasn't envious of that at all.

—from the memoirs of Joseph "Katipo" St. George

2

HAIL VICTORY

Tuesday, October 18, 1938

He was coming.

Joe dared not say his name. He dared not even think it.

They had been let out of school early for the parade and had practically fallen over one another scrambling to be first to the route to get a good viewing position. They were careful not to step onto the road itself, however, as that was forbidden, and the Brownshirts of the Sturmabteilung—the SA—who policed the route had long batons that dealt swiftly and painfully with anyone who stepped out of line.

Joe straightened his school cap and lined up the toes of his carefully polished shoes exactly with the edge of the cobblestone footpath. Not a fraction over. Beside him, his best friend in the world, Klaus Bormann, did the same, although Joe knew Klaus's big clodhoppers had a mind of their own and would not stay in that position for long.

He was closer now.

The sound of drums reverberated from around the corner, and the paving beneath their feet began to vibrate, reaching up from the very ground on which they stood, through their shoes and shins to their knees, their bellies, their hearts. Joe stared for a moment at his fingertips and wondered if it was the vibrations or his nerves that was making them quiver. Embedded in the noise was another sound, a mechanical clanking, grinding. Although it was still distant, Joe recognized it immediately and beamed with excitement at Klaus, standing tall as a young tree beside him.

Klaus, at fourteen, was older than most of the boys in their class as a result of having been held back a couple of times along the way. Only Joe—still twelve but tall and lanky like his father—matched Klaus for height. Klaus wasn't the brightest child in the class, but he had friendly eyes, a broad grin, and a flop of unruly black hair that no amount of hair cream could hold in place.

Joe glanced around behind them. The boys from Kreuzberg Park Realschule had not been as lucky as those from St. Andreas. They had farther to come and arrived after Joe and his schoolmates had already lined the route, so they formed a second row behind. Most of them could still see well enough, but the boy behind Joe and Klaus was going to have a problem. He was a small, mousy boy Joe knew only by his nickname: Ratte. Blocked by the tall shoulders of Joe and Klaus, he would see little or nothing.

Joe turned. It was a great day. A day to be excited. A day to be generous of spirit. He would offer the boy a position at the front, then they would both see.

"Get out of the way," Ratte said poisonously before Joe could utter a word. "You don't even belong here."

Joe turned away, a little taken aback. Klaus, who'd heard, shook his head in good humor.

"You're not even German," Ratte snarled behind them. "The parade is not for you!"

They could hear music now, a brass band, the sound merging into the throb of the engines and the sharp thrum of the drums.

"You look more German than me." Klaus grinned, and it was true. Klaus had dark hair whereas Joe's blond hair gave him a regal, Aryan appearance, despite his British father and New Zealand mother. Glancing behind, Klaus continued, "And a lot more German than he does."

Joe could almost feel the expression on Ratte's face burning into his back and shook his head with a quick ironic smile. If only Ratte hadn't been so hateful, he would have been standing at the front of the crowd right now.

The crowd surged and murmured, and Joe saw the first elements of the parade turn the corner at the end of the plaza. It was the Hitlerjugend—Hitler Youth—smart and important in their brown shirts, black shorts, and white knee socks, shoes stomping in perfect unison.

Klaus was in the Deutsches Jungvolk, the junior Hitler Youth, and he couldn't wait till he turned fifteen and could join the Hitlerjugend, with their smart uniforms and shiny knives. Joe's father wouldn't let him join and wouldn't even give a reason why, which Joe thought was really unfair.

The front row of the Hitlerjugend were flute players, the high-pitched notes of their marching melody spiraling out across the road. The next row were the drummers, their arms flailing high in the air with each beat. Behind the drummers came rows of serious young men, their arms and backs rigid, their heads high and proud. Next year Klaus would be marching there, thought Joe enviously, *and* he had long pants!

There must have been over a thousand Hitlerjugend in all, ten to a row. Behind them, looking tough and dangerous in their black uniforms with the bloodred splash of the Hakenkreuz armband, marched the soldiers of the Waffen-SS. They came in clusters: ten rows, a small gap, then the next ten rows.

From out of nowhere a smattering of light rain arrived, the drops sparkling like fireworks in the afternoon sunshine—a sun-shower. It stopped almost before it had begun, barely enough to discolor the road dust. Not even the sky itself would dare to rain on this parade.

A tall bronze statue of a soldier on horseback, greened by the elements, watched down from a pedestal behind a circular wire fence on the other side of the street. The soldier's expression was awestruck, proud. Joe imagined that he would rear up on his metal steed, bound over the fence, and join the parade. But he didn't.

The second- and third-story windows of the buildings that lined the route bulged with people, like some giant hand had grabbed the buildings and squeezed, and the people were oozing like toothpaste out of the openings. From the top of every building huge banners dropped almost to street level. On each one, in bright red, burned the Hakenkreuz, the hooked cross of the National Socialist Party.

They could hear cheering now and distant chanting. *He* was almost there.

The Waffen-SS passed blackly by, and now there were soldiers. The Wehrmacht, the regular German Army. First came the officers on horses—magnificent, haughty animals that stared disdainfully down at the thronging humanity on either side of the street. The battle dress of the horses was swathed with flowers, and even as they watched, young women darted from the crowd and added to the foliage. Then came the soldiers themselves, steel-helmeted, dark green ranks—a sea of them, no, an ocean. From one side to the other of the square they stretched, rifles at attention. Wave after wave after wave in rigid, uniform rows, emotionless, relentless. More and more of them until it seemed that even the air was thick with the sound and the color of the marching men.

Joe stared, dizzy, his jaw open wide. He didn't know there were so many soldiers in the army. He didn't know there were so many soldiers in the world! And still they passed. Line after line. Platoon after platoon. Regiment after regiment.

The crowd was a living creature now, moving and breathing as a single entity. Muttered words merged into a common voice.

Except for Ratte. "Out of the way, Engländer," he spat. "You're blocking the view."

Joe and Klaus glanced at each other.

"Definitely not German-looking," Klaus said with a grin. "Jüden maybe."

There was a sudden, sharp intake of breath from the boy behind them.

Joe glanced back. "Could be," he agreed, and childishly poked his tongue out at the boy.

Ratte went white, red, then purple in the space of a few seconds. His fists clenched, unclenched. His nostrils flared. To be branded a Jew! On this day, of all days. In this place, of all places.

Joe turned away. He braced himself for a punch in the back but didn't really expect it. There was a Brownshirt a few feet away. Ratte would not want to get into a fight with either Joe or Klaus, let alone both at once. Especially in front of the SA.

The crowd drew in its breath, and Joe looked to the end of the road to see why.

The armor had arrived. Artillery pieces, small at first, pulled by teams of horses, but soon followed by massive truck-towed cannons that looked as though they could fire a shell all the way to Moscow. Behind them came the tanks: huge, mechanized beasts with massive snouts and clawed tracks.

The crowd roared with excitement and delight, but the sound swirled around into the blue-gray fumes and clanking rumble of these massive metal creatures and was lost. Countless rows of them passed, two abreast, the nearest so close that Joe felt its breath, and inhaled its scent as it growled along in front of him. He could almost reach out and touch the heavy black cross emblazoned on its hide.

A giant, metal, fire-breathing dragon, Joe thought. Heaven help anyone who ever attacked Germany. They would have to face that!

The tanks passed by, and the sound began to fade as they

turned another corner. The crowd quieted too, anticipation muting its excitement.

There was a gap, then a Mercedes staff car turned the corner at the end of the platz.

The chancellor was about to arrive.

This was not *him* though. Joe could tell from the reaction of the crowd at the end of the street; they were silent, unmoving, waiting.

Another car appeared, then another. Still the crowd was silent, ignoring the assembled dignitaries in their open-top limousines.

"There's my uncle," Klaus said breathlessly as one of the cars drew near. A broad-faced, tight-lipped man in his late thirties. Klaus threw his arm upward in the Nazi greeting, but the man did not see and merely stared expressionlessly forward as the car passed them.

There was a new sound now breaking the hushed silence. "Heil Hitler!"

The chant started at the very end of the platz and spread like wildfire along both sides.

"Heil Hitler!"

Thousands of small paper flags appeared from within the crowd, small red triangles decorated with the Hakenkreuz in a white circle.

Joe leaned forward, trying to see past the rest of the throng. Behind him he sensed, rather than saw, Ratte struggling to catch even a tiny glimpse of the great man.

The car neared, traveling slowly, and finally, there he was.

The chancellor. Standing in the front passenger seat of the Mercedes open-top car. All around Joe arms were thrust stiffly outward in the Nazi greeting, the Hitler salute. Herr Hitler returned the salute in an off-handed, almost-bored manner.

"Heil Hitler," the animal that was the crowd roared, breathlessly, raucously, uncontrollably.

A few people had cameras, holding them high in the air and aiming them without looking, hoping to catch a good shot through pure luck. Schoolgirls on the other side of the platz were crying, Joe saw. One fainted and was sucked into the maw of the crowd. He hoped she would be all right. A pretty young woman in a fashionable polka-dot dress with a young child in her arms broke free from the crowd and was alongside the car before the guards could react. The car stopped, and Joe watched in amazement as the child, a girl of three or four, handed Herr Hitler a small posy of flowers and then raised her chubby little arm in a perfect Hitler salute.

The chant changed. "Hail victory!" they roared. "Hail victory!"

Somehow above it or through it, another sound penetrated: a high-pitched, ratty snarl from behind him. "Go home, Engländer!"

Joe stuck out his chin and thrust himself forward, tiptoeing on the edge of the pavement.

"Hail victory!" he shouted, louder than the rest. His salute was higher, stronger than the rest. "Hail victory!" he yelled again. "Hail victory! Hail victory! Sieg Heil!"

The chancellor turned toward him, his eye caught by the

sheer energy of Joe's movement. For a moment the great man caught Joe's eye, and a half smile of acknowledgment crossed the Führer's lips, then another short, self-conscious salute and the car moved on.

The crowd remained where they were until long after the car had turned the corner at the end of the street. Slowly the people quieted and began to dissemble into a group of individuals, no longer a single living mass. Klaus turned to leave. Joe turned with him, only to be confronted by the surly face of the boy called Ratte.

"You'll get what's coming to you," Ratte said in a low voice.

"You and what army?" Klaus snarled and stepped toward him. Ratte spun around and was quickly lost in the crowd. Joe and Klaus looked at each other and laughed, the laugh as much a release of their exhilaration as anything.

The two of them drifted along, flotsam on the ebbing tides of the gradually dispersing throng. The only thing Joe wasn't sure of was whether it was he or Klaus that Ratte had directed his threat at.

They caught up with Lukas and Kurt on Goebenstrasse, and Ompah joined them by the canal. Ompah's real name was Johan, but he played tuba in the school orchestra and he looked a bit like a tuba himself, so everyone called him Om-Pah-Pah, or Ompah for short.

They walked together, lost in the sights, smells, and sounds swirling around inside their heads. Joe walked on the narrow curb, stepping between the cracks, one foot on each stone, holding his arms out to either side for balance.

Ompah and Kurt started playing soldiers, darting from the corner of a building to the next, peering carefully around for the enemy, and firing the occasional burst from their Schmeisser machine pistols at snipers concealed in the parapets of the buildings across the canal. They must have been good shots because there would always be a whistling noise, followed by a thud, to let the others know that the sniper had fallen from his perch.

Klaus had a photo of Dorothy Lamour, the beautiful American actress, leaning against a stair rail and wearing not very much at all. He had been given it by a boy in the Hitlerjugend. Lukas was trying to grab it off him, but Klaus was holding it high above his head and Lukas couldn't reach.

Kurt eventually asked, "Hungry?"

Joe was. There was something about the excitement that had used up all his energy. "There's a good bakery on Bissingzeile," he said. "My mother gets breakfast rolls there."

There was a murmur of agreement, and the five of them set out in that direction.

Lukas started singing the Horst Wessel song, the anthem of the Brownshirts, and Kurt and Ompah joined in.

"What do you think Ratte is planning?" Joe asked Klaus as they walked. "You really riled him up."

Klaus shook his head. "He'll have forgotten all about it by tomorrow."

Joe nodded, although he wasn't quite as confident.

Lukas stopped at the door to the bakery. *Reinsgart Bäckerei* it said in large red letters outlined in white on the shopwindow.

Like most bakeries, it had a hanging sign by the door in the shape of a large wooden pretzel. The window display itself was tantalizing. Bread rolls and loaves of every description, peppernut cookies and pound cakes, hutzelbrot and pumpernickel rounds. The smell of baking drifted through vents at the front of the shop, winding around them and drawing them inside.

Joe had a few coins in his pocket, saved from his pocket money, and could see a particular rugelach cookie that seemed to be beckoning to him.

But Lukas said, "I'm not going in there."

Joe looked where Lukas's eyes were fixed. A large yellow star was stuck to the corner of the shopwindow, by the door.

"They're Jewish, so what?" Ompah shrugged. "Still smells good to me."

Klaus seemed uncertain and looked at Joe for guidance.

Inside the shop Herr Reinsgart moved to the window display and retrieved a lemon tart for a customer. He was a tall, silver-haired man, his back ramrod straight. He was quite military in bearing, although he walked with a cane. Joe's father said he had given part of his left leg for Germany in the Great War. Another yellow star was attached to the lapel of his white bakers' coat.

"My father would kill me," Lukas said. "And I don't care how good it smells, I don't want to eat food that dirty Jewish hands have touched."

"It's probably poisoned!" Kurt exclaimed.

"If the food was poisoned, his customers would all be dead," Joe pointed out.

"He's half Jewish," Ompah contributed. "I know because my father delivers his flour."

"I'm not going in there," Lukas declared again.

"Me neither," Kurt agreed.

Joe shut his mouth. They learned all about Jews in German lessons at school. But somehow that had never seemed to apply to the tall, distinguished figure of Herr Reinsgart, despite his yellow star.

"Dirty Jew," Lukas said, then called it out again: "Dirty Jew!"

On the other side of the street, a couple of passersby stopped to watch.

Ompah began to march up and down the footpath outside the shop, goose-stepping like the black-clad troops of the SS they had seen a little while before. Kurt and Lukas joined in, forming a line in front of the shop, marching and giving the Hitler salute.

Joe found himself going along with it, without quite meaning to. "Jews out!" he shouted, and heard Klaus's voice join in.

The door to the shop opened with a rattle and the sound of a bell, and suddenly Herr Reinsgart was there, cane in hand, and waving furiously at them.

"You urchins!" he shouted. "Get away from my shop."

"Jews out!" There was time for just one more chant before Herr Reinsgart took a step forward, and the five of them ran for it, skipping along the pavement and roadway past the shop, yelling "Pig Jew" back over their shoulders, laughing as they ran.

"I know you!" Herr Reinsgart shouted after them. "I know

you, little St. George boy! Don't think I don't know who you are—your mother will hear about this!"

"He wouldn't dare," Ompah said pompously as they slowed to walk along the canal path. "He's just a Jew. He has no rights."

"If he does, we'll smash his windows," Kurt said. "See how he likes that."

Joe walked silently. It would earn him a spoonful of castor oil or a couple of belts from his father's razor strop if Herr Reinsgart did complain to his mother.

"Let's smash his windows anyway!" Lukas said brightly. "Serve him right for trying to sell his stinking Jew food in our neighborhood."

"He'll know it was us," Klaus warned, "then there'll be more trouble."

"I don't care," Lukas said. "It'll teach him not to mess with us!"

"When?" Kurt asked, excitement gleaming in his eyes.

"Tomorrow," Lukas announced, "after the shop shuts at five. We'll give him another half hour or so to lock up and go home, then we attack!"

"A lightning raid!" Ompah punched the air.

Klaus grinned, a bit vacantly.

"We could leave something at the scene, like a cap from another school . . ." Joe was getting caught up in the idea now. "He'll think it was somebody else."

The cap was a good idea, if he could get hold of one. Otherwise the repercussions would be worse.

"Okay, men, tomorrow night." Lukas as usual was the

general, marshaling the troops. "Rendezvous in the park after school at fifteen hundred hours. Synchronize your watches."

That was a bit silly, Joe thought. They always met in the park after school for soccer or piggyback wrestling or marbles anyway.

"I don't have a watch," Klaus said.

Ompah gave the Hitler salute. "Hail victory," he said.

"Hail victory," the others chorused.

"Sieg Heil!"

3

THE GREAT SOCCER WAR

Wednesday, October 19, 1938

Klaus was late for the rendezvous.

He had been kept back after class. Erik von Deisenberg had persuaded him to put glue in Herr Uhl's pipe as a practical joke. It hadn't taken Herr Uhl long to find the culprit. Nobody else would have been dumb enough to risk such a stunt. So Klaus had to spend an hour after school scrubbing the floor of the school cafeteria.

If it wasn't for the fact that Klaus's uncle was Martin Bormann, the personal secretary of the Führer, the punishment would have been much more severe.

Joe, Kurt, Lukas, and Ompah played soccer while they waited for him, using just one goal at the far end of the field in the center of the park.

Just a few years earlier the park had been a moldy, old dump site of rotting garbage and thigh-high weeds, home to a number of vagrants and feral cats. But the National Socialists had changed all that and the park was now a modern, clean garden with flower beds of orchids and tulips. There were climbing bars at one end and an ornate marble fountain at the other.

In the center was the soccer field, which was the playground for many of the St. Andreas students each day after school.

Joe was goalie, his long arms and legs making him a natural for the position. Ompah played defender, as that meant less running. Kurt and Lukas were the attackers, dribbling and passing the ball between each other as they circled in toward the goal.

At the far end of the field another group of boys were shooting goals using the other goal net, and in the center of the field a small group of kids were playing jacks in the center circle.

Joe and his friends had been kicking the ball around for half an hour, during which time neither Kurt nor Lukas had managed to score a goal, when Ompah said, "Hang on, look at this . . ."

Joe glanced up, having just saved another goal, and saw Ratte marching onto the far end of the field, a soccer ball under his arm, followed by a gang of his schoolmates.

Kurt ran over and stood next to Joe. "What are they doing here?" he asked. "They've got their own field in Kreuzberg Park."

"Dunno," Ompah said. "Let's go and tell them to clear off."

Lukas walked over, dribbling the ball slowly between his feet, and said doubtfully, "There's eight of them."

"Yeah, leave them alone," Joe said. "They're just looking for a fight. Let's not give them any reason to start one."

"Especially when we're outnumbered!" Lukas agreed.

Ratte was gesticulating at the St. Andreas boys, who slowly picked up their ball and trudged off the field, where they sat on the sideline and watched as Ratte and his friends began their own game of soccer at the far end of the field.

"Hey! They've kicked the juniors off the field," Ompah said indignantly. "*Our* field. That's not fair!"

"Leave them alone," Joe repeated. "They're trying to pick a fight and we don't want any of it."

"As long as they stay down that end," Lukas the general said, "we'll leave them alone. But if they try to come up this end . . ."

What? thought Joe. What will you do? There are eight of them!

Lukas hooked the ball up with his toe and began juggling it with one foot. After a moment or two he lobbed it higher in the air, over Joe's head and into the goal.

"Goal!" he called.

"Not fair," Joe protested. "We weren't playing!"

He ran after the ball and tossed it back out to Kurt, who dribbled it downfield a way. Then he turned around and charged back at the goal, side-slipping the ball over to Lukas as Ompah raced up to tackle him. Lukas fired the ball at the top right corner of the goal and swore loudly, using words that Joe hadn't learned yet, when Joe's long arms plucked the ball out of midair.

"Now what?" Ompah said.

Ratte and his friends were having a heated argument with the jack players in the center circle.

"It's our field," Joe heard one of the St. Andreas boys say. They were about ten years old, and there were four of them, but no match for the eight bigger kids who were now towering over them.

"What are they up to?" Kurt wondered.

"I'm not putting up with it," Lukas said. "This is our field. If they don't clear off, they can deal with us." He looked around. "Who's with me?"

Joe nodded. "We can't let them get away with this."

Ompah looked scared but was trying to cover it up.

Kurt just shrugged. He never minded a good scrap.

"Okay," Lukas said, "let's go."

The smaller St. Andreas boys in the center circle were getting up to leave, somewhat reluctantly, when Ratte pushed one of them over and a handful of jacks scattered across the field.

"Leave them alone!" Ompah called out.

"And get off our field!" Lukas shouted.

Ratte smiled malevolently and said, "It's our field now. *You* get off the field."

"You've got your own park!" Ompah sounded aggrieved.

"Well, now we've got yours too," one of Ratte's friends sneered, a big boy named Tomas.

The ranks of the two sides closed on each other. The four smaller children shuffled off to one side, sensing that violence was looming.

"Get off, or we'll make you," Joe said softly.

"You and what army?" Ratte laughed and spat at him. He was too far away and the spit just landed on the ground at Joe's feet.

"You're dead, Ratte," Lukas said, his voice rising.

Joe looked around. Even if the smaller children joined in, which they probably wouldn't, it wasn't a fair matchup. He wished Klaus were there. He was big and strong and good in a fight.

"That's your last warning," Joe said evenly. "Leave now or you'll get it."

"You leave, Engländer, or—" That was all Ratte got out before Joe's fist caught him on the underside of his jaw, snapping his mouth shut. He went over backward in a flail of arms and Joe dropped on top of him, his knee driving into the boy's stomach, winding him. That would keep him out of it for a few minutes, Joe thought, which evened up the odds just slightly.

A fist caught Joe on the side of his head, but he half saw it coming and turned his head with the punch, so it just grazed him. He spun off Ratte, who was gasping for air, and dived at the new attacker, tackling him around the midriff and knocking him over. The boy sat down on his backside, hard. Joe pushed him to the ground and took a couple of fists to the face before landing one of his own, a wild roundhouse punch that drew blood from the boy's nose.

Then strong hands ripped him off the boy and two more attackers were on him, punching and kicking with the ferocity of wildcats.

From the corner of his eye, Joe saw Ompah wrestling with one boy on the ground, using his weight to pin the other down. Kurt was trading punches with a thick-necked boy a few centimeters taller than him, but seemed to be getting the best of it. Lukas had his arms pinned behind him by one boy, while another was pummeling him with heavy blows.

Joe roared and grabbed the leg of one of his attackers as he kicked again. He pulled, and as the boy came down toward him, Joe brought his own knee up. There was a nasty-sounding thud as his knee met the boy's face and the boy screamed like a baby, which was quite encouraging.

But the other two were on him again now, and he fell back to the ground, trying to protect himself with his hands. Even Ratte had got some of his breath back and was darting around, trying to land a kick on Joe's head.

They were everywhere. There were just too many of them. Joe tried to grab Ratte's ankle but missed, and the hard tip of a school shoe smashed into his forehead.

He was on his stomach now, with someone sitting on his back, pinning him down, while two others grappled with his legs and Ratte ran around trying to get another kick in at his head.

Then suddenly there was a grunt from above and the weight was gone. The grip on his legs loosened, and he rolled over just in time to see Klaus crack the heads of his two attackers together. They spun apart, shrieking and clutching at their temples.

Joe grabbed for Ratte's ankle again and got it this time, pulling the boy's feet out from under him and hearing with satisfaction the hard thud as Ratte hit the ground.

Klaus had moved on to the two boys beating up on Lukas, and they turned to face him, but backed away slowly as Joe jumped to his feet and stood by Klaus's side, the two of them blocking the low afternoon sun, their long shadows stretching over the Kreuzberg Park boys.

The boys broke and ran, and behind him Joe heard Ratte and the others scrabbling off backward as well.

Lukas jumped to his feet, blood and snot streaming from his nose and down the front of his shirt, but otherwise none the worse for wear. "Get them, men!" he shouted, and began to run after the fleeing boys.

Ompah let out a war cry and also gave chase. They all joined up, yelling and whooping and hurling insults at the backs of the other boys.

At the park gates they stopped, watching the Kreuzberg Park boys run for their lives up the road.

Lukas was wiping at his nose, laughing and shouting all at the same time. "You fight like Catholic boys!"

"Don't come back!" Ompah yelled, but they were probably out of hearing range.

"What the heck did they do that for?" Kurt wondered out loud.

Klaus told them. "At the parade, I said Ratte looked like a Jew."

"Hey, look what I got," Joe said brightly, holding up a Kreuzberg Park Realschule cap.

At 5:00 p.m.—1700 hours, according to Lukas—the boys started collecting stones, big heavy ones from around the low rock wall that encircled that park. The mission to smash the baker's windows was underway.

"If they're too small, they'll just bounce off the glass," Lukas told them, as if he did this all the time. "And too big is hard to throw. But it has to be heavy enough to smash the pane, not just crack the glass."

Joe found four good-sized ones that filled the pockets of his pants and threatened to bring them down around his ankles. He hoisted his pants up a little and adjusted his suspenders. The largest of his stones was about the size of an egg, and he was sure it would make a merry mess of Herr Reinsgart's lemon tarte display.

"Let's do it!" Ompah shouted.

"Show the dirty Jew!" Lukas yelled.

"Dirty Jew!" Klaus echoed.

Joe had time to wonder before they were off on their mission if they would have been brave enough to go through with it if they hadn't still been full of steam and fire from the fight with the Kreuzberg Park boys.

"Hold it, men," Lukas ordered as they approached the corner of Bissingzeile. "We need a forward scout. Volunteers?"

Before anyone had time to volunteer, he continued, "Okay, St. George, it's you. You lead. We'll be a few paces behind you."

"Yes, sir." Joe snapped a salute. "And, sir . . ."

"Yes?"

"If I don't make it back—"

Lukas nodded grimly. "We'll tell Blondie that you loved her."

Ompah and Kurt cracked up at that, and so did Klaus a second or two later.

Joe tucked the Kreuzberg cap under his sweater and slipped around the corner, still laughing.

The shadows had disappeared now as the sun had slipped

below the jagged screen of buildings that was the western quarter of the city. The streets were dim, but there was plenty of light left in the sky yet. Electric street lights flickered into life along the length of Bissingzeile, adding a muted yellowish cast to the twilight.

It was plenty light enough to see that the street was not as quiet as they had expected it to be.

Joe fingered the egg-sized stone in his pocket and casually walked in the direction of the shop. There was some kind of activity going on outside the bakery, he saw, although he couldn't quite make out what it was.

He slowly drew nearer . . . then tensed, drawing in his breath.

The men in the street were SA. The smart brown shirts looked quite different in the dusky light. There was something unsettling about the deep shadows beneath the dark caps and the dull red of the Hakenkreuz armband—the swastika armband his father always called it—like a tight ribbon of dried blood around their upper arms.

There was a squad of these storm troopers, at least six of them, leaning over some shapes on the road.

Joe kept putting one foot in front of the other as though he had somewhere to be at the other end of the street.

He could see the shapes now. They were people. Herr Reinsgart and a lady he had often seen in the back of the shop—Frau Reinsgart, the baker's wife. They were on their knees.

Scrubbing, Joe saw. They were scrubbing at the stones of the road with damp rags. Cleaning the road. In the gathering darkness.

The leader of the SA squad stood over Herr Reinsgart with a stick in his hand, Herr Reinsgart's cane.

Blood was flowing from the baker's forehead and dripping onto the road as he worked. As it dropped, the SA leader would gesture at it with the cane, and Herr Reinsgart would quickly rub it away with the cloth, then continue scrubbing at the road.

Joe looked around in horror at Lukas and Kurt, a few yards behind.

"Dirty Jews, clean streets," he heard Ompah say with a quiet snicker. Nobody laughed.

Joe walked past the bakery, earning nothing more than a quick glance from the Sturmführer.

It wasn't until he was well past that he stopped. The others caught up with him quickly. He stood still for a moment with his eyes shut, and then with a horrible sick feeling in his stomach, he turned back.

"What are you doing?" Lukas hissed.

"Don't be an idiot," Ompah said.

Klaus just watched.

Joe ignored them and took another step.

Kurt grabbed him by the arm, but Joe shook it off and took another couple of steps. "Leave them alone," he said quietly.

The Brownshirts turned in surprise, and the leader looked up, glaring at Joe from under the short peak of his uniform cap.

"Come here, boy," he demanded.

"Leave them alone," Joe said again, walking steadily toward the officer.

Kurt retreated with a terrified look.

"Why do you care? Are you Jüden perhaps?" The man asked quizzically, glancing around at his men. "But I see no yellow star. Jude liebhaber, I think." A Jew lover.

"Neither," Joe said steadily, closing on the officer. "But this man"—he pointed at Herr Reinsgart—"is half German."

"And half Jew." The officer looked around at his men with a surprised laugh. "Go home, Jew lover."

Herr Reinsgart took his eyes off his work and looked up at Joe with a warning shake of his head. *Go away,* his eyes pleaded.

"He's half German," Joe said quietly. "German like you. He fought for Germany in the Great War. Why are you doing this to him?"

The officer's expression changed instantly from bemusement to anger. He stepped toward Joe, raising the cane.

"Leave the baker alone" came a new voice. Klaus's voice. Suddenly he was by Joe's side, standing square, facing off with Joe against the SA man. The other storm troopers started to move, gathering in a tight semicircle around Joe and Klaus. Joe could see his other friends gathered at the far end of the street.

"Leave him alone," Joe repeated, and braced himself for the slashing whip of the cane.

But then a voice came from the squad. "That's Bormann's kid. Martin Bormann's nephew."

There was a sudden hush among the storm troopers.

The leader took a step backward. He seemed undecided.

"We are finished here," he said after a long awkward pause, and a moment later the storm troopers were gone.

Joe walked home with Klaus, the others having scattered to their own homes.

It was strange, he thought later. Never once during the fight in the park, despite the punches, the kicks, the blood, and the pain, never once had he cried. Joe was twelve. He was too old to cry.

But walking through the darkening streets with his friend, for reasons he didn't fully understand, he bawled like a baby.

4

BLOOD BROTHERS

Wednesday, October 26, 1938

"You have to get the angle right."

The knife in Klaus's hand had a black, checkered handle with the swastika emblazoned on a red-and-white diamond in the center. The handle was protected by a shiny steel finger guard and the heel of the knife was also steel, also shiny. The blade was about fifteen centimeters long, wide and flat. Klaus had borrowed the knife from one of his friends in the Hitler Youth. It looked sharp and angry.

He demonstrated again with the knife, drawing it carefully down his right cheek at a thirty-degree angle. "Understand?"

Joe nodded and accepted the knife back from Klaus. "Yes," he said. "First *with* the direction of the bristles, and the second stroke against."

Klaus nodded.

"But . . . when you don't have any bristles, how do you know which direction they are growing?"

Klaus tapped the side of his own cheek. "Here the direction is always downward."

Blondie sniffed excitedly around Joe's feet. He nudged her to the side and concentrated on the face in the mirror. Joe had no need to shave, but Klaus said that he might as well learn so that when he needed to know how, he would know. Which seemed to make sense, but staring at his frightened face in the bathroom mirror, he was beginning to feel less sure.

The glass in the mirror was crystal clear and sparkled like a diamond around the edges. The bathroom bench was a deep rich wood, elegant and ornate, if a little dulled on the edges where it had worn from constant use. The porcelain bowl that steamed with water in front of him was rose-patterned and traced with gold leaf around the edges. The room smelled faintly of Joe's mother's favorite perfume.

Joe lathered more soapy foam onto his face with his father's shaving brush and gently touched the knife to his cheek. He didn't dare touch his father's razor. It was bad enough using his brush, but the razor was sacrosanct.

"Is this angle right?" he asked.

"Looks good to me," Klaus replied.

Joe brought the blade slowly down his cheek, barely touching his skin, leaving a thin blade of soap. He rinsed the knife in the bowl and brought it back to his face.

"Ouch!"

A drop of blood welled from a small cut and ran down the edge of the blade before dropping to the floor, where it made a dark rosette. Blondie scampered over and licked at it.

"Eww! Yuck!" Klaus laughed. "Your dog's a cannibal!"

"If she were a cannibal," Joe pointed out, pressing one hand against his face while he rinsed the knife with the other, "she would eat other dogs."

"So she's a man-eater, then." Klaus laughed.

"I think I've had enough shaving for now," Joe said. "I'll practice again later."

He washed the soap from his face with a flannel and pressed a pinch of cotton wool against the cut. "You know the other day," he said, "at the bakery . . ."

Klaus looked uncomfortable but nodded.

Joe asked, "Why did you stick up for me?"

"I told Lukas," Klaus said, a little embarrassed. "I already told him. And Kurt and Ompah too. I don't know why they . . ." He trailed off.

Lukas hadn't spoken to Joe for a week. In fact, it seemed that he had gone out of his way to avoid him. Ompah too, who gave Joe embarrassed sideways glances when they passed each other in the hallway. Kurt hadn't really cared, but he mainly hung around with Lukas, so Joe hadn't seen him much either.

Something had changed in the world since that day outside the bakery on Bissingzeile. The soldiers' uniforms seemed a little less smart, the buttons of their tunics a little less shiny. Even the air he breathed seemed thinner somehow.

When he closed his eyes at night, he saw the brave face of Herr Reinsgart warning him not to get involved. Joe had ignored the warning, and he was still not sure why.

He waited for Klaus to continue.

"Well . . ." There was another pause. "I told Lukas—I told him it didn't matter if I agreed with you or not. You are my friend. And friends stick up for each other no matter what."

Joe thought, not for the first time, that Klaus wasn't as dumb as everybody made him out to be.

"Thank you, Klaus," he said softly.

"It's what friends do," Klaus said. "We're best friends, and the Hitlerjugend teaches us about honor and loyalty to your friends."

Joe winced a little at the mention of the Hitler Youth, which caused a drop of blood to escape from under the cotton wool. He saw it in the mirror and wiped at it, then pressed the swab back to his face.

"We should be blood brothers," Klaus said. "That's what really best friends do, so they'll be friends forever."

"Yes, I'd like that," Joe said.

Klaus picked up the knife from where Joe had left it beside the bowl and dried it carefully on a small towel. "Okay, you ready?" he asked.

Joe nodded and held out his hand. The dab of cotton wool was sticking to his face by itself now. Klaus brought the tip of the large blade delicately down and quickly made a series of small cuts in Joe's palm.

Joe shut his eyes and drew his breath in sharply on the first one but didn't flinch, and the other cuts didn't seem as bad as the first. He was a little surprised at how many cuts Klaus made though. A large glob of blood welled up and dripped from his hand onto the wooden bench, away from Blondie's reach. He opened his eyes and pressed his palms together for a moment.

"Want me to do yours?" he asked.

Klaus shook his head. "I can do it."

He swapped the knife to his left hand and held his right over the porcelain bowl. He worked away for a moment on the palm of his right hand. Blood dripped steadily as he did so, making red strawberry splashes in the milky water of the bowl.

"What do we do now?" Joe asked.

"We shake hands, to mix our blood, and say the Blood Brothers' Oath," Klaus answered.

Joe held out his hand, blood dripping. Blondie pounced, but he ignored her. Klaus took his hand, and they solemnly shook.

Joe asked, "What is the Blood Brothers' Oath?"

Klaus gripped his hand tightly and stood tall, his other hand across his heart. "My brother, with . . . um, blood . . ." he fumbled.

Joe thought for a moment, then recited in a reverent tone, "For he to-day that sheds his blood with me shall be my brother; be he ne'er so vile, this day shall gentle his condition."

"Wow," Klaus said, still shaking Joe's hand. "Did you make that up just now?"

Joe shook his head and slowly released Klaus's hand. "William Shakespeare. *Henry V.*"

"It was good," Klaus said, "my brother."

"Thank you, my brother," Joe said. "So this means that we are bound by the bond of blood to fight each other's fights, aid each other in times of need . . ."

"And take care of each other's children if one of us dies," Klaus added.

"I think that's a godfather, not a blood brother," Joe said. "But still. If I died, that means you would take care of Blondie for me, right?"

"Blondie the cannibal dog?" Klaus laughed, and then corrected himself before Joe could do it for him. "I mean Blondie the man-eater!"

The man-eater, hearing her name, jumped up on Klaus's leg. She scrabbled frantically at the fabric of his trousers with her soft puppy paws. Klaus scratched her behind the ears, and she licked at his hand.

"My mother would never let me have a dog," he said. "She's allergic. Besides, nothing is going to happen to you. You have a blood brother to look after you now."

"But if anything did . . ."

"Then of course I will look after this man-eater dog of yours."

Joe rolled his eyes and laughed.

There was no more cotton wool so Joe pulled out a slightly grubby handkerchief from his pocket to clean up his hand. It quickly stained bright red. But as it did, the series of cuts that Klaus had made in his palm became clear.

The cuts were in the shape of the Hakenkreuz.

A swastika.

Two days later, probably due to the dirty handkerchief, the cuts got infected. That drew the attention of his mother and subsequently his father too. No amount of explaining or apologizing seemed to work, and Joe had to swallow not one but two spoonfuls of castor oil, followed by a session with his father's heavy leather strap that left his bottom red and numb.

Dr. Winslow from the embassy gave him some antiseptic

cream for his hand, which took away the redness and the burning within a couple of days, but it was clear that there was going to be a scar.

His hand slowly improved, and so did the rift with his friends, although neither was quite as it had been before. Certainly, neither was fully healed on a cold November night just two weeks later: November 9, 1938.

Kristallnacht. The Night of Broken Glass.

I think there comes a time in every child's life
when you realize that your mother and father
are people, in addition to being your parents.
They have lives outside of the world they share
with you and which existed long before you did;
they have done things they would rather you did
not know about; they have secrets that are not
for your ears. It's then that you find out your
parents are not who you thought they were.
In my case, that's a colossal understatement.

—from the memoirs of Joseph "Katipo" St. George

5

KRISTALLNACHT

Wednesday, November 9, 1938

The sound of jackboots faded on the concrete steps outside the front door. Low echoes that rippled out into the night. The boy didn't move, he couldn't move; he stood frozen, rigid, except for the sobs that racked his chest. The Gestapo, and his father, were gone. They didn't even bother to close the front door.

From outside, a truck engine roared, then there was a flash of headlights before a fierce gust of wind howled down the street, grasping the door in its icy breath and sucking it back into its frame with a crash that shook the house.

His mother's hand came down gently on his shoulder. Her voice was steel. Calm, flat, and emotionless. "Joe, I need your help."

Why didn't you do something? Why didn't you stop them? Why didn't you scream at them? The boy said none of these things. He sucked back a sob and turned to face her.

"What do you need me to do?" he asked instead, as if she needed a hand with the housework.

She stared directly into his eyes, and this was suddenly not his mother talking. Not the same woman who had sung him to sleep when he was small and there was thunder. Not the same woman who had scolded him for traipsing muddy shoes across the parlor floor. This woman was icy, distant . . . mechanical almost.

She was *professional*, he thought, and wondered why that word had occurred to him.

"Joe, I need to do something, but I have to be sure I won't be interrupted," she said. "I need you to watch the street for me."

"What? How?"

His mother beckoned for him to follow her. She led him up the stairs—squeaking in all the usual places—and into the front bedroom, the one that looked out over the roadway. His parents' bedroom.

The lights were off, but when Joe reached for the switch, his mother's hand was already there and stopped him.

"Don't turn the lights on—and don't touch the curtains," she said in the same matter-of-fact voice. "That can be seen from the outside. Come and stand here."

Joe stood next to her. The heavy velvet drapes that covered the window were closed except for a small slit in the center. From where he stood, he could see a sliver of the street.

"Move slowly, very slowly, toward the window," his mother said. "Any quick movement will attract an eye. Stay a hand's width away from the drapes. That way, in this dark room you will be all but invisible. I need you to watch the street. There will be at least two men out there somewhere."

Joe looked. The street was empty, and he said so.

"No, it's not," his mother said. "Look more carefully."

Joe scanned the other side of the darkened street. The streetlights had gone off when the banging and the screaming had started across the city. A small park—more of a flower garden really—was surrounded by a low wooden fence. A tall tree, an oak, grew up through the cobblestones on the footpath, its branches spreading out across the fence into the park. He paid close attention to the tree, but could see nothing.

"Nobody," he said.

His mother moved alongside him in a long, slow, fluid movement. She said nothing, but stared intently out through the gap in the drapes for a long while before moving slightly to survey the other end of the street.

"There," she said after another long moment.

Joe looked. "Where?" he asked.

"At the edge of the house, the Werners' house—see where it meets the park, just to the left of their doorway."

Joe stared intently at the wall. "There's nobody there," he said.

"Follow the lines of the brickwork . . ." his mother said, "the mortar between the bricks. You can just make it out in this light."

Joe narrowed his eyes and found the tiny, thin smudge that was the mortar line between two rows of bricks. He traced it back to the left. It suddenly stopped. So did the row above it and the one above that.

By tracing the end of the mortar lines he found that he was staring at the shape of a person . . . A man, Joe thought, dressed in dark clothing, with his face covered. You could not actually see him, you could only deduce his presence by what was not visible behind him.

"I see him," Joe breathed.

"Good. Now watch him. There'll be others too—at least one. I need you to watch them without them seeing you. If they make any attempt to approach the house, I need you to do something—make some kind of loud noise—to alert me."

"I'll slam the bedroom door."

"Good."

"What are you going to do?"

"I have to make an important call," she said, and quietly, slowly, she moved away from the window.

Joe watched her walk down the upstairs hallway, past his room to the spare bedroom at the far end of the hall. She went in and shut the door. Joe turned back to the window.

Why had she gone in there? The telephone was in the hallway downstairs. And how did she know all this stuff anyway?

The black blob shape huddled against the brickwork of the house opposite moved slightly. Enough that he could discern the man's height. He was tall, and a hat made him appear taller again.

In Agent Troy's adventures the bad guys always hid behind a tree, or stood by a lamppost, but gave their position away by carelessly lighting up a cigarette. The reality, he now knew, was quite different.

He turned his attention back to the tree. Where was the second man his mother said would be there? He couldn't be behind the tree, as it was too close to the fence . . . And he wasn't beside the tree either, not that Joe could see anyway . . .

A tapping noise intruded from the back bedroom. An irregular pattern that he recognized immediately as Morse code. All good spies knew Morse code and Joe was learning it, but this was much too fast for him to comprehend. So that's what his mother had meant about an important call. The Morse key must be well hidden, Joe thought. He had been in that room many times and had never seen the slightest sign of it, or of any place it could be hidden.

Many things in this household were apparently not as they seemed on the surface.

A car was parked a few meters along from the tree, and he examined it carefully. Could the person be crouched behind it? Possibly. There was nobody in the car . . . He could see dimly through the windows to the paving behind, and . . .

There he was! The second man. He *was* in the car. But he was sitting in the rear seat, not the front seat, with his head back behind the window post. That was a trick that wasn't in any of Joe's books. The dark shape of the man's head moved slightly, confirming it.

On an impulse, Joe moved slowly away from his vantage point, then ran quickly along the hall to his own room. Twenty seconds later he was back in position, with the finderscope from his telescope clutched firmly in his left, unbandaged hand.

First he checked that the two men were still there. Keeping half an eye on the man by the wall, he brought the finderscope to his eye and focused in on the man in the car. It didn't help. In fact it made things a bit darker, but he kept the scope directed at where he knew the man's face would be.

The tapping sound continued from the back bedroom, and an explosion sounded in the distance to the east.

Finally came the sound he was waiting for.

A car turned the corner and yellow streaks of headlights illuminated the street.

For a moment he thought it was going to stop at their door, and he made ready to kick the bedroom door shut, the signal to his mother, but it just passed by.

For a long moment though, the headlights lit up the inside of the black car on the other side of the road, lit up the man's face in the dark circle of the finderscope. The focus was not perfect, but it was enough for Joe to be able to identify the man if he ever saw him again.

It was a thin face with sunken cheeks, not unlike Herr Goebbels, the Minister of Propaganda, but with a toothbrush mustache like Adolf Hitler. A scar ran from the man's forehead to his cheekbone across his left eye.

The image in the finderscope darkened as the car passed by.

The tapping had stopped now. A moment later his mother was back with him.

"Still there," Joe said, "and his friend is in the back seat of that car down there."

His mother took care to keep her distance from the drapes. "Well done."

"Did you get your message through?" Joe asked.

She looked at him for a moment before nodding.

"Good," Joe said. "So when will we see Father again?"

"Soon," his mother said, drawing him away from the window. "Soon."

But Joe knew she was lying.

6

THE DARK MEN

Thursday, November 10, 1938

On Thursday, the boy stayed at home. School was closed anyway because of all the violence and unrest of the previous night, but he wouldn't have gone even if it were open. He felt sick, and in a much deeper way than if he just had the flu or a stomachache. It was a sickness of his heart, a sense that the world had turned upside down and would never be the same again. An ache that he felt from his toes to the hairs on his scalp.

On Friday, however, at his mother's insistence, he did go to school. He'd had no intention of going and kicked at the walls and shouted when his mother said he must. At first his mother tried to hug him, to reassure him. But he wouldn't let her near, thrashing around like a cornered animal when she approached him. He knew he was being silly, but inside, the feelings were too overwhelming to deal with.

Eventually that cold steel look came over her face again, that *professional* look. Joe had ceased to be her child, her son, and instead had become a problem that had to be managed.

For some strange reason, that reassured him, and he calmed himself and listened carefully to what she said.

"Joe, I need to do some things today. I need to go to the embassy. There are letters to write and phone calls to make. Some of which I can't do from home."

He nodded his understanding. "But . . ."

"Joe, I can't leave you at home alone. There are bad people watching this place. I need you to be somewhere safe, and I think school is the safest place right now. If these—" She caught her breath and closed her eyes for a moment. Her hands were not steady. "If these people were to kidnap you, then I would be forced to cooperate with them in ways I do not want to cooperate. Do you understand?"

He did. She just had to explain it in logical terms like that, and it all made perfect sense. Besides, he reasoned, at least school would take his mind off things.

"Go and do what you have to do," Joe said quietly to his mother. "I'll go to school and I'll see you afterward."

"I'll pick you up from the gate myself," his mother said. "Do not leave the school with anyone else, even if they say I sent them. All right?"

Joe nodded his understanding again.

School was alive with rumors and stories, whispered in the corridors and relayed in hushed voices in the classrooms when the teacher's back was turned. Joe moved through the day in a daze. Hardly anyone spoke to him. News of his father's arrest had made it to the school and spread like a disease through its veins.

Only Klaus stood by him, which was brave of him. Klaus

didn't want to discuss the arrest, except to say, "Sorry about your father."

Jacob and Benjamin, the Rabinowitz twins, were missing from class. It was at morning break that Joe found out why.

He was sitting with Klaus on the floor of the corridor outside the music room. There were no music lessons on a Friday so this part of the hall was deserted, which suited Joe just fine. The corridors were long, dark places, with their dark floorboards and dark wooden paneling. They were lined with wooden pegs for schoolbags, coats, and caps, but where they sat, the pegs were empty except for an old lost sock that had never been claimed, and which now dangled sadly from the last peg on the row.

Joe was sitting the usual way, with his bottom on the floor. Klaus was standing on his head, his feet against the wall, his elbows making a V-shape around his head. Someone had told him that you don't blink when you are upside down and he was trying to test out this theory.

"Jacob and Benjamin's whole family was taken away last night," Klaus said. "They were stupid. Stupid Jews. They should have left Germany months ago. They knew they weren't wanted here."

"Where were they taken to?" Joe asked, thinking of his own father.

"Concentration camp," Klaus said. "They really should have got out before all this started. They could have, you know." He shifted his eyes to look at Joe. "It was their father's fault, if you ask me. Just because he had a good business here.

It was making money, so he didn't want to give it up."

Joe stared at the old sock on the wall. A small spider on a delicate thread dropped slowly down from the ceiling, near the sock, and he watched that for a while too.

Klaus continued, "Typical Jew. All they care about is money, you know."

"What's a concentration camp?" Joe asked.

"Just a camp," Klaus said. "They concentrate people into a place with others of the same kind. All the Jews go into one camp, and all the Romani into another. Like that."

"Is it like a prison?" Joe asked.

"Well, they're not allowed to leave, so I suppose in a way. But my uncle says they get plenty of food and water and games and exercise, so it's more like a holiday camp in some ways. He says it is the best thing for people like Jews because all the rest of Germany hates them, and at least in the concentration camps they will be safe."

Joe nodded. That didn't sound too bad, then. That was a bit of a relief, as he quite liked the Rabinowitz twins. They were soccer players too, and good goal-scorers. He wondered if his father was in a concentration camp. Probably not. He had been arrested, and so was probably in a prison somewhere.

His mind wandered as he watched the spider slowly make its way back up the shimmering thread. Maybe he could blow up the walls of the prison with a bomb and help him escape! Maybe that was what his mother was doing right now. No, he thought, she was probably doing exactly what she said she was going to do: write letters and make phone calls to try and get his father released.

"I learned a new swear word last night," Klaus said, changing the subject. "Dad said it to some Brownshirts who came into our street last night looking for Jews. They'd got lost."

"What is it?" Joe asked.

Klaus said, "I asked Hans what it meant on the way to school this morning." Hans was an older friend of Klaus who was in the Hitlerjugend.

"So, what is it?" Joe asked.

"It's really bad," Klaus said mock-seriously. "I'd get in trouble if a teacher heard me say it."

"But what is it?"

Klaus looked at him sideways. "I can't tell you, Joe. It's only for people who wear long pants."

Joe told him what he thought of him with a few choice swear words of his own.

The bell sounded for the end of morning break, and walking back to class, Joe thought to himself that the whole swear word business had just been a trick to take his mind off his problems. That was kind of Klaus, he thought. And it had worked. For a few moments anyway.

There was no news about his father that afternoon when his mother picked him up from school. She just shook her head, a single slow shake, and Joe didn't ask again.

They spent the evening just like any other evening. Joe did his homework before dinner, even though it was Friday and he would have the whole weekend to do it. Dinner was a huge affair, with pork bellies and sauerkraut and ice cream for dessert. His mother went to a lot of trouble for just two people, and Joe suspected it was her own way of taking her mind off things.

After dinner they sat together in the front parlor with the fire roaring. She passed the time crocheting a scarf. Joe read a book, forcing himself to concentrate on the pages. Word by word. Line by line.

It felt like just an ordinary evening, except for the regular glances that his mother made at the hallway. Where the telephone was.

Saturday passed slowly. His mother would not let him go out anywhere, and she didn't have to explain why. Sunday was more of the same, until well after bedtime.

The telephone rang, jolting Joe awake. He didn't have to look at the clock to know that it was quite late. After 11:00 p.m. at least.

He heard his mother stir in her room, but before she could get up, the ringing stopped. Just one single ring.

Strange, he thought.

The telephone rang again. Two rings this time, then stopped again.

His mother was at his bedroom door by the time the telephone rang for a third time. This time just one ring, then silence.

This was the professional mum, the cold steel mum, and she had a flashlight in her hand.

"Joe, we're leaving," she said with a dark urgency that chilled

Joe's soul. "Grab just what you can carry in your schoolbag, and get dressed. Don't turn on any lights."

"Why?" Joe asked, but she was already gone, back to her own room, and he heard the sounds of her drawers opening and closing.

He was dressed in moments—in his warmest clothes, as he felt that was going to be important. He emptied his schoolbag on the floor, not caring about the mess, and threw in a clean pair of underpants and an undershirt.

What else should he take? he wondered. The telescope, of course, but that wouldn't fit. He unclipped the finderscope and put that in instead. Six of his favorite tin soldiers followed, and *Hutchinson's Adventure-Story Magazine.*

Socks, he had forgotten clean socks. He found some and laid them on top of the finderscope in case it got bumped.

Blondie snuffled at him from her basket, and his heart suddenly froze. He couldn't take Blondie, could he? But surely she didn't expect him to leave the puppy behind.

"Come on, Blondie," he whispered, and she trotted over to where he stood.

He looked around his bedroom but couldn't see anything else he couldn't leave behind. Except for his soccer ball of course. He tucked it under one arm and quietly joined his mother in the front bedroom.

As quick as he had been, she had been quicker. She was fully dressed, wearing her warmest coat, and had a small suitcase in one hand. She was standing by the drapes, gazing intently outside.

"What is going on?" Joe asked, although he already had a pretty good idea.

"Downstairs," his mother ordered. "Now. If there's any room left in your bag, fill it up with biscuits, or dried beef from the pantry. Nothing perishable. Wait for me in the scullery." Then almost as an afterthought, she answered his question. "The Gestapo are coming to arrest me tonight. We can't let that happen."

In the scullery, Joe found Blondie's leash and fastened it around the leg of the table, clipping the other end onto her collar. She whimpered, realizing that something was not right, and he patted her head softly.

He found a pencil and a sheet of paper and left a quick note for Klaus, then he moved near the back door and waited.

It was when his mother joined him in the scullery that she noticed the soccer ball. "Leave the ball, Joe," she said.

"No, I'm taking it," Joe said. "I'm not leaving it." It was hard enough to leave Blondie behind. He wasn't leaving the soccer ball too.

"You're leaving it," she said.

"They'll be looking for us, but they won't suspect a boy carrying a soccer ball, will they?" Joe reasoned. "Nobody on the run would be carrying a soccer ball." He stared at his mother in the dim light of the pantry and thought he detected surprise, and possibly a little pride among the concern on her face.

"You're right, Joe," she said. "Good idea. Now wrap your scarf around your face like this and pull your cap down as low as you can."

She showed him, wrapping her own scarf around her face so that only her eyes were visible. In the dark of the night, they would be like ghosts.

"What are we waiting for?" he asked, but even as the words left his mouth, it became suddenly clear. A diversion.

A car engine sounded from the front of the house, revving, roaring, racing along the narrow lane. Then came a series of flat bangs that Joe instinctively knew were gunshots. There were answering gunshots too, and he thought of the dark men huddled against the wall and in the black car.

From the back of the house, footsteps sounded, running, and he knew that there were men out there also, running now toward the front of the house. His mother waited a second or so longer until the running footsteps had faded, then quickly unlocked the scullery door and they slipped out into the darkness.

It was cold, bitterly cold. That was the first thing Joe noticed. His breath hung in white clouds in the air in front of him, and his skin stung from the tiny icy needles in the air. It wasn't as dark as he had expected. That was the second thing he noticed. There was a dull, yellowish glow from a lamppost at the end of the service lane. The third thing he noticed was the man in the black leather trench coat, a fedora hat pulled low over his eyes, who detached himself from the wall of the alleyway to intercept them.

There was just enough light in the alleyway for Joe to make out that one of his hands was in his pocket and the other was rising up in a "halt" sign.

"Stop—" the man began, but that was all he got out before Joe's mother shot him.

It took Joe a long moment to work out what had happened.

He'd seen out of the corner of his eye his mother's hand coming up toward the man's chest, then the lightning-bright flash from the end of her fingers and the clap of thunder that made him jump, but it was such an unthinkable occurrence that he could not believe it was a gun until the man fell down.

It was nothing like the Hopalong Cassidy Western movies that he loved. Nothing like the descriptions in *Detective Yarns.* The man didn't go flying backward with his arms flailing. He didn't say anything. His body just shuddered once as the bullet entered his chest, convulsed, and dropped in a small heap where he had been standing.

"Come on, Joe," his mother said firmly, "They will have heard that."

They stepped over the body, where it had fallen on the concrete path, and began to run through the service alleyway behind the houses.

Joe looked back once, the sound of the gun still crashing in his ears, to see an accusing finger of inky liquid reaching down the path from the body toward them.

He clutched his soccer ball tightly and ran with his mother.

They reached the end of the service alley, and his mother stopped running. They were on the road now, and running would attract attention, so they walked—briskly, but still a walk. After twenty or thirty meters they turned into another service alley behind another row of houses. Joe found he was sweating despite the cold night air. It was uncomfortable; it made him damp inside the thick woolen clothing and he knew it would make him feel colder later, when they stopped.

They turned again, into another street, and so it continued for the next half an hour, moving, turning, moving again in a process his mother called "quartering." The aim, she told him, was to put the maximum distance between them and the house without moving in a straight line.

Several times cars traversed the street they were on, but the headlights gave them plenty of warning and they would flatten themselves into a doorway or behind a hedge until the car had passed.

One car passed slowly, a bright flashlight shining from the rear window. That was a Gestapo car for sure. He tucked himself into a tight, dark ball behind a small shrub as that car passed. His mother, just ahead of him, flattened herself on the grass of a small garden, turning her face away from the road. "Don't breathe!" she whispered harshly, and Joe sucked in his breath to avoid exhaling the white mist that would shine in the flashlight's beam and give away their position. His mother became nothing but a shapeless mass on the ground, and the car passed without incident.

They avoided the wide swathes of the main roads and kept as much as possible to the smaller back roads and alleys. Minutes became half an hour, and that turned into an hour.

The progress was slow with the constant need to duck and dive for cover, along with the indirect route they were taking . . . to where? Joe was not sure.

They stopped at the end of Verbenastrasse and peered

carefully from behind a thicket of head-high shrubs that decorated the corner of a group of townhouses.

His mother hesitated, and even Joe's untrained eye could see the danger. It was a long, straight street with no side roads or alleyways to duck into. The houses were narrow townhouses built in long rows fronting onto the street, with no gardens or shrubs to hide behind. Once they entered the street they would be in a long shooting gallery until they reached Vaderhoffestrasse at the end. There would be no place to hide, and no escape.

But there was no alternative, so, after checking carefully both ways down the street, Joe's mother grabbed his hand and stepped out onto the footpath. There was no caution, no furtive scurrying in her movements. Having committed to the action, she took it boldly, striding rapidly down the street in an effort to get out of the rattrap quickly.

A curtain moved slightly in a window, and Joe had the sense that, despite the late hour, the street was awake, alive, watching them as they hurried toward safety and freedom. He hoped that whoever was watching would not alert the Gestapo, but he suspected not. Everybody was afraid of the Gestapo.

There were perhaps two or three hundred meters to the end of the street, and fifty of those slipped by before Joe knew it. Nerves started to set in after that as he realized just how exposed they were. All it would take was just one patrol, just one car to turn into the street, and they would be lost.

As if confirming his fears, from the far end of the street ahead of them came the sound of truck engines and bright lights appeared.

Joe and his mother froze, watching as the trucks maneuvered into a roadblock.

His mother's hand was on his arm, but Joe had already stopped. The headlights of the trucks were pointing sideways and the light was not strong enough to reach them, but the way ahead was now completely blocked.

Slowly, very slowly, they turned, lest a sudden movement attract the eye of the soldiers. In step, they began to retrace their footsteps toward the other end of the street.

More lights. More noise. This time from a group of soldiers on foot, talking and searching the street with flashlights.

Joe froze and sensed his mother's rigidity beside him. To the left and right the high frontages of the tightly packed brick houses rose like the walls of a prison. Behind them the lights of the roadblock beckoned them, like a flame attracts a moth.

And in front of them, the sound of the boots and the waving torches spelled doom.

Joe's mother hesitated, for the first time indecisive, and Joe felt her fear.

She drew him back a few steps, then up a small block of steps into a recessed doorway.

It wouldn't help. The searchers were scanning the doorways with their flashlights as they passed each one. Desperately Joe looked up and down the street. From the roadblock at one end to the searchers at the other. There was no way out.

He looked across the street, but the houses on that side of the road were identical in their short flight of steps leading to a recessed doorway. There were no gaps between the houses. There was nowhere to hide.

He gripped his mother's arm tightly, suddenly terrified for the first time. What would the Gestapo do to his mother? What would they do to him? Visions of torture and death appeared to him, and it no longer seemed like a big game.

"Stay very still and cover your face completely," his mother whispered. "There's a chance they won't notice us."

There was no chance of that, Joe knew; his mother was just trying to calm him.

The searchers grew closer. Joe could hear the tromp of their boots on the cobbles of the street. He shuddered.

The searchers were only a few houses away now, flashlights blazing into doorways. Not even a rat would escape their inspection. And that's what he and his mother were. Rats, caught in a giant rattrap that was just about to spring shut.

Two houses to go, and there was a soft click behind them. He stifled a cry, just in time, then there was a gentle hand on the back of his collar, drawing him back.

The door snicked quietly shut in front of him, and they were standing in the entrance parlor of one of the long, thin houses. An elderly woman stood with them, one gnarled finger raised to her lips. Thin and sinewy, her skin had deep crevices that showed in the dim light that crawled in from a rear room. The sound of boots grew closer, and the crack of the doorway glowed for a moment, framing the door in a thin line of fire.

The glow faded, and the boots passed. A moment or two passed in silence.

Joe began to speak, but his mother's finger touched itself to his lips. She put a hand to her ear, and Joe understood immediately. He strained his ears but could hear nothing.

He bent and put his eye to the keyhole of the door. He could just make out the road, and the houses on the opposite side of the street, and there . . . He recoiled suddenly as a dark shape passed in front of his eye. There was another man, following the search team. A dark man in black clothing. A man who traveled in darkness and silence behind the noise and bright lights to catch the hunted when they emerged from hiding, thinking they were safe.

The old lady motioned them toward the rear of the house, not uttering a sound. They passed a small table decorated with candles, and a large Star of David was mounted on the wall above it.

A small passage led them to a scullery and a boiler room with an outside door, which she opened cautiously.

"Thank you," Joe's mother whispered, but the lady shook her head and gestured again at the open door. They were to go now. The lady had risked enough already.

They made their way down a short flight of wooden steps into a courtyard shared with a house on the next street over. The rear door of the other house was already ajar, just a fraction, and they pushed it open cautiously.

A young man silently greeted them and led them through another winding, narrow house to the front door.

"Eighty-three," he said, pointing across the street.

The number was embossed on the door of the house across

the road in bold brass letters. That door also opened as they swiftly but cautiously crossed the road, and they slipped inside.

For a while they traversed the streets of Berlin in this manner. Sideways across the streets, in through front doors and out through courtyards or cellars. From street to street to alleyway they hopped, as the marching boots and bright lights of the searchers cut swathes down the length of the streets just behind them.

Occasionally they saw cars crossing at intersections, and once they were nearly surprised by a dark car with no lights, cruising quietly along the street in front of them, but ducked into the waiting doorway just in time.

At the last house, a young couple led them quickly to the back door, and actually embraced them both, before pointing them down the street in the direction of the city center. There were no more open, welcoming doors after that, but by now they were well beyond even the widening scope of the search.

Eventually they reached a small retail district, deserted at this time of night. His mother led them around the back of a block of shops. She had a key that opened a small courtyard. Another key opened the rear door of one of the shops.

"We'll be safe here," she said, and Joe for the first time noticed the fatigue in her voice. "There is a small apartment upstairs. We'll stay here tonight and make for the train station in the morning."

Joe was too exhausted to ask any questions about that. A clock on the wall told him that it was nearly one.

There were two hard flat mattresses on the floor of the

upstairs apartment, and he gratefully laid himself down on one, took off his coat, cap, and scarf, then spread his coat over himself like a blanket, and drifted into an unsettled sleep in which he dreamed, over and over, of a bright flash of light, a clap of thunder, and inky liquid on the path . . . pointing at him like an accusing finger.

His mother was already up when he awoke. The sounds of her moving about had not disturbed him, which was unusual and showed how tired and deeply asleep he must have been.

She was seated in a wicker chair by a small desk, watching him. This was the mother he knew. The loving woman who had made his breakfasts and bandaged his knees when he skinned them. Who had cradled him through sickness and marveled at the paintings he brought back from school. When she saw he was awake though, the cold professional was suddenly back.

"The shop opens at nine," she said. "We'll leave then. For now, have something to eat. You will need the strength."

She crossed to the window as he took a couple of biscuits from his schoolbag and crunched them dryly.

"It's raining," she said quietly. "That's good."

Joe wondered why it was good as she moved back to her suitcase and opened it. On the top were two small black umbrellas.

"Here," she said, handing him one.

Joe looked at the umbrella closely. It seemed very ordinary, and he wondered about its secrets. Secret Agent Troy had a lot of amazing gadgets like knives and guns concealed in everyday objects such as umbrellas.

He opened it and examined the inside of the fabric but could see nothing.

"What does it do?" he asked.

His mother gave him a strange look. "It's an umbrella; it keeps you dry," she said. "It's raining outside."

"But doesn't it, you know, do something else?" Joe insisted.

"Like what, for example?"

"Fire bullets?"

She laughed. "I think you've been reading too many books. It's just an umbrella." Then she relented a little, shrugged, and said, "But there are ways to use an umbrella."

Joe nodded eagerly. She came and took the umbrella, holding it up just in front of him.

"Look at the shaft," she said. "What do you see?"

"Just a metal shaft," Joe replied, puzzled.

"But it's shiny, right, and it's a good, thick, old-fashioned shaft—so look at it again and tell me what you see."

He looked, and suddenly realized what she meant. "I can see behind me. It's like looking in a mirror. A curved mirror."

She nodded. "If someone is following you, you will be able to spot them, without turning around, or looking in shop windows, or any of the other things that would let a watcher know that you are worried about being followed. But there's more."

"Bullets?" Joe said eagerly, but she laughed again, a little deliberately he thought.

"Let's say you see a Gestapo or SS officer standing nearby. All you need to do is to tilt the umbrella slightly toward them. Just a little. Just until you can't see their face. If you can't see their face, then they can't see your face. It is the ideal disguise, because it isn't a disguise."

Joe practiced, tilting the umbrella until he could not see his mother's face.

"Anything else?" he asked, and could tell by her hesitation that there was something. "What? Tell me."

She still hesitated, but eventually said, "There is one thing. You're not trained to use this, so I shouldn't show you."

"What?"

"All right. Look at the end of the umbrella, the tip."

Joe looked but could see nothing odd. It was an ordinary wooden umbrella tip. He said so.

"It's not wood. It is ceramic, painted to look like wood."

"Why?"

"I'm getting to that. Inside the ceramic tip is a sharp pointed blade."

So there *was* a knife hidden in the umbrella! Joe caught his breath.

"To use it, you just crack the end of the umbrella sharply on the ground. That will smash the ceramic cover and leave just the blade. But you have to know how to use it."

"I'll cut their throats!" Joe said in a harsh whisper. "I'll stab them in the heart!"

"No, you won't!" his mother said firmly. "That is the very last thing you will do."

She took the umbrella from him, folded it closed, and showed him how to hold it in a two-handed grip.

"If a Gestapo officer stops you, and you need to escape, you crack the tip, then stab the man in the upper thigh. Here." She touched the tip of the umbrella lightly on his leg. "He will defend his face and his upper body with his hands, because that's what he will be expecting. But he won't expect you to attack his legs. You stab, then twist, like this," she said as she showed him. "Then you run. I don't care what you've read in your books or seen in the movies. If you stab a man in the thigh and twist the blade, I promise you he won't be running after you."

Joe nodded silently, awestruck. He had known this woman his entire life, and yet he knew nothing about her. It was a terrifying thing to realize.

"When we leave the shop, we will be pairing," she said. "That means we will be traveling together, but apart. We will keep in sight of each other at all times, but to any observer we will be two separate travelers, not a mother and child traveling together. Here . . ."

She rummaged for a moment in the suitcase and came up with a pair of glasses. "Here, put these on. They will make it harder for anyone to recognize you."

She found a dark-haired wig in the suitcase and put it on, completely covering her own blond hair. She carefully combed it and then pushed two flat rubbery-looking objects into her mouth. They pushed her cheeks out a little, changing the shape of her face. Two small, quick things, Joe thought, but only someone who knew her well would recognize her at a quick glance.

From down the stairs came the sound of a key in a lock.

"You can do this," his mother said reassuringly.

"I know," Joe replied, hoping it was true.

The shop owner was a tall, balding man with a long mustache combed and waxed into a Prussian style. He wore a smart woolen jacket and a tired expression. He appeared at the top of the staircase and handed Joe's mother a thick brown envelope, then disappeared just as quickly back down into the shop.

Joe's mother opened it and handed Joe a passport.

He examined it. It was a photo of him, but to his surprise he was wearing glasses—the exact glasses his mother had handed him a moment ago. He couldn't ever remember a photo like that being taken. His name, he read, was now John Graham. He was fourteen years old and American.

"How did—" he began, but his mother cut him off.

"Don't worry about it now," she said. "I'll explain later. You have been staying with your aunt in Berlin and are traveling back to your parents in Frankfurt." She gave him a letter addressed to his parents from his aunt. He read it carefully, memorizing the names without having to be asked.

"You've been in Germany for less than a year, and you don't speak the language very well. Remember that, it can be quite useful not to understand what they are asking you."

Joe looked again at the bespectacled photograph of himself and slowly shook his head in amazement.

They descended into the shop together. The balding man with the big mustache pretended to show Joe's mother a pair of brightly colored pumps, then held the door open for her as she left. A moment later Joe followed, opening his umbrella as soon as he was outside the shop.

The rain was light. Just enough to justify the umbrella. He practiced looking for tails and hiding his face with the umbrella as he slowly followed his mother toward the Lehrter Bahnhof, the central Berlin train station.

When I look back now, I think it was at the train station that I first started to realize that I had what it took to be a spy. I don't mean clever or brave. I mean heartless and ruthless.

—from the memoirs of Joseph "Katipo" St. George

7

RUN RABBIT RUN

Monday, November 14, 1938

The boy followed the woman through the crowded streets of central Berlin, toward the train station. An unremarkable boy. An ordinary woman. Both carried umbrellas, but that too was unremarkable with the ever-present threat of rain. The pavements were crowded. Morning shoppers, businessmen, and uniformed soldiers mingled in the morning mists of the city.

It was cold. The kind of chill that came in the late autumn when the air was moist and the wind was brisk, finding its way through chinks and gaps in Joe's overcoat and scarf. His knees stung from the cold and he wished again that he were a little older and allowed to wear long trousers.

Still, as long as he kept moving, the blood kept flowing and the cold remained nothing more than pins and needles pricking at his skin.

It was a strange feeling, moving among all the normal people. People with jobs to go to and groceries to buy. People whose biggest problem was whether the food market would be out of eggs.

Did any of them have a father who had just been arrested by the Nazi's secret police? Were any of them running for their lives? He thought not, and looking at their faces—calm, impassive, unemotional—he tried to emulate their thoughts and feelings, to project the same air of indifference.

As they turned the corner into Scharnhorststrasse, his mother stopped and examined some fruit in a wooden case outside a shop. Joe kept walking and saw, in the shaft of his umbrella, that she fell in behind him as soon as he was a few meters past.

Together, but alone. "Pairing" she had called it. A pair of travelers, not a couple.

He changed his soccer ball from one arm to the other and stepped onto the street for a moment to get around a lady pushing a pram.

There was an urgent blare from a truck horn, and he stepped back onto the footpath as an army truck whooshed past, close to the curb. A spray of dirty water dampened his bare legs and trickled down into his socks. Idiot, he thought. He was supposed to be alert and aware of his surroundings, and he had the umbrella to help. There was no excuse for what had just happened. If he had been hit, even if mildly injured, then their escape would've almost certainly been over.

He knew his mother would be disappointed in him, and he forced himself to focus on what he was doing. He stopped for a moment, pretending to check his shoelace, and let his mother take the lead once again. She turned the corner of Scharnhorststrasse into Invalidenstrasse, and now, straight ahead, he could see the huge curved roof of Berlin's central station, Lehrter Bahnhof.

• • •

A Mercedes-Benz saloon car pulled to a halt in one of the bus stands outside the train station. Two identical cars pulled up behind it. A bus driver, blocked from the bus stop, raised his hand to sound his horn, but then saw the black coats and the red armbands on the men who emerged from the cars and thought better of it.

A tall boy was with the men. He had black hair and long trousers. He seemed reluctant to be there, and one of the men kept a firm hand on his arm as they moved briskly into the covered hall that led into the station.

Joe's mother arrived at the gates to the platform just a few people in front of Joe. She passed without incident, but the guard wanted to check Joe's documents a second time. He was an elderly man in an ill-fitting uniform, with a few wisps of straggly gray hair leaking from under his hat.

"American?" he said twice, despite Joe nodding each time.

You don't speak German well, Joe told himself. And your papers are in order. There is nothing to worry about here.

"Why do you carry the soccer ball?" the man asked. "American boys play baseball, don't they?"

Joe grinned, as innocently as he could manage and tried his best to mimic the rolling vowels and throaty *r*'s of the Americans he had met, while mangling the German language. "No, no, I loving for the soccer ball."

"Really," the man asked. "Who is your favorite player?"

"Fritz Szepan," Joe replied automatically, and regretted it at once as the man's eyes narrowed.

"American, you say, but your favorite player is the German captain?"

Joe fought a rising panic and said quickly, "Szepan is best most player in world! Famous to California from New York."

The man smiled, revealing crooked and missing teeth. "World famous he is! The best player in the world. This is true. The Hungarians, the Italians, pah!" He all but spat on the ground. "We would have the World Cup if not for Austria."

Joe nodded. Germany had annexed Austria eight months before. After that, the German coach had been required to include five Austrian players on their World Cup team. Germany hadn't made it past the first round.

"I think Germany played against both Switzerland and Austria that day," Joe said, forgetting to mangle his German, but the man didn't notice.

"An American who understands soccer!" Now it seemed they were great friends.

There was a cough from behind Joe, and the old guard quickly handed back his papers and waved him through saying, "One day America perhaps? You will play in the World Cup?"

Joe just laughed and kept moving. He was glad he had brought the soccer ball. Already it was bringing him luck.

His ticket said platform three, but that was currently deserted—of trains, at least. There was a train on one of the other platforms that appeared nearly ready to depart, but on his platform the people waiting to board milled around in small circles, talking quietly in groups or just standing silently.

Here and there were mothers with children; everywhere

there were soldiers in the gray-green uniform of the Wehrmacht, the German army.

He had lost sight of his mother in the kerfuffle at the gate but saw her standing with a tall businessman, a cheerful-looking fellow with a double chin and a protruding belly. She was laughing at something he was saying. Looking at the way he was standing, and the way she was responding to him, it was clear that the man found her quite attractive, and that she was inviting the attention.

It made Joe feel quite uncomfortable, with his father gone for just a few days, even though he understood the game she was playing. The Gestapo were looking for a blond woman with a young boy, not a brown-haired woman traveling with a fat man.

It was all about appearances.

He had been inside the train station before, but each time it filled him with awe. It was a huge structure, with a high, rounded roof—so high that the steam and smoke from the train engines could billow up and dissipate without choking the passengers. The roof was crisscrossed with thousands of massive beams, grimy and blackened from years of locomotives. The overall effect was like that of a long, dark tunnel, at the end of which the entrance glared like the sun itself, despite the gloom and persistent rain outside.

The walls were made up of hundreds of brick pillars, each with a huge electric lamp set well above head height. At this time of the day they were not needed, as large arched windows ran the length of the station on both sides.

The odd feeling was back, as if he were acting a part in a play—which in a way he was. He was playing the part of a boy who had been visiting his aunt, and was heading home to loving parents and a warm fire, and probably American hot dogs and Coca-Cola to drink. He dwelled on that thought for a moment, partly to try and make it real in his mind, in case he got questioned, and partly because it was so much more appealing than the reality.

A young soldier and his girl crossed in front of him, arm in arm, giggling over some intimate joke. He wondered what their story was. Everybody had a story. Perhaps they were childhood friends who had grown up together, never knowing their true feelings for each other until he was called up to the army. When he returned, would she be waiting, or would she have run off with his best friend . . . er . . . Wolfgang, whose father was the mayor of the small town they lived in?

Joe smiled inwardly. Everybody *did* have a story, and it was a good game to play, to keep his mind off his own.

A family appeared on the platform beside him, hustling and bustling with a huge load of suitcases. They made a small mountain of the cases in the center of the platform and stood in a line in front of them, waiting, like everyone else, for the train to arrive.

There were three children, a boy about Joe's age and two older sisters. The parents had that harried, browbeaten look that Joe had seen many times, which came from trying to organize a family on a long trip. The mother was brushing at her hair with one hand, trying to tame some wild curls that kept escaping from her headscarf. The father tugged subconsciously at his tie, loosening it, then retightening it with a slightly puzzled expression as though he couldn't understand how it had come loose.

The two sisters, both in their teens, were studying a handsome young sailor in the uniform of the U-boat service and giggling behind their hands, saying things that Joe could only guess at.

The boy glanced a couple of times at Joe's soccer ball, then looked at him and smiled. Joe smiled back. The boy had happy eyes. There was a quick sparkle to them that told whole stories about his harried parents and giggling sisters. *Look what I have to put up with!*

On impulse Joe dropped the soccer ball onto one toe and lobbed it in the boy's direction. The boy trapped it deftly and returned it with a rather flashy around-the-leg pass.

Joe trapped the ball and flicked it into the air, heading it back to the boy. That got the attention of the boy's parents, who gave him a disapproving stare. The boy ignored them, caught the ball, and bounced it off his knees a few times before dropping it and rolling it across the floor to Joe. Joe flicked it up again with his toe, caught it, and tucked it back under his arm. Best not to draw too much notice to himself.

He wandered over to the boy and asked in his purposefully bad German, "Who for do you play?"

"B-B-B . . ." The boy with the happy eyes stammered, stopped, took a breath and tried again.

"B-Berlin West Rangers," he said.

"Hah." Joe laughed. "St. Andreas Knights. We beating semi-finals you last year!"

"Only because the r-r-r-ref had lost his sp-sp-sp-spectacles," the boy responded immediately.

"But for the linemans who were cousins from your coach," Joe shot back.

The boy grinned.

Joe stuck out a hand and the boy shook it.

"Jo . . . hn Graham," Joe said with only a slight pause.

"M-M-Max Schell," the boy said, and started to say something else but it was lost in the shriek of a train whistle as a locomotive pulled into the opposite platform, a dense cloud of smoke puffing up into the domed ceiling of the station.

Even before the train had stopped, there was another whistle and a second train appeared from the opposite direction, the locomotive wheezing alongside Joe's platform in a blast of smoke, steam, and the squealing symphony of its brakes.

The boy's family started to organize their cases, and Joe stayed with them. There was no harm in appearing to be part of a large family, he decided.

The train pulled to a halt and a flood of humanity emerged. People of every shape and size, from ruddy-faced farming women to elegant ladies, from gritty-fingered laborers to smartly suited businessmen, all hurrying to places they had to be, on the other side of the low metal fence that separated the disembarking passengers from the embarking passengers.

The dim doors of the train beckoned to him. Within their

shadows lay the promise of freedom. Of more and more miles between him and the Gestapo.

The last few stragglers appeared, an elderly woman in an old wooden wheelchair, escorted by a nurse and a man in a dark suit.

Just a few more seconds, Joe thought. He forced himself to breathe slowly and calmly. And then it all went wrong.

From nowhere appeared a small group of Gestapo officers, instantly recognizable in their long black leather coats and red armbands, standing in a small group at the end of the boarding fence, where the passengers had to pass to get on the train.

"What's going on?" Joe heard Max's mother ask.

"Gestapo inspection," Max's father replied. "Looks like they're checking everybody's papers before letting them board. Probably routine."

On the other platforms Joe could see similar groups of Gestapo men doing the same for the other trains.

Around him everybody looked suddenly nervous, and he wondered how many other people had something to hide. He supposed it was just general edginess about the inspection and the presence of the Gestapo.

Joe himself was terrified and trying his best not to show it. A Gestapo inspection! Surely it was him and his mother they were looking for. He kept breathing deeply to calm himself. He had good papers, a passport, and a cover story. Besides, he reasoned, they wouldn't have a decent photo of him, so they wouldn't know what he looked like.

That thought cheered him a little, and he straightened his

shoulders and tried to look as much as he could like part of Max's family.

Way ahead of him in the line he saw his mother, now arm in arm with the fat businessman, slowly approaching the Gestapo checkpoint. It was hard to believe this was the same woman who would not let him call his dog Betty, because she didn't approve of Betty Grable.

He looked a little farther ahead and saw with shock, and rising horror, the sunken-cheeked face and the thin mustache of the man who had been in the car outside his house. Worse, standing next to him was Joe's best friend, his blood brother, Klaus Bormann.

His mother edged behind someone else in the line, hiding her face. Clearly she too had seen Klaus. If Klaus was here, with the Gestapo, there could be only one explanation. It was because he could identify them.

Joe desperately looked around for a way out. If they ran for it, they would be chased and caught. If they reached the inspection point, they would be recognized and caught.

He thought desperately for a moment, and then it came to him. Just like the other night at his house. What they needed was a diversion.

He tapped Max on the shoulder and held up the soccer ball and his umbrella. "Would be you holding these for me? I need going to toilet."

"Of c-course," said the boy with the happy eyes.

There were still plenty of disembarking passengers milling around on the platform. Joe took advantage of a small bit of cover provided by a group of workmen in grimy coveralls and slipped across to the gentlemen's toilet near the newsstand.

He peered cautiously from around the side of the pillar by the newsstand. The front of the stand was covered in newspapers. Just off to one side was a trash bin, and in that, among other assorted litter, was a discarded newspaper.

He inched forward until he could just see the owner through a small crack in the wooden side of his stall. The man was focused on the Gestapo inspection, not paying any attention to his stand.

Joe stretched out a steady hand to a small pile of matchboxes, lined up next to a display of French cigarettes. With slow, small movements that would not attract the owner's eye, he slid a box off the top of the pile and secreted it in his palm.

With his toe, he slowly shuffled the trash bin to one side, edging it closer to the front of the stand. It made a low, scraping sound, but that was easily muffled in the hissing and blowing sounds that came from the three trains waiting to depart.

He extracted a single match from the box and tossed the rest into the bin. With a quick check around to make sure no one was watching, he struck the match on the wooden side of the stall, cupping his hand to conceal the small glow, and when he was sure it was well alight, he dropped it into the trash bin.

It landed on a crumpled piece of paper and some discarded train tickets and began to slowly spread.

Joe shuffled sideways away from the stand and glanced over at the inspection point. His mother was just four people in the line away from Klaus and the Gestapo man.

He dared not turn around to look at the newsstand, but there were no shouts, no screams. Nothing. Perhaps it had just petered out.

Joe shut his eyes for a moment, feeling sick and faint. What would he do if she got caught? Run for it? If they found her, they would know he was there somewhere too.

Perhaps if he . . .

The whoosh and the roar from behind him exceeded his wildest expectations. Joe looked—he couldn't help himself. Everybody looked.

The fire in the trash bin must have hit the discarded newspaper and that had gone up in a sheet of flames, licking at the newspapers on the front of the stand, which had burst into a nice little inferno.

There were shouts and screams from the passengers and the owner himself ran around the front of the stand, waving his hands at the flames as if that would do anything.

The elderly guard who had quizzed Joe about the soccer ball appeared at a rapid lurch carrying a bucket of sand, which did little to stop the conflagration.

The trainmasters' whistles sounded the all-aboard and the engines started to huff as they built up a head of steam. Clearly the first priority, in the case of fire, was to get the trains clear of the station.

If the fire created a small panic, the whistles created pandemonium.

Embarking passengers began climbing over—even hurdling—the embarkation fence, running toward the trains.

Disembarking passengers who had not yet found their way off the platform began running for the exits. Somehow everybody managed to get in everybody else's way, and the resulting muddle was a riot of confusion and noise.

Joe started running for the train, which had already begun to move, keeping one eye on Klaus. He ran between groups of individuals, trying to keep as many people as possible between himself and the checkpoint.

The Gestapo officer now had a pistol out and was waving it futilely in the air.

Joe took another step toward the train, his eyes on Klaus, and collided with someone. It had no impact on the mass of flesh in a tight blue dress that ran into him, but it sent Joe flying. His schoolbag slipped from his shoulder and went sliding across the floor, while Joe hit the ground hard in the opposite direction.

Feet were all around him now, and when he tried to get up, a knee collected him in the side of his head, knocking him back down. Somebody trod on his leg, and he yelped.

Finally a small gap in the traffic allowed him to get back on his feet, and he scrabbled after his schoolbag.

It got kicked out of his reach, but on the second go he got a hand around one of the straps and hauled it back close to his body.

Around him the maelstrom continued as people, unable to get out of the gates because of the crush of people there, headed back in the opposite direction, looking for another exit.

Joe darted through a small gap between two heavy-suited

businessmen, running like schoolboys, and hurdled the fence without slowing.

There were fewer people on this side of the barrier, most of them now having boarded the train. Still a few people darted here and there, either trying to board, or just running in circles as some people do when they are scared and confused.

Open doors beckoned from several of the carriages, and Joe ran toward the nearest. The train was starting to gather speed now though, and in running to keep up with it, Joe found himself running directly toward Klaus and the Gestapo man who were now standing at the head of the platform.

Their attention was on the milling crowd and the fire, which still blazed away nicely against the wall of the station, but Joe knew that any second they could glance around and there he would be, running straight into the embrace of the secret police.

He put on a burst of speed and reached the doorway of a carriage. The train was faster again now, and he needed every ounce of speed just to keep up with it.

He tossed his bag through the doorway and leapt after it. His fingers scrabbled for a handhold, and his body slipped backward, his feet dangling out of the doorway, his shoes scraping along the rough concrete of the platform.

His fingers slipped again and the drag on his feet hauled him backward as if the platform were unwilling to let him go.

One hand came loose and he spun around, desperately clinging to a small metal ridge with his other hand, watching helplessly as he was dragged closer to Klaus and the Gestapo officer, their eyes, fortunately, still fixed on the blazing fire.

Then his other hand slipped, and he braced himself for the impact with the platform, but he did not fall, his wrist caught in a vicelike grip.

He felt himself being hauled bodily into the train and tucked his feet up into the doorway just as the outside wall of the platform flashed past and the train jolted out of the station.

Joe scrambled to his feet in the shuddering doorway of the train and looked up to see who his savior had been.

"If you hadn't m-m-made it, I was going to keep your s-s-soccer ball!" said the boy with the happy eyes.

BOOK TWO

LONDON

I was in Paris for only a couple of hours and, to my dismay, never got to see the Eiffel Tower. (I would see it a few years later, but under far more dangerous circumstances.)

I did get to see some landmarks in London, but only for a few days, before my mother shipped me off to live with her relatives in New Zealand.

New Zealand was everything I expected it to be, and nothing like I expected it to be. I had left the country when I was just three, and my memories of it were vague, to say the least. It was a wild, untamed country in those days. At least compared to the sophistication of London and Berlin.

My new home was a sheep farm near a country town called Masterton. I grew up on that farm. In every possible way. As I lost my childish innocence, so did the world. The threat of war loomed like a huge dark wave and then broke over us with a horrifying thunder. Poland, Denmark, and Norway fell quickly. The Netherlands, Belgium, and France were next in the German sights.

The British government seemed ineffectual and their prime minister, Neville Chamberlain, nothing but a lame duck, according to my uncle Jack.

I have three overriding memories of my time back home in New Zealand as the war slowly spread its tentacles across Europe.

The first is of my terrible, terrible yearning to be back there, to get into the war any way I could. To be "doing my part" to defeat the Nazis.

The second was my heartache at being so far away from my mother, and having no idea whether my father was dead or alive, or being tortured in some Gestapo dungeon.

My third memory is of Millicent Jackson's lips. In fact, I don't think it is overstating the truth to say that the world as we know it today was very nearly a vastly different place because of Millicent Jackson's lips.

—from the memoirs of Joseph "Katipo" St. George

8

U-BOAT

North Atlantic Ocean, February 22, 1941

The water is colder than the boy expects. Colder than it has any right to be, colder than the bitter wind that gusts above it. The water saves his life. It puts out the flames on his clothes and hair. It cushions his fall. It embraces him.

And then it begins to kill him.

Far away—so far away—he sees the SS *Hampton Claire* and its vital cargo reeling, aflame but not yet sunk. There is no sign of the crew abandoning ship. Instead, dark figures silhouetted against the flames are running with fire blankets and buckets of sand. His mind, shocked to numbness, cannot at first comprehend why. Surely the ship is on its way to the bottom of the Atlantic.

The hole is huge: blackened, jagged metal edges twisted like putty by the force of the explosion, revealing the gaping entrails of the vessel. But it is also high, he notices. The ship was heeling over, hard into its emergency turn, when the torpedo struck. As it straightened, it raised the wound in its side above the waterline. That precious cargo of food might yet reach the hungry mouths of the British.

The fog in his mind gradually clears. He is freezing. Already he can barely feel his fingers. He raises his hands to wave and begins to shout, but before the words can form on his lips, the water beneath him brightens, silhouetting his feet and his body. It is as if the sun has risen, but suddenly, and beneath the waves of the ocean.

Then the shock wave strikes: a hammerblow that leaves him gasping as a huge balloon of water erupts barely a hundred meters away. It is as if he has been hit by a train, a jolt so fierce that it smashes the air from his lungs. For a moment he is sure his heart has stopped.

Before he can begin to make sense of what has happened, there is another glow, another eruption of water and once more the terrible, teeth-jarring shock.

Again it happens, and again, although growing more distant each time; the glow not so bright, the shock not so shattering.

Time passes, but in the aftermath of the explosions, and the brain-draining cold, he has no idea how long. He floats, his life saved by his inflatable Mae West, but his life force and his energy are seeping away into the arctic frigidity of the water. He begins to feel warm, but somewhere in the recesses of his mind he remembers that feeling warm is a sign of advancing hypothermia. Who taught him that? Wilfred, he thinks.

More time passes and there is a swelling in the water near him, a heaviness, a darkness, then a great black shape emerges from the depths. The U-boat broaches, tailfirst, spewed from the belly of the beast. It seems to hang for a moment, suspended in the air, and Joe can see a long gash along the side. The rudders look mangled and useless. It crashes down, sending a shower of spray into the cold air and creating a wave that submerges Joe.

He emerges, gasping and spluttering, seawater and snot streaming from his nose, but the cold water brings him back to his senses.

The sleek hull of a destroyer is cutting through the water and searchlights crash on, converging on the stricken submarine as it wallows in the heavy seas.

There is a pause, a hesitation, a drawing in of breath . . . Then a deck cannon opens up, shells smashing into the conning tower of the submarine, clanging off the hull, some missing the U-boat and sending up spouts of water all around Joe. He dives beneath the waves, swimming desperately down as the heavy projectiles zip past him.

The firing stops and Joe surfaces to see the U-boat crew emerging from the conning tower and through a hatch on the deck.

A large gun is mounted on the deck just forward of the conning tower, but none of the Germans are foolish enough to make a move toward it. It would be suicidal for them and for all their crewmates. Probably deadly for Joe as well, who is still in the target area.

Several of the submariners appear to have been injured. Some are supported by crewmates, others are hauled up out of the hatches and carried. A long line of men are standing on the hull of the U-boat when it begins slipping back below the waves, the buoyancy that has brought it rushing to the surface now leaking away.

Already tenders from at least two ships are approaching the stricken sub, with armed seamen on board. The submariners are jumping off the side of the boat, swimming clear of the sinking vessel as they wait for rescue.

Joe looks back at the SS *Hampton Claire* to see it steaming away in the moonlight. They will think him dead, Joe knows, and he soon will be if he doesn't do something about it.

That is when he finally begins to wave his arms and shout.

London was a bit of a shock. Having left it barely two years earlier, I was amazed to see how much it had changed. Barrage balloons, bombed-out buildings, rubble in the streets, and people with that wide-eyed stare of too many sleepless nights burrowed into their Anderson shelters or scurrying down into the Underground stations as German bombers rained death from above.

But the biggest shock of all had nothing to do with any of that. All the courage or bravado that had sustained me as I ran away from New Zealand, snuck onto a ship, and stowed away across two great oceans now failed me, as I realized with horrible certainty that, for the last two years, my mother had been lying to me. About everything.

—from the memoirs of Joseph "Katipo" St. George

9

STAY PUT

London, February 28, 1941

There is a zebra in the middle of Camden Town, trotting up the center of the road as if it were home on the plains of Africa. The boy has never seen a zebra other than in books, but its black-and-white coat is unmistakable. It is smaller and stockier than he expected and he certainly did not know they ran wild in Central London. It stops at a tiny patch of grass on a traffic island and begins grazing.

A few people start to gather around, staring, so Joe guesses that zebras probably don't run wild in Central London. Something spooks the animal and it takes off without warning, galloping away up the street.

A few moments later a pair of men in zookeeper uniforms appear with ropes and nets and chase after it.

Joe wanders aimlessly in the opposite direction. He has no idea where to go.

There is no Lindemann Street. The address on the letters his mother has been sending for the last two years does not exist. It isn't that she doesn't live at that address, or that there is no house with that number on that street. It isn't even that it has been bombed out of existence by the Luftwaffe. Lindemann

Street in Camden Town in London simply does not exist—and never has, according to a steel-helmeted policeman directing traffic on a corner.

27 Lindemann Street, Camden Town, London. That was at the top of every one of his mother's letters. Each letter was a lifeline, a link to his family, to the real world, a window out of the dreary, rural landscape he found himself in in New Zealand.

But there is no 27 Lindemann Street. The "real world" he was desperately craving to get back to has turned out to be a fantasy.

Joe does not have any of those letters. Not anymore. All he has now are the clothes on his back, and a ratty navy greatcoat to replace his oilskin coat that was badly burned during the torpedo attack. He was taken aboard the tender from the destroyer HMS *Havelock*. After some initial confusion about how he had come to be in the water with the German U-boat crew, he was given dry clothes and a bunk and completed the passage to London on the *Havelock*.

He wanders uncertainly for a while and passes the policeman again on a corner outside the ruins of a church. Clearly the good Lord offers no divine protection against German bombs.

From there it is a short walk to a large, tree-filled park: *Regent's Park,* according to a sign. Other signs point to a zoo.

Why would his mother lie to him about her address? In her letters she also spoke about the efforts the British government was making to locate his father. Was that a lie too? Is his father dead? Is he being tortured by the Gestapo? An image comes to mind of his father tied to a chair as black-coated Nazis administer electric shocks and remove his fingernails with pliers. He tries to banish the image from his brain, but it keeps returning when he least wants it to.

He makes a home that night in the bombed-out ruin of a terraced house. The entire row of half a dozen houses has been badly damaged. The upper levels of one of the houses has partially collapsed, creating a remarkably snug, wedge-shaped space in the cellar that Joe fits out with blankets and pillows salvaged from other rooms. Being belowground, he feels he is safe from all but a direct hit.

On the other side of the street from his new digs is the wreck of a double-decker bus, large, red, and wallowing on its side in a small park like some great beached whale, all its windows smashed. The rear of the bus is just a tangle of twisted metal. An advertisement on the back declares that Dunlop tires are the only tires with teeth. To Joe's eyes, it looks like the bus itself has been chewed up and spat out, probably by the same bomb that destroyed the houses.

The entire street is cordoned off with ropes and patrolled by an air-raid warden. But the warden is easy to avoid and the rope is a warning, not a barrier.

Joe eats food from tins he scavenges from among the smashed bricks and timbers, opening them with a kitchen knife because he can't find a can opener.

A leaflet, one of many scattered through the rubble, is titled "If the Invader Comes" and gives a series of instructions of what to do if (when) the German army invades. The main advice seems to be not to be surprised (which seems self-evident), not to panic (easier said than done), and not to run away. The order from the commander-in-chief is to "stay put." That part is no problem. Joe has nowhere to go.

He uses the leaflets for toilet paper.

That night, the bombers come. As they did the previous night and the multitude of nights before that.

London was different on those nights, however. Joe wasn't there.

The HMS *Havelock* was delayed coming into port, chasing after another U-boat. So they arrived a day after the rest of the convoy and thus avoided a devastating bombing raid on the Liverpool docks.

This is Joe's first night in London.

This is his first blackout.

This is his first bombing raid.

He has heard about the bombings. He has read newspaper reports of the Blitz and listened to newscasts on the radio. None of that, however, has prepared him for the sound of the planes and the eerie squealing of the bombs raining from the sky.

As the light fades, the darkness of the city rises, like a black fog drifting up from the ground.

Cities are full of lights. Streetlights, car lights, lights from windows. But not this city. London is blacked out, a dark blanket hugging the ground, nestled around the River Thames.

Light has become the enemy. The only real light comes from stars, and there are few of those, flickering in gaps among dark clouds.

The raid begins with the slow, rising wail of an air-raid siren in the distance, a cry that is echoed again and again, taken up by one air-raid post after the other, creating a banshee-like cacophony of sound.

It seems so loud that no other sound could possibly intrude, but one sound does, a low, constant drone at the very edge of hearing that gradually solidifies into a solid wall of noise. One plane? A hundred? A thousand? The entire Luftwaffe? Joe has no idea.

The antiaircraft guns sound distantly, getting louder and louder, punctuating the sound of the oncoming planes with bangs, like fireworks or a car backfiring, only much, much louder.

Joe is drawn to the entrance of his hideout, creeping slowly up the stairs from the cellar. The night sky is alive. Long fingers of searchlights probe the darkness, reflecting off clouds and the ungainly shapes of barrage balloons. There! Is that the tail of a bomber? Is that a wing?

Peppering the dark sky like huge instant stars are constant explosions of flak. A crescent moon is up, watching over the proceedings with a Cheshire smile.

Then comes the long squealing of the bombs, louder and louder, followed by the *crump* as they land. It is awful and entrancing at the same time. But the sounds are getting nearer. The droning is louder, the *ack-ack* sounds of the antiaircraft guns closer.

A bomb strikes . . . only a few streets away, Joe judges, by the flash of light and the roar of the explosion. Another, even closer. Smoke and dust whirl up his street, and he shuts his eyes against it as he scrambles back inside his shelter, almost falling down the stairs in his haste to get underground.

The next explosion seems right outside and the collapsed floor that is the roof of his cellar shudders, dust sifting down. A timber cracks.

That is when the screaming starts. A woman's voice. It is high-pitched and dreadful. A scream of terrible agony or unbearable loss. Or both.

He climbs slowly back to the top of the stairs and stares out in the direction of the sound. It is close by. The woman must be in the house that has been hit, just down the street. He waits for the clang of an ambulance bell, but it doesn't come. He waits for the sound of running footsteps, wardens, anyone. But that doesn't come either.

There is only him. He inches forward out of his shelter, one foot, then another . . . Then he stands up to start running but drops to the ground after just a few paces and scuttles backward as the squealing of bombs comes again from overhead and the flash of explosions lights up the neighborhood.

The screaming continues. Still nobody comes. Joe creeps forward once more, then scrambles back again at the sound of more bombs.

A third time, and this time he gets to the center of the road before a single squeal overhead makes him turn tail and run like a rabbit for the safety of his burrow.

He crawls back down the stairs to the crushed and ruined cellar. The woman's screaming penetrates, and he puts his hands over his ears to try and shut it out.

It helps. A little. And after a while, the screaming stops.

Not long after that the all-clear siren sounds. As it slowly winds down, waves of shame and guilt at his own cowardice wash over him, and he begins to slap himself in the face with one hand and then the other, until the pain fades into an uneasy sleep.

He is woken up by a low growl, an animal of some kind. Two eyes glow in the darkness of the cellar, reflecting the flashes of light from the sky. The sirens are wailing again, the *ack-ack* guns are blasting, the bombs are falling, yet somehow he has slept through all that cacophony only to be woken by the sound of a wild animal.

A dog, he tells himself. Just a mutt seeking shelter, safety. Just like him.

The animal growls again.

Joe reaches slowly to pick up a candle he has placed to the side of his makeshift bed. He lights it with a matchstick. The soft glow fills the small space.

It is a dog. Its teeth are bared, a dull white in the gloom of the cellar. It's not a mutt though. A beagle, if he isn't mistaken, with floppy ears and large, expressive eyes. Someone's pet. Or she was.

He holds out a hand, palm down, and lets the dog move to him and sniff it. She growls again, but he keeps his hand outstretched.

"You're not angry," he says. "You're not vicious. You're afraid. Like me."

Another explosion sounds nearby.

The dog stops growling and begins to lick his hand. He curls his fingers around her neck and begins to scratch behind her ears.

"Come here, girl." The dog comes to him, curling up and nestling into his stomach. She shivers and whimpers softly at every loud sound from outside.

"It's all right, girl," Joe says, although it isn't.

The bombers come again the next night. If a bomb were to hit, he is not sure he would care. The world as he knew it is gone. Before, everything seemed so black-and-white. Now it is just gray.

Except for Grable. That's what he'd called the beagle. She's the one splash of color in his life. She has stayed. Perhaps she has nowhere else to go either. Perhaps her house was destroyed, her owners killed. Or maybe this was her house. It makes Joe wonder how many other pets have suffered during the Blitz.

He feeds her from tins and collects water from broken pipes for both of them. Later he will look back and think that, as much as he helped her, it was Grable who helped him get through those first few days.

The bombers come each night without fail. He quickly learned the sounds. The bombs came in a pattern: five blasts. Each explosion closer and louder than the last, and he felt sure the next one would be a direct hit, but always it passed just overhead, the remaining bombs receding into the distance. Perhaps there was some truth in the old saying about lightning never striking twice. Perhaps this mess of broken bricks and pipes is safe. It is certainly as safe as anywhere else in London. Which is to say, not at all.

By the third night he is thinking about how he can get back to New Zealand. Its green meadows and rolling hills no longer seem boring or distant. They seem peaceful and safe.

He would have presented himself back to the captain of the *Hampton Claire* and asked for a return passage working on board, except that the ship, her captain, and the precious cargo of desperately needed food were gone. After weeks of braving German U-boats and the frozen fury of the Atlantic, she had been hit by a stray German bomb in the mouth of the River Mersey before she had even had time to dock. That bomb did what the torpedo could not. It ripped apart her boilers and sent her to the bottom.

He could try and stow away on another boat, but security at the docks in London is twice what it was in New York, and ten times that of New Zealand. Armed soldiers patrol constantly. Passes are checked. Trespassers are arrested.

Coming to London was a huge mistake, and one that will probably cost him his life.

For the first few days he hides in the broken building, crawling up out of the cellar to one of the crumbling upper levels and watching people going about their lives as if nothing was happening.

Life is going on. All around him. The Nazis are bombing the heart out of this city and people keep living their lives, going to work, going to restaurants and nightclubs, even motion pictures. The world is a crazy place, and it is slowly driving him insane.

10

WOMAN IN A KHAKI SKIRT

London, March 5, 1941

When the boy finally does see his mother, it is by accident.

The night they arrived from Paris two years earlier, desperately tired, they were picked up from the train station by a large man with a handlebar mustache, driving a big black car. Joe's memories of that night are vague and mainly of the mustache. It fascinated him. It was long, gray, drooping, tobacco-stained, and twisted into tight pointy ends that stuck out sideways. It looked like a small, furry, horned animal that came to life when he spoke.

That entire night is now no more than a dark blur, but wandering randomly around London, Joe feels a surge of recognition as he approaches a large stone monument. Three words are bleakly etched into one side: *The Glorious Dead.*

Those words trigger something in his memory. He *knows* this road. He recognizes the monument. It is the same street he was driven down by the mustachioed man two years earlier. He remembers thinking that there was nothing glorious about being dead.

He stayed in the car as his mother and the man went into . . . where? Which building was it?

He walks the length of the street trying frantically to remember, without success. Undeterred, he returns the next day, and the next.

The sky is dark with heavy, threatening clouds. The air smells like rain mixed in with the ever-present stench of smoke and rot. The Blitz bouquet.

He sees a woman he thinks is his mother wearing a white blouse and khaki skirt, sipping tea at a table in a small tearoom within sight of Big Ben. If not for Big Ben, he might never have found her. It begins to chime just as he passes the window of the tearoom, glancing in through the crosses of tape stuck on the windows. The woman looks around at the sound, momentarily distracted from her conversation, then turns back to the man sitting across from her at a small wooden table.

Out on the street, Joe stops in his tracks, earning a "harrumph" from the bowler-hatted man following along behind, who has to step aside to avoid him.

Joe stands there like an idiot. Like a statue. Like a statue of an idiot . . . staring in through the window. This woman looks like his mother, but her hair and clothing are different from how he pictures her in his mind. The man she is with is tall and thin with wire-framed glasses. He does not recognize the man—and why would he? He is not even sure he recognizes the woman. It has been two years. Can you forget someone in two years?

Can you forget *your own mother*?

His hands are suddenly shaking. His heart is racing. He fights the urge to rush in through the door of the tearoom and fling his arms around her, to hear her voice and see her smile. To feel her softly stroke his hair, as she did whenever he was ill or upset. That is what a little boy would do, and he is no longer a little boy.

Is this her? He has to be sure. He finds a place to wait, near the entrance, seated on an empty crate that has been discarded on the footpath.

A few moments later the woman and her companion stand up, pulling on coats and slipping canvas gas mask bags across their shoulders, before stepping outside.

There is something about the way she walks, the way she turns her head. Her hair color is different, her makeup more . . . obvious. But it is her.

He stands also, on the verge of running to her, shouting, weeping. He even draws the air into his lungs but holds it there as she does something odd. She slips her arm through the arm of the tall man.

Joe stops, shocked, the words frozen on his lips, the air jammed solidly in his chest. This can't be his mother. *But he was so sure!*

He thinks desperately back to the letters she sent. She was working as a secretary, she said, in the typing pool of a financial firm. Something to do with the stock market. She didn't elaborate in her letters and he didn't inquire in his. That information seemed boring and irrelevant. She had certainly not mentioned a boyfriend.

Why would she? How could she? His father is still alive as far as either of them know. Isn't he? And if he is alive, then what is his mother doing, walking so romantically, arms linked with this other man?

Unless it isn't his mother. Just a woman who looks like her. A doppelgänger.

Is he going mad? Is he so desperate to see his mother that he is seeing her where she doesn't exist?

In the ruins of the houses he had found a tweed newsboy-style cap. He brought it with him but hadn't been wearing it as it rubbed on the raw, burnt patches of his scalp. He takes it out now, puts it on, and pulls it low over his eyes, turning up the collar of his ratty navy greatcoat as the couple draw near. He pretends to examine his shoes as they pass, while watching them out of the corner of his eye.

He notices every detail. The weave of her khaki skirt, surely part of a uniform. The stiffness of her starched white collar. The way she loosely knots the belt of her coat, rather than buckling it. The missing stud fastener on her gas mask bag and how the loose flap swishes as she walks. The wave of her hair. The color of her lipstick. Everything.

It *is* his mother. Without question. And her feelings for the tall stranger are clear, from her cheerful laugh and the brightness of her eyes as she chats with him.

He waits a moment after they pass, then follows them, acting casually, just a boy with errands to run and in no particular hurry. Around a corner, into a side street lined with tall, important-looking limestone buildings with grand entrances. They stop at the top of a flight of stone steps by a statue of a soldier on a large plinth.

The man says goodbye to her there, with a warm embrace, but—Joe is glad to see—no kiss, before heading back the way he came.

She descends past the statue, turns left, and disappears into an unmarked entrance guarded by two armed soldiers. Joe saunters down the steps and across a courtyard to a park where he loiters, trying not to attract attention from the guards.

He is surprised a few minutes later to see a short, stout man wearing a homburg hat emerge from the same doorway, followed by a tall, strong-featured man, half a pace behind. The tall man is a bodyguard. Joe can tell by the way he moves, the way his eyes dart around, examining everyone and everything in the vicinity.

The short man is someone Joe knows from newspaper photographs: Winston Churchill, prime minister of Britain.

Now the questions are piling up in his mind.

What is going on?

What is this place?

What is his mother doing in the same building as Winston Churchill?

Is it really his mother?

Is he going mad?

He waits, leaning against a tree in the park. The morning passes without incident, or any further sign of his mother.

By noon he is hungry. He has no money to buy food and doesn't want to return to his cellar in case he misses her.

"What you up to, then?" a voice asks.

Joe turns to see a stocky boy in an oversized but torn jersey, with a gas mask bag slung around one shoulder. Younger than Joe, perhaps twelve years old. He has come up behind Joe, through the park. He is solidly built with fiery red hair and a "chin bum," which was what Joe's best friend, Nikau, always called a cleft chin. Thinking of Nikau, who was Māori, makes Joe think of New Zealand and that makes him feel a little homesick for the place he had been desperate to leave.

"Why do you want to know?" Joe asks.

"You look like a Kraut," the boy says. "We know how to deal with Nazis around here."

A knife appears in his hand. Joe did not see where it came from.

"I'm not German," Joe says quickly as a girl and a much larger boy emerge through the trees.

The girl has the same fiery-red hair and chin as the boy, so has to be his sister or cousin at least, although she is taller, skinnier, and older—about Joe's age. Her gas mask bag is decorated with a crude crayon drawing of Mickey Mouse. At least Joe thinks it is Mickey Mouse. It might be a frog on a bicycle.

The bigger boy is quite stout, a difficult feat in these days of rations and food shortage. He has his hair slicked flat with Brylcreem and parted in the center. His eyebrows are too heavy for his face, which makes his forehead seem to protrude. He needs to shave, which reminds Joe of Klaus.

"He's a spy," the girl says. "See how he was watching that building?"

Was it that obvious?

"That's the War Rooms, innit," the girl continues. "Churchill's War Rooms. Why are you spying on Churchill's War Rooms?"

"I wasn't," Joe says, which is technically true. It is his mother he is spying on, and he didn't even know these were the Cabinet War Rooms.

"So answer my question, Schweinehund," the boy says, waving the knife. "What you up to?"

"Yeah, Schweinehund," the girl says. "That means 'pig dog.'"

"If I were German, I'd know that already," Joe says mildly.

"Where you from?" the boy asks, now pointing the knife directly at Joe's face.

"New Zealand," Joe says.

"He don't look like he's from New Zealand," the girl says. "He looks like a Nazi with that luverly blond hair."

Joe's hair is far from "luverly." It's a mess of ragged ends, some blackened, some parts shaved entirely where the explosion burned it right to the skin. A steward on the destroyer tried to give him a crew cut, but the result was like something out of a horror show.

"I'm from New Zealand," Joe insists. "Everybody in New Zealand has blond hair."

"What about that cousin of your friend Margo?" the boy says, turning to the girl. "Ain't he from New Zealand?"

"Hugo," the girl says. "Yeah. But he don't have blond hair and neither does his dad."

"They must be from the South Island," Joe says. "I'm from the North Island."

"How do we know you're for real?" the boy asks.

The big boy has done nothing so far but stand beside the other two, cracking his knuckles and looking threatening.

"Yeah, he could be a German spy," the girl says, and adds "Schweinehund" for good measure.

"Get Wild Bob to beat 'im up," the boy says. From his sideways glance, it is clear that Wild Bob is the knuckle-cracking brute.

"How will that tell us anything?" the girl asks.

"Well, if he's a German spy, he'll know secret spy fighting stuff. So if Wild Bob can bash 'im, then he's not a spy."

They all consider that for a moment. Especially Wild Bob who is looking quite pleased at the opportunity to bash someone. He takes a step toward Joe.

"Except if I were a spy, I might let Wild Bob beat me up just to fool you," Joe says.

"He's tricky this one," the girl says. "Gotta be a spy."

"What happened to yer hair?" Wild Bob asks. For all his intimidating looks he has a quiet, hesitant way of speaking. "You get bombed?"

"Torpedoed," Joe says.

Now they all seem to notice his naval greatcoat.

"You a deserter?" the girl asks, narrowing her eyes.

"He's too young to be a deserter, idiot," the boy says. "You can't desert if you can't enlist."

"You're the idiot," she says. "He might be older than he looks."

"Not a deserter." Joe shakes his head. "Stowaway."

That seems to raise his status in their eyes for some reason. The knife disappears as rapidly as it appeared.

"Where were you going?" the girl asks.

She thinks he was trying to get *out* of London! Joe wonders if they will believe that he actually stowed away *to* London. He shrugs. "Anywhere."

"Don't blame yer," the boy says.

"Ever seen a cannon shell?" Wild Bob asks.

Joe shakes his head.

"I got some," Wild Bob says. He reaches into a pocket on his oversized trousers and pulls out a large bullet-shaped object about fifteen centimeters long.

"Don't show the spy," the girl says. "I still think he's a spy."

Wild Bob either doesn't hear or doesn't care.

"Yes, I might report you to German high command," Joe says. "They'll be wondering where their cannon shells are."

"They're not German; they're British," the boy says. "Don't you know nothin'?"

"Where'd you get them?" Joe asks.

The boy jerks his head back in a direction that could have been anywhere. "Spitfire came down in the street. Pilot was proper dead an' all."

"Some other kids beat us there," the girl says. "But there was still a few shells left and they run away when I showed them my fists."

"When you showed them your face, you mean," the boy says. He winces as she kicks him in the ankle.

"We're gonna cook 'em off tonight in the park," Wild Bob says in his hesitant way. "Wanna come?"

The other boy sighs with exasperation. "What you inviting him for? We don't even know 'im."

"They're Bob's shells," the girl says. "He can invite bloody Princess Elizabeth if he wants to."

Joe is fairly sure that bloody Princess Elizabeth would not be interested in going with Wild Bob and his friends to a park at night to "cook off" some cannon shells. But then again, he has never met her, so she might. "What about the blackout?" he says.

The girl laughs and the boy snorts so loudly that snot ends up hanging from his nose. Joe watches it swing back and forth as the boy says, "That's not for the likes of us."

"We're Blitz rats," the girl says.

Joe does not get to find out what that means. The woman who looks like his mother emerges from the café entrance at that moment, her head down, mostly concealed by a wide-brimmed hat.

"I gotta go," he says.

"You comin' tonight?" Wild Bob asks.

"Maybe."

"Six o'clock, meet back 'ere," the boy says. "We won't wait for yer."

Joe nods as if he has any intention of coming back to watch them cook off the Spitfire shells and hurries after the woman. She strolls away in the direction of the river. Joe trails her, checking behind to make sure the Blitz rats aren't following him.

The woman also glances back regularly, perhaps to make sure she isn't being followed.

Joe keeps a careful distance and at least a couple of people in between them at all times. Even so, once or twice she nearly catches him and he has to duck quickly out of sight.

She strolls along Thames Street beside the river for a ways, and he stays in the adjacent parklands, using the trees as cover.

She walks past bridges and jetties, ending up at Blackfriars Bridge, a low, flat bridge consisting of a number of graceful cast-iron arches in between piers topped by pulpit-shaped bays. After a quick look around, she begins to cross.

Joe crosses to the footpath on the other side of the road. It is a lovely afternoon. The threatening rainclouds of the morning have been blown away by a firm breeze, leaving virtually cloudless skies. The wind has also taken with it the acrid fug of smoke that lay over the city since his arrival. Even the people of London seem brighter, a sense of hope and determination returning with the sunshine, although he knows they will all be praying for heavy cloud cover that night.

Pigeons coo from the railing of the bridge. Two young children skip along, hand in hand in front of their mother, who is pushing a pram. All his ideas suddenly seem so silly, so childish. All he has to do is to walk up to the woman and say hello. Then he'll know for sure. It is that simple. If it is his mother and if she is having an affair with the thin man, that is her business. He can live with it.

He steps to the curb, waiting for a black cab to pass. The woman stops, halfway across the bridge at one of the pulpits.

She slips off her gas mask bag with the missing stud fastener and places it on the stone bench seat running around the inside of the wall while she gazes out at the river, admiring the view. A man in a tan suit and a fedora hat stops nearby, also slipping off his gas mask bag. They do not speak. They do not even glance at each other, which seems a little odd to Joe.

A horse pulling a milk cart passes in front of Joe, blocking his view for a moment. When it clears, the man is leaving the pulpit. His gas mask bag is back over his shoulder. It is missing one stud, Joe notices. The woman continues over the bridge in the opposite direction. Her gas mask bag now has two studs. *They have swapped bags!*

On impulse Joe turns and begins to discreetly follow the man. What is so important about that gas mask? he wonders. What is really in that bag? After a few twists and turns the man ends up at a long stone building. A glance at the wall tells Joe this is the Temple Tube station, part of the Underground. He follows the man into a concourse, busy but not crowded at this time of day. The man purchases a ticket from a vending machine and presents it to an inspector at a barrier, before descending a flight of stairs to the platform.

Joe waits for the inspector to be busy clipping tickets, then ducks around behind a group of uniformed soldiers, through the barrier and down the stairs.

He sees the man standing on the platform, waiting for the train. The man glances up as Joe descends, but Joe is mostly hidden behind another group of servicemen, air force officers this time.

The next handoff is even smoother. The train arrives and the doors open. People pour out. One moment the man is carrying the gas mask bag over his shoulder, the next moment he is not, although Joe cannot see where it has gone. There are hundreds of people on the platform, all of them with gas mask bags. Any one of them could be the one he is looking for.

It doesn't matter. Not really. He doesn't need to know where that bag was going, or even who has it. The carefully orchestrated walk, checking behind to make sure she wasn't being followed, the double switch of the gas mask bag. This is exactly the sort of classic spy stuff he has read about in his books. Which means that the woman he thinks is his mother is a spy. That is all he really needs to know.

No!

It is not his mother. He can't accept that.

But then he thinks about his father. Captured by the Gestapo. The image of the electric shocks and pulled fingernails comes back to mind, and he shakes his head to clear it.

His father. That has to be it. They must have threatened to kill or torture him if his mother didn't do exactly what she was told. Didn't become a double agent. And if she *is* a double agent, where does that leave him? What will happen if he contacts her?

More importantly though, if she truly is a double agent feeding secrets to the Germans, *what is he going to do about it?*

Joe makes his way back to the park in Whitehall and waits some more, watching the doors to Churchill's War Rooms.

Around five o'clock the woman emerges again from the doorway and begins to walk in his direction. He pulls on his hat and turns up his collar, sliding behind a tree. He puts a hand to his face and scratches his nose as she walks straight past him. He has a clear view of her face.

This time there can be no doubt. This is not some woman who resembles his mother. This is not his imagination playing tricks on him. This *is* his mother.

He follows her, noting the street signs as they pass so he can find his way here again later. Waterloo Place, past a number of statues of brave soldiers and kings, then onto Pall Mall. Left onto Haymarket and right onto Coventry Street.

The center of the roadway here is cordoned off. A bomb has ripped up the fabric of the road, leaving a crater into which mucky water trickles from broken pipes.

A short way along Coventry she pushes open a set of double doors and disappears inside. The sign above the doorway, in elaborate gold lettering, gives the name of the establishment: *Café de Paris.*

When she does not emerge after a few moments, he too pushes open the door and steps in. A short passage takes him to a flight of steps leading down to a landing on a mezzanine floor, from which two flights of stairs descend to a dance floor, well underground.

He'd assumed that the café would be a kind of tearoom, but from the look of this, it's more like a restaurant and dance club. It is deserted, except for a number of uniformed staff moving tables and chairs around on the ground floor and on the mezzanine level. A band is practicing on a small stage between the two flights of stairs.

There is no sign of his mother.

Does she work here? Is she meeting someone here?

He takes the stairs on the left, moving slowly, aware that she might be watching him. If she is, does she recognize him?

"Can I help you?"

Joe turns to see a tall black man up on the stage, casually dressed and with his sleeves rolled up. In his hand he holds a conductor's baton.

Joe thinks quickly. What *is* he doing here? What would a boy his age be doing in a place like this, at this time of day?

"Looking for work," he mumbles.

The man smiles, a broad flash of white teeth in the dark face. "Ain't you a little young to be working in a nightclub?"

"I'm older than I look," Joe says, although that isn't true.

"And I'm younger than I feel." The man sticks out a hand. "I'm Ken. But people call me Snakehips."

Joe shook it. "Joe."

"What do you do, Joe?"

"I'm a musician." Joe says the first thing that comes into his mind.

"Well, that's just swell, Joe. What do you play?"

"Play?"

"What instrument?"

"The mouth organ," Joe says. He'd once played Klaus's mouth organ, although he wasn't able to get much of a tune out of it.

Snakehips nods. "Well, we don't need no mouth organ. How about the drums?"

"I could learn," Joe says.

"Well, we already got a drummer," Snakehips says. "Can you lead a swing band?"

"Absolutely!" Joe says with conviction.

Snakehips laughs. "Well, that's my job. So it looks like we got no work for you. But I admire your spunk. Go down the street; there's a baker on the corner. He's looking for a new delivery boy because . . . well . . . You know how it goes."

"Thanks," Joe says with genuine warmth despite having no intention of visiting the baker.

"Good luck," Snakehips calls as Joe makes his way back up the stairs, still scanning around him for any sign of his mother.

The bright light of the sky outside has him blinking as he pushes back through the double doors of the club.

Where is his mother? He hadn't seen her leave the club, and there seemed to be no other way in or out. Perhaps she went to the bathroom?

He finds a place on a corner from where he can watch the entrance without attracting suspicion and waits. In his adventure books, spying always seemed so exciting, but he seemed to be spending most of his time waiting.

He waits for a very long time. It begins to rain and he takes shelter in a shop doorway, but still she does not appear.

Only after dark and having been twice moved on—once by a policeman and once by a white-helmeted air-raid warden—does Joe return to his makeshift home.

Grable is sleeping and does not wake as he enters. He takes off his wet hat and overcoat and hangs them on a broken hatstand to dry. He curls up next to Grable, and she wakes up enough to wriggle closer to him, sharing his warmth. He pulls blankets over both of them and sleeps, dreaming of New Zealand.

He had not told anyone in New Zealand that he spoke German. It wasn't something to be proud of. Not in those days, in the colonies, in the lead-up to the war. But the local school taught both French and German. Preparing children for the coming domination of the world by the Nazis, according to Nikau.

One day during their German lesson, Joe's teacher had made a fairly serious error. A dumb mistake that a lot of English speakers make with the German language. Before he could help himself, Joe had corrected her.

"You are both wrong and *stupid," replied the teacher, a bad-breathed, middle-aged dragon named Mrs. Hughes-Bottomly. (Huge-Bottom, the way Nikau pronounced it.)*

Joe had been tired that day, irritable, homesick too. And he didn't like to be called stupid. When the teacher repeated her mistake, he corrected her again and this time told her why she was wrong. This was not the right thing to do.

The dragon threatened him with the strap if he didn't apologize.

"Why would I apologize when I am right?" he had asked.

That had brought out the strap. It would have brought a visit to the principal in a larger school, but there was no principal. Only a dragon.

"Hold out your hand," Mrs. Hughes-Bottomly had demanded.

He held out his left hand bravely.

"Your other hand," she had insisted.

And the scar on his palm, that he had always taken pains to keep hidden, was suddenly there, in plain view. A swastika etched in a raised white line.

"A Nazi," she had said, barely able to talk through her horror and disgust. She raised the strap.

"A German boy did this to me," Joe said, which was true, although it made the incident seem worse than it was. But that just brought all the memories flooding back and his eyes filled with tears and a small voice emerged from his throat and said, "And not long after that the Gestapo arrested my father."

The strap had remained there, suspended in midair, until he had reached up and taken it from her, without resistance.

After that he had walked outside and the doorway suddenly seemed too small and the sky seemed too big and the ground seemed to swell like a big green balloon, and the next thing he knew he was lying on his back in the sick bay.

And that was where the dream ended.

Most of it was true.

11

BLITZ RATS

London, March 6, 1941

The boy is up early the next morning, marching through the smoky orange light of the after-dawn as rescue workers and firemen scurry around, cleaning up the mess and chaos of the previous night.

A blanket has been pulled over a shape in the gutter, but as Joe nears, a policeman comes and removes it, revealing the body of a small girl in a daffodil-patterned dress. Her hand clutches a string of rosary beads. There is no indication of how the girl might have got there. The police officer picks her up gently and carries her away. His face is rigid.

Near a Tube station, the boy sees a massive crater, bigger than any others he has seen. The bomb must have collapsed part of the Underground. A double-decker bus has driven into the crater and has been all but swallowed by it. The body of the driver is still at the wheel.

The boy sees these things without any kind of emotion. No anger, no sadness, no sense of injustice. There is simply too much destruction, all around. He is becoming immune to it.

He makes his way to a grassy, tree-lined park from where he can watch the entrance to the Café de Paris. He sits directly opposite a secondhand shop with a sign saying: *We buy anything—except broken glass, we have plenty.* He smiles at that and realizes it is the first time he has smiled since coming to London.

He could buy something, if there was anything he wanted to buy. A chance discovery in a broken chest of drawers had yielded a small ceramic bank in the shape of a cow. After not inconsiderable debate with himself, he broke it open, finding a treasure trove of pennies and halfpennies mixed in with quite a few threepence and even a small number of shillings. He promised himself that if the owner of the house turned up, he would return it. If they didn't, they probably didn't need it anymore. The coins are of limited use without a ration book, and he has not yet found one of those, or really knows what to do with it if he does find one.

When his mother hasn't emerged by midmorning, Joe walks back to Whitehall, to watch the doors of Churchill's War Rooms.

There are plenty of comings and goings of service personnel and secretaries and important-looking men in dark suits and bowler hats, but no sign of his mother.

For lunch he buys a bagel for a penny at a busy Jewish bakery on a corner, the very bakery where Snakehips suggested he ask for work. Here there is no yellow star. Here he does not see the baker and his wife cleaning the road in the gathering darkness as storm troopers look on. That world seems so distant now, in both place and time, yet the memory, once it has come to him, is as fresh as if it were real, here and now.

Back to Whitehall and more waiting, and watching, and waiting. His mother finally emerges midafternoon and he follows her as before. She makes several unnecessary turns into side streets and stops regularly, looking into shopwindows that, taped up as they are, still act as mirrors. Joe anticipates this each time, however, and ensures that she does not catch his reflection. She does not seem to be going in any particular direction and her route often circles back on itself.

He waits as she enters a small, shadowy alley between two large buildings. It is mostly deserted, and there is no way to avoid being seen if she looks around in there. The lane is old, the bricks of the buildings on either side dark with soot, their few windows opaque with age and grime, staring blindly down at ancient, ill-fitting cobblestones. It feels like the kind of alley that Jack the Ripper may have lurked in before slicing up his victims, except that had been Whitechapel, not Whitehall, if Joe remembered the stories correctly.

His mother turns left at the end of the lane and only then does he hurry down after her, but when he reaches the end, she is gone. The street is bustling, and she is nowhere to be seen. He scans both directions, then hurriedly turns back into the lane, worried that she has positioned herself in a place where she can observe anyone who is following her. That's what a spy would do.

A man is halfway down the lane, wearing a black overcoat and a homburg hat, not unlike Churchill's. His eyes seem fixed on some distant spot at the end of the lane, as if he is deliberately *not* looking at Joe. After he passes, Joe turns and continues up the alley, walking backward so he can watch the man, with just an occasional glance behind to make sure he doesn't bump into anything.

As the man reaches the end of the alley, he turns, glancing back at Joe. It is a mean face, Joe thinks, weather-beaten and craggy, with pronounced jowl lines. His left eyelid droops, perhaps the result of some old injury. The man quickly looks away and hurries out of the lane.

Just a random stranger? Joe has a disquieting feeling that this is not the case.

His mother has thrown him off the tail, he is sure of that, and it was deliberate. Did she know he was following her? Or was this just good "craft" to make sure that nobody was following her.

He wanders back to St James's Park, from where he can watch the entrance to the building in Whitehall.

By the time night falls, Joe is sure his mother is not returning. He is about to leave when he sees the tall, redheaded Blitz rat girl emerging through the trees. He tries to conceal himself behind a lamppost, but she sees him and bounds over.

"'Allo, 'andsome," she says brightly, scratching the cleft in her chin.

"My name's Joe."

"Peggy," she says. "And me brother's called Eddie."

Her brother is just coming over toward them now, followed by their large friend.

"The big kid is Wild Bob," Peggy says.

"I remember," Joe says.

"His real name is Milton, but we always call him Wild Bob and he kinda likes it," she says. "He talks a bit slow, but if you make fun of him, I'll bash you up meself."

"I wouldn't want that," Joe says mildly.

"You taking the mickey?" she asks, her cheeks reddening, her fists clenching.

"No," Joe says. "Sorry, no. I wasn't." He was, but it seems best not to admit it.

"So you gonna make fun of Wild Bob?"

"I really won't," Joe says. "I give you my word."

That seems to soften her. Her fists unclench and her cheeks lose their color.

"Torpedo boy has a name," she says as the others arrive. "Joe."

"I 'spected it was Hans or Fritz," Eddie says.

"Call me Adolf if it makes you feel good," Joe says, earning a sideways glance from Peggy. "How did the Spitfire shell cooking go? Did Princess Elizabeth show up?"

Wild Bob shakes his head. Peggy gives Joe a deadly look, and he shrugs an apology.

"It were raining," Eddie says. "Not much fun cooking off shells in the rain. We're going tonight instead."

"Why don't you got a gas mask?" Wild Bob asks. "Everybody got a gas mask."

"Even Wild Bob's baby sister got a gas mask and she's only three," Peggy says.

"She got a Mickey Mouse one," Wild Bob says.

"I wanted a Mickey Mouse one, but they said I was too old," Peggy says. "They don't actually look nothin' like Mickey Mouse anyway."

"So where's yours?" Eddie asks.

"I don't know where to get one," Joe says.

"Didn't your mum or dad give you one?" Peggy asks.

Joe is silent, unsure what to say, which they must have misinterpreted as meaning his parents have been killed, judging by their sideways glances at each other.

"Don't matter," Peggy says sympathetically. "We'll find you one somewhere. There's plenty of 'em lying around." *Belonging to dead people,* she does not say.

It only now belatedly occurs to Joe that by not carrying a gas mask he is making himself conspicuous. People will notice him because of that, and the first rule of spying is not to be noticed. If Peggy doesn't come up with one, he will have to find one himself somewhere. Then it occurs to him that being conspicuous is the least of his gas mask problems. He knows about mustard gas and other gases they used during the Great War. He has seen ex-soldiers, blinded and scarred, breath whistling in their throats as they begged on the streets of Berlin. Those were the ones who had got off lightly.

The idea of clouds of blistering, choking gas drifting through London streets is suddenly very real and absolutely terrifying.

"We're going to Regent's Park to cook off the Spittie shells," Wild Bob says.

"Come with us," Peggy says. "It'll be smashing."

“I’m not sure,” Joe says evasively.

“Ain’t ya got the nerve for it?” Eddie asks.

“Just hungry,” Joe says.

“We’ll get a feed at the rest center after,” Peggy says.

“Aren’t those for homeless people?” Joe asks. He has seen posters to that effect.

“’Course,” says Peggy, “but they never check. Long as you got tuppence for the meal and a penny for dessert.”

If Joe wasn’t convinced before, he is now. The idea of a meal that doesn’t come out of a dusty tin is extremely appealing, although he vows to remember to slip something into his pocket for Grable.

“Won’t it be dark by the time we get there?” he asks.

“Told you he ain’t got the nerve,” Eddie says.

“Gotta be dark,” Wild Bob says. “No fun otherwise.” He turns abruptly and heads off. Eddie and Peggy glance briefly at each other before skipping off after him.

Joe watches for a moment, then shrugs and follows them.

“I still think you should save the shells for the invasion,” Peggy is saying when he catches up. “We can kill some Krauts.”

“Jerry ain’t never going to come,” Eddie says.

“Took ’em eighteen days to conquer Poland,” Peggy says. “Six weeks to take France. And those countries had armies.”

“We have an army,” Joe says.

“Not much of one,” Peggy says. “Just the flotsam and jetsam from Dunkirk. Got no equipment, no big guns. What are we going to do against the Blitzkrieg?”

"Just one problem," Eddie says. "It's called the English Channel."

"Ever heard of boats?" Peggy says.

"Ever heard of the Royal Navy?" Eddie says.

"Surely Eddie's right," Joe says. "As long as the Royal Navy protects the Channel, the Nazis can't cross."

"Not until they knock out our air force," Peggy says. "Then they can use their Stukas to blow up our ships—and then who's going to guard the ditch?"

"So you really think Hitler will invade?" Joe asks a little nervously. He hadn't thought about that when he had stowed away, but here in England, the threat hung over the city like a dark cloud.

"It's just a matter of time, innit," Peggy says assuredly. "What are you going to do when they come?"

"Not be surprised, not panic, and stay put," Joe says.

Peggy laughs. "Lot of good that'll do."

"I hope Hitler comes with them," Eddie says. "I'm going to get a gun and shoot him meself."

"I'd punch 'im in the face," Wild Bob says. "Then in the guts. Then in the face again."

Hitler deserves more than just a punch in the face or the guts, in Joe's opinion, but he has never been punched in the guts by Wild Bob and is quite sure it wouldn't be very pleasant.

Eddie kicks at the side of a trash bin as they pass, rattling the metal lid and scaring up a cloud of flies that had settled over it like a blanket. "I'd shoot 'im, then I'd cut him into pieces and stick him in one of those," he says.

"How would you even get near him?" Joe says. "He has the entire SS as his bodyguards."

"I'd find a way," Eddie says confidently.

They continue on, and it's almost dark by the time they reach the park. Joe looks nervously at the sky.

Peggy notices. "They don't come this early," she says. "They tried that during the Battle of Britain, but the Spitties and the Hurricanes kept shooting 'em down."

"Now that's a sight I'd like to see," Joe says.

"Well, you might be lucky. Maybe Jerry will decide to come early tonight, just for you." Eddie laughs.

"What do we do if there is an air raid?" Joe asks. "We're all out in the open here."

Suddenly he is craving the comforts (or lack of them) of his cellar.

"We dance." Peggy sighs and starts to twirl with an imaginary partner. "Don't you so love dancing?"

"You're bleedin' bonkers," Eddie says.

"At least I'd die happy," Peggy says.

"That's the plan?" Joe asks. "We all start dancing?"

"Nah, only her," Eddie says, "coz she's stark ravin' mad. Rest of us lie down."

"That's your plan?" Joe asks. "To lie down?"

"No point in hiding down holes," says Eddie. "If a bomb's gonna hit yer, you're dead anyway. But if a bomb comes close and you're lying down, the shrapnel flies over your head. Don't hurt ya. Oh, and stick a cork in your mouth—that's for the percussion." He reaches into his pocket and pulls out a grubby wine cork, with visible teeth marks. "Here, I got a spare."

"Um, thanks." Joe takes it, gives it a quick wipe, which does nothing to make it seem cleaner, and puts it in his pocket.

A thought occurs to him and he asks without thinking, "Don't your mum and dad wonder where you are?"

"No need to wonder," Peggy says with a glance upward. "They're watching over us."

"Oh," Joe says, also glancing at the sky. "Isn't there . . . I mean, shouldn't you . . ."

"Go live in an orphanage in the countryside?" Eddie scoffs. "Not me. Not likely."

"Me neither. We're squatters," Peggy says proudly. "Plenty of abandoned houses around. We got a luverly one. Live like a king and queen. Proper posh we are."

"What about Wild Bob?" Joe asks. "Why's he wandering around with you?"

Wild Bob answers, carefully enunciating each word. "We got an Anderson shelter in the garden. I don't like it."

"Makes him cluster-phobic," Peggy says.

"Cluster-phobic?" Joe suppresses a grin.

"She means closet-phobic," Eddie says. "It's an irrational fear of being stuck in a closet."

"So Wild Bob tells his dad that he's going to the Tube shelter," Peggy says. "But really he don't like that neither, so he just wanders around."

"That's how we met him," Eddie says. "And now he hangs out with us. Hold up." He held a finger to his lips.

A pair of tin-hatted police officers are patrolling the edge of the park. Joe and the others hide among the trees until they pass.

Cooking off Spittie shells turns out to be illegal, exciting, and potentially deadly. They find a remote area of the park, well away from the zoo because Wild Bob doesn't want to frighten the animals (though Joe thinks the animals would be frightened enough by all the German bombs and a few cannon shells would hardly make any difference).

Wild Bob carefully embeds the shells into the ground, nose first "so they don't kill nobody," while Eddie and Peggy build a little fire pit around them using stones. They make a fire using scrunched up pages of the *Daily Mirror* and twigs, which Wild Bob sets aflame with a match that he lights with a flick of his thumb.

Nothing happens at first. The paper catches and the twigs begin to smoke, then burst into flames. The outside casing of the shells seem to start glowing in the heat.

"Is that it?" Joe asks.

In the middle of his sentence the first shell explodes. Smoke billows and a sheet of flame envelops the fire pit. The casing of the shell goes spinning into the air, spewing out sparks. It is still in midair when the second shell explodes, which unfortunately knocks over the third so that it is aiming almost directly at Joe. He skips sideways just as it goes off, the projectile whizzing past his left hip, hitting a tree behind him where it explodes, showering him with shards of tree bark.

Joe hears Eddie whooping with excitement as he checks himself for injuries, feeling lucky to be alive.

"Cor! That was smashing!" Peggy cries.

"Yeah, brilliant," Joe says. "Really brilliant. Now what?"

"Run!" says Wild Bob.

Through the trees, Joe can hear shouts and police whistles.

"So who's that woman you been spying on?" Peggy asks a little later as they lie on their backs in the middle of Waterloo Bridge, watching the searchlights play across the night sky, a thousand strands of brilliant cotton, searching for enemy bombers that always somehow seem to be just out of view.

The *ack-ack* sounds of the antiaircraft guns punctuate the almost constant rumble of explosions, and the flashes of flak seem more like a fireworks display than a deadly barrage. The smell of cordite drifts across the water from nearby batteries, mingling with coal smoke and the acrid smell of smoke from the fires. The bridge itself vibrates under Joe's back whenever a bomb strikes nearby.

"You sure we're safe here?" Joe asks.

"Safe as houses," Eddie says. "Actually, much safer than the houses. Bomb goes to the left or the right we get a free shower, but that's about it. Like I told ya before, we're safe as long as we're lying down."

"What about all the shrapnel from the flak?" Joe asks. "That must land somewhere."

"I ain't never heard of no one being killed by no falling shrapnel," Eddie says.

"That's because nobody else is dumb enough to lie in the middle of Waterloo Bridge during a bombing raid," Joe says.

Peggy makes chicken-clucking sounds and Eddie laughs.

"So, come on, then . . . Who's that old woman you been leering at?" Eddie asks.

"My mother," Joe says.

Eddie laughs. "Nah, I mean really."

Joe says nothing, creating an uncomfortable silence, during which all three of the others sit upright and stare at him.

"I thought your parents was dead," Eddie says awkwardly.

Joe shakes his head.

"You're spying on your own mother?" Peggy asks incredulously. "Why?"

"Aren't you supposed to be lying down?" Joe says. They all ignore him.

"Why you spying on your mum?" Wild Bob asks.

"I think she might be passing information to the enemy," Joe says. It sounds stupid, but both Peggy and Eddie gasp and even Wild Bob raises his eyebrows.

"Your mum is a Nazi spy!" Eddie blurts.

"Possibly," Joe says.

"What . . . I mean how . . . I mean, who—" Peggy stumbles over her words.

"Why?" Wild Bob asks.

Joe gives them the only answer he can. The one he has been agonizing over since this all began. "My father was captured by the Gestapo when we used to live in Berlin."

"I thought you was from New Zealand," Eddie says.

"I am. My parents were diplomats in Berlin," Joe says. "But my father was arrested and taken away. My mother and I only just escaped in time."

"So why would your mother . . . ?" Eddie begins.

"Don't be daft," Peggy says. "The Krauts will be using Joe's dad to force his mum to spy for them."

"I don't know for sure," Joe admits, "but that's what—"

"Got one!" Eddie shouts, jumping to his feet and pointing at the sky.

A bomber is spiraling down in flames.

"Take that, Nazis!" Peggy shouts, leaping up beside Eddie.

"It's a Dornier," Eddie yells. "We got a Dornier!"

"How do you know?" Joe asks, trying to make out the shape of the rapidly spinning, burning aircraft.

"See how thin it is?" Eddie says, his voice still raised with delight. "The Flying Pencil, they call it."

It is long and thin, Joe notes, although he can't help thinking that he is watching young men burning as they fall to their deaths.

The plane hits the ground somewhere in the distance with a huge fireball as its bombs detonate.

Eddie and Peggy hug each other, and Wild Bob is shifting on his feet in what Joe thinks is a little dance of happiness.

Only after the long plumes of flames die away do they all sit back down.

"We could help you spy on your mum," Peggy says.

Joe looks at her, thinking about the offer.

"What could we do?" Eddie asks.

"We're Blitz rats," Peggy says proudly. "We know London better than anyone. And we're invisible."

"We're not invisible," Eddie says.

"Yes, we are," Wild Bob says.

"We are," Peggy says. "Nobody sees us. Nobody notices us. Tell us what you need us to do, Joe, and we'll help you."

Joe thinks about that for a while longer. "I think she carries secrets out of the War Rooms in her gas mask bag. I saw her swap her bag with a man on Blackfriars Bridge. He gave the bag to someone else. But I don't know what's in the bag, or who these other people are. I can't prove anything. What I really need is a camera. Get some evidence. Take it to the police . . . or somebody."

"I can borrow a camera," Wild Bob says. "A good one. I know how to use it an' all."

"He does," Peggy says. "His dad owns a photo studio."

"Brilliant," Joe says as a brace of bombs lands downriver with a muffled underwater *crump* that reminds Joe of the depth-charging of the U-boat. The bridge shudders beneath him. Water erupts into the air, and a little of the spray drifts over them.

"Men, we have a mission," Eddie says.

"I'm not a man," Peggy says.

"You can pretend to be a man," Eddie says.

"*You* can pretend to be a man," Peggy says.

Eddie ignores her. "I'm the mission leader. First we're going to need a code name for the operation—"

"I want to be the mission leader," Peggy says. "I'm the one with the brains."

"Girls ain't leaders," Eddie says. "That's man's work."

"Oh yeah? Tell that to Cleopatra," Peggy says. "And Queen Victoria, and Catherine the Great, and—"

"Joe should be leader," Wild Bob says. "It's his mission."

The siblings stop squabbling and look at Joe.

He shrugs. It is what he was thinking anyway. "Onion," he says, picking a random word out of the air.

"Eh?" Eddie says.

"Onion?" Peggy asks.

"The name of the operation," Joe says.

"Operation Onion," Eddie says. "All righty, but we'll need disguises. I just so happen to have a false mustache."

Peggy bursts out laughing so hard at this that Joe can't get a word in for a moment, and after a while the image of little redheaded Eddie in a too-large fedora with a long, droopy false mustache, plus Peggy's infectious laughter, become too much and he begins to laugh too. Wild Bob joins in and soon all four of them are giggling away as planes drone, search-lights probe the sky, and London explodes all around them.

"It might be dangerous," Joe adds when he can catch a breath. He thinks of the man in the trench coat who followed him in the lane.

"Better be," Eddie says. "Or it won't be any fun."

When Joe gets home, Grable seems unwell. She hasn't eaten the bowl of food he left her. Her nose is hot. He wets a cloth and drips water into her mouth, which she swallows weakly, looking up at him with her big beagle eyes. He wants to get some milk for her, but that is impossible without a ration book, which he still does not have. Perhaps Peggy or Eddie can get some for him. He will ask tomorrow . . . if Grable survives the night.

12

OPERATION ONION

London, March 7, 1941

The boy dreams of New Zealand again, although this dream is different. He is back on his uncle's farm, lying in the paddock down by the stream with Millicent Jackson, fascinated by the soft curls of her hair and the gentle curve of her lips.

Wind is whispering along the surface of the water and pukeko stalk the bank, calling their peculiar squeaking cry. Other native birds answer from the trees. The dark shape in the sky looks like one of those birds at first, but it is falling, not flying. The rounded metal nose and the angular tail fins are suddenly as clear as if he was watching through binoculars. It falls and falls... seemingly right toward them... And now he hears the high-pitched squeal of its fins. But where is the bomber? The sky is clear.

The bomb lands in the middle of the stream, sending up a huge spout of mud and water and dead birds and frogs that splatter over and around them. The aftermath is silence. The birds are silent, the trees are silent, even the gurgling of the stream has been silenced.

There is no sound at all until Millicent starts screaming. He clasps her hand, slippery with mud and water, hauling her up off the ground, and now they are running back toward the farmhouse, but a glance upward shows the clear blue sky awash with the deadly black shapes, hundreds, perhaps thousands of them falling and falling and falling and the world is exploding and he wakes up sweating.

During the night a bomb has fallen in his street. He didn't even hear it. Or did he? Perhaps it was the bomb in his dream.

A woman half a dozen doors down on the other side of the street is busily sweeping her doorstep with a wicker broom. Her hair is bound up in a scarf that is knotted on the top, turban style, as is the fashion. Her plain gray dress is torn in a number of places although she does not seem to be aware of this. The doorstep is intact. The house it belongs to is gone. There is just a jumble of broken bricks. As Joe watches, someone takes her by the arm and leads her away.

He solves his milk problem that morning, quite by chance. A white-jacketed milkman wearing an apron and peaked hat is picking his way through the rubble from his cart, where his horse waits, flicking its tail impatiently.

Joe catches up with him in the middle of the street and holds out a few pennies. "Could I buy some milk, please, sir?"

The man stops and looked at Joe over broken spectacles mended with tape. He shakes his head. "My milk is all accounted for," he says. "Got just enough for my deliveries, no more."

"It's not for me," Joe says. "It's for my dog."

The man shakes his head again and starts to turn away.

"Truly, sir," Joe says. "She's a beagle, her name is Grable, and she's sick. She won't eat, but I thought she might drink some milk."

Now the man turns back. He looks Joe up and down. "Come with me," he says.

When they get to the cart the man hands Joe a half-pint bottle. "Bit of a shame," he says. "I tripped on some debris. This bottle broke."

The bottle looks perfectly intact to Joe, and he smiles as he takes it. "Thank you, sir."

"I had a dog," the man says, refusing the proffered coins. "Part Labrador. Beautiful boy he was."

"What happened to him?" Joe asks.

The man lowers his eyes. "You don't want to know. Now g'arn with yer, before I change my mind."

Grable laps gratefully at the milk when Joe pours some into her bowl. She finishes it, licking at the bowl long after it is empty, then begins licking his hand, looking plaintively at him with those big eyes.

"Not now, girl," Joe says, softly stroking her ears. "Let's see if you keep that down."

He gives her some water instead. After an hour when she doesn't vomit or get stomach cramps, he gives her the rest.

Peggy has brought him a gas mask. It looks new; at least the canvas bag it comes in does. He thanks her, and means it, for a variety of reasons. She smiles and hugs him, only letting go when Eddie looks around to see what is happening.

Wild Bob has brought a camera. That looks new also.

"It's a Leica II, with a M39 lens mount and a Zeiss telephoto lens," Wild Bob says.

It is the most words Joe has heard him say in a single sentence.

They are encamped in the ruins of the church near Regent's Park. The roof is completely gone and the floor is a mess of smashed pews and colored glass, along with the remains of the ceiling and pillars. The walls are still standing, however, shielding them from prying eyes.

This is apparently where Eddie, Peggy, and Wild Bob usually meet before setting off on their adventures through Blitz-ravaged London.

The apse, behind the altar, is the least damaged part of the church. It is there that they sit in a small circle around a low table.

"Leica?" Joe says. "Isn't that a German brand?" He remembers seeing that name on cameras in shops in Berlin.

Wild Bob nods. "So is Zeiss. Best cameras in the world are German."

"Not very patriotic though, is it?" Eddie says.

"So you think we should use some crappy, old, cheap camera to spy on Joe's mum just because it isn't German?" Peggy snaps.

"That's exactly what I think," Eddie says. "Death to the Nazis!"

"Seems to me that using a Nazi camera to catch a Nazi spy is sort of ironic," Joe contributes.

"It's *moronic* is what it is," says Eddie.

"So what's the plan?" Peggy asks.

She is looking at him. He is the leader of the mission. He should have a plan. But he doesn't have one.

"I guess we go and wait in the park till she comes out," he

says. "Then we follow her. She'll be watching for tails, so we'll take it in shifts. If she stops or turns off suddenly, then the person behind her carries on, and the next person takes over."

"Right, and the first person goes to the back of the line," Eddie says.

"We should all bring a coat," Joe says. "Reversible if you have one. And a hat. We can put on coats and swap hats to change our appearance."

"Ain't it going to look a bit suspicious?" Peggy says. "The lot of us hanging about in the park, watching the War Rooms."

"Yeah, we thought you was a spy when we saw you doing it," Eddie agrees.

Joe nods thoughtfully. "We should bring something to do. Play cricket or something."

"We don't have enough for cricket," Eddie says.

"Yes, we do, you moron," Peggy says. "Bowler, batter, catcher, fielder. You only need four."

"That's not proper cricket," Eddie says.

Wild Bob stands and walks over to the side of the church. He moves a couple of bricks and a broken timber panel to reveal a metal lockbox. He brings it over and puts it in the middle of the table, then unlocks it with a key from a string around his neck.

The box is full of what must be Wild Bob's treasures. A ball of string, a pewter mug, a rubber ball, an air-raid warden's whistle, a silver pen engraved with the initials AMMW, a paperback called *The Mystery of the Blue Train* by Agatha Christie. There is more: a set of jacks missing one piece, a gold pocket watch, a pair of men's spectacles with a cracked lens. And more.

"Wow," Joe says. "Is this all your loot?"

There is a sudden strained silence. Peggy is looking daggers at him. Wild Bob looks uncomfortable.

"He's not a looter," Eddie says rigidly. "It's just stuff he finds lying around. It's not looting if you find stuff."

By that definition he is a looter, Joe thinks. He has stolen food, clothing, and coins from the ruined block of houses he is living in.

"I didn't mean that," he says quickly. "I meant loot like pirate treasure. Is this like your treasure chest?"

Wild Bob suddenly looks a lot happier. He nods. "My treasure chest." He seems to like the sound of those words.

He rummages around in the box and pulls out a pack of playing cards.

"Brilliant," Peggy says. "That's better than cricket."

"It's not cricket with four people," Eddie mutters.

Wild Bob finds a rubber ball in the box and hands it to Eddie.

A few more items from the box disappear into Wild Bob's voluminous pockets before the treasure chest gets reburied under the rubble.

They wait in St James's Park, across the courtyard from the War Rooms. They sit on the grass among old brown and yellow oak leaves.

They are supposedly playing gin rummy, but nobody is

concentrating. They each hold a handful of cards and randomly pick one up from a pile in the middle, discarding another without even looking at their hand.

Joe couldn't have concentrated on the cards even if they were playing properly. His focus is on the doorway. He doesn't want to miss her.

Per his instructions, they have all brought coats and hats with them. Peggy has two hats and a reversible coat, blue on one side, green on the other. Eddie has a school cap and Wild Bob has a trilby. Joe has brought his newsboy cap.

Eddie also has his fake mustache, which seems to be made of real human hair glued onto a piece of sticky tape. He stuck it on and winced when Peggy pulled it off, saying how ridiculous it looked. It looks all right on Wild Bob though, from a distance. It seems to complement his thick eyebrows.

Two women emerge just before noon, but Joe shakes his head and picks up the cards to deal another round.

"What's that on yer hand?" Wild Bob asks as Joe is shuffling.

Joe winces and closes his hand. He normally takes great pains to keep the palm of his hand hidden.

"Giz a look," Peggy says.

"It's nothing," Joe says.

"Come on, show us," Eddie says.

Joe slowly unfolds his fingers to reveal the crooked scar that Klaus had carved.

"What's all that about, then?" Eddie asks suspiciously.

"I, um, it's—" Joe stumbles.

"What's going on?" Peggy asks, narrowing her eyes. "Why do you have a Nazi sign on your hand?"

They are all staring at him now.

It is Wild Bob who asks, "Who did that to you?"

Joe sighs. "A German boy. I thought he was my friend. He *was* my friend. We were doing a blood brothers thing. I didn't know he was making a swastika."

"I bet your dad gave you a hiding when he seen it," Eddie says. "Mine would have."

"He did," Joe says, remembering the day vividly, and surprisingly fondly.

"Is your dad still alive?" Wild Bob asks.

Joe put down his cards and takes a deep breath. "I think so," he says. "I hope so. He was arrested by the Gestapo in 1938."

"Cor blimey," Eddie says.

"I haven't heard anything of him since," Joe says. "Nobody has, as far as I know."

"That's tough," Peggy says, touching him on the arm.

Eddie notices the gesture. "Least he's still *got* a mum and dad," he says.

Peggy's hand falls away.

"What happened to your parents?" Joe asks gently. It seems wrong not to ask, but he doesn't want to open deep wounds.

"Dad was killed in France, at Dunkirk," Eddie says. He says it proudly, chin raised. Proud, not of his father dying, Joe thinks, but the fact that it had been at Dunkirk.

"Mum was killed by a bomb," Peggy says.

"From a Heinkel," Eddie adds as if it mattered what kind of plane dropped the bomb that killed their mother.

"Direct hit, 'undred pounder," Peggy says. "Right on our Anderson."

Joe looks confused, and Peggy clarifies, "Anderson shelter. Like a big metal box. You dig a hole in your backyard and stick it in there as a bomb shelter."

"I know what an Anderson shelter is," Joe says. "But how did you not get killed too?"

"Just lucky," Eddie says quickly. Too quickly. He and Peggy look at each other.

"They weren't in it," Wild Bob says. "Just their ma. By herself."

"Why?" Joe asks, curious despite himself.

Peggy and Eddie are still looking at each other. The moment lasts a little too long. A breeze ruffles the old fallen leaves and flips over a couple of the playing cards. Nobody moves to fix them. A gray squirrel is watching them from the base of a nearby tree, a thin twig clutched in its tiny hands. It is chewing off the bark. It looks like it is playing the flute. Its tail is twitching.

"We hated the thing," Eddie says eventually. He and Peggy break eye contact, and both stare at the ground. "Cold and wet it were."

"Smelled like moldy cheese," Peggy says.

"Every night we got woke up by Wailing Winnie, and Mum would drag us down to the shelter," Eddie says. "So this night Peg says she ain't going. So I says I ain't going neither."

"You said it first," Peggy says.

"Nah, you did," Eddie says.

"It were you," Peggy says.

Joe draws in a deep breath. He looks at Wild Bob, but the big boy is watching the squirrel.

"Your mum left you in the house and went to the shelter by herself," Joe says slowly.

"Yeah, and then the shelter got a direct hit and she was killed and it serves her bloody right for not staying with us," Peggy says, furiously wiping away tears.

"How dare you," Eddie says, jumping to his feet. "How bloody dare you!"

"It's true," Peggy says.

"Don't you blame her," Eddie shouts. "She didn't want to die, just because of us. She did the right thing. We just got lucky, is all."

"Oh yeah, real lucky," Peggy sobs.

There is a click from the camera. Wild Bob has taken a photo of the squirrel. It must be camera shy because it drops the twig, spins around, and scurries up a tree.

They all watch it for a moment, and Eddie slowly sits back down. Peggy wipes her nose on a sleeve.

"An' that's why you won't find us skulkin' down some shelter during raids," Eddie says quietly. "Rather take our chances above ground."

"Joe, is that your mum?" Wild Bob asks.

The others turn to look, and Joe confirms it with a nod.

His mother, hatless and wearing a dark coat, has just left the War Rooms, gas mask bag draped carelessly across one shoulder. Wild Bob takes a picture as she climbs the steps past the statue.

Eddie jumps to his feet, crosses the courtyard, and follows her up the steps.

Peggy follows Eddie, well back out of sight, and Wild Bob follows Peggy. Joe brings up the rear.

Joe's mother is not even halfway down the short road that leads to Parliament Street when she abruptly reverses course, retracing her steps. Eddie carries straight on, and the others duck back around the corner, huddling in a group until Joe's mother passes them, crossing the road and turning to walk alongside the park.

It is Peggy's turn to follow her, while Eddie catches up to the rear of the line, at the same time taking off his coat and swapping hats with Joe. When Joe's mum makes another abrupt turn, this time into one of the pathways that lead into St. James's Park, Peggy walks right past, and Wild Bob is the one who turns in after her.

Outside the gates of Buckingham Palace, which are well guarded by both Beefeaters and soldiers in battle dress, all heavily armed, Joe's mother circles right around a large monument with a statue of Queen Victoria topped by some golden angels.

Wild Bob continues on, and it is Joe's turn to follow, waiting until she has completed her circuit of the monument before falling in behind her.

A respectable distance back, Eddie follows Joe.

Joe's mother heads toward the Wellington Arch, where a

number of policemen are standing in a tight group in front of a small police station. She skirts around them into Hyde Park but, apparently satisfied that she has not been followed, makes no further moves to evade possible tails.

She makes her way to a park bench in front of an old octagonal bandstand. Joe stays in a clump of trees, peering out through some low, leafy branches.

His mother is waiting for something. Some*one*, probably.

Eddie arrives, then Peggy. They have changed coats and hats. Eddie takes the rubber ball from a pocket of his coat, and he and Peggy start to throw it back and forth. Just two kids playing in the park. Invisible, as Peggy says.

Wild Bob positions himself carefully in the trees next to Joe and takes a photo with his long-distance lens, while Joe checks around for anyone who might be watching them watching her.

They wait. The sun moves a little in the sky, and the shadows in the trees shift slightly.

A man in a tan-colored suit and a fedora appears at the far end of the clearing in which the bandstand sits. He walks over to the bench, sits on the opposite end to Joe's mother, unfolds a newspaper, and starts reading it.

"They're talking," Peggy says quietly, deliberately missing a catch and trotting over near Joe to recover the ball.

"How do you know?" Joe asks. He cannot see the faces of the man or the woman, and if he can't, neither can Peggy.

"By the way they're breathing," Peggy says, pretending to look for the ball. "And the way they are deliberately ignoring each other. Ordinary people glance around sometimes."

She "finds" the ball and trots back to toss it to Eddie.

Peggy is right, Joe sees. His mother and the man in the fedora keep their heads turned slightly away from each other, and if he looks carefully, he can see what Peggy means about their breathing.

The man reaches inside his jacket and takes out something—a package of some kind. He places it on the seat beside him, and with a casual flick of a hand, nudges it toward Joe's mother.

A man in a black overcoat enters the scene so quickly that it is as if he has suddenly materialized.

With alarm, Joe realizes that the man is walking up behind the bench seat where his mother and the stranger sit.

A lot of things happen very quickly.

Joe's mum reaches out to pick up the parcel.

The man in the tan suit folds his newspaper and slowly gets to his feet.

Both are oblivious to the man behind them.

A sound comes sharp and hard, like a loud clap of someone's hands.

Wild Bob's camera clicks.

The man in the tan suit lurches forward, dropping his newspaper. His hat flies off. He collapses as the man in the overcoat turns toward Joe's mother, and now Joe can see the pistol in his hand.

Joe is frozen, unable to move, unable to speak.

It is Peggy's voice that rings out across the clearing. "Oi!" she yells. *"Oi!"*

The man spins around to look at them.

Wild Bob's camera clicks.

The man turns back toward Joe's mother just as her gas mask bag, spinning on the end of its strap, catches him full in the face. He staggers backward, tripping over his own twisted feet, and goes down, the pistol skittering away from his hand.

Joe's mum is sprinting now, away through the park, heading for the Wellington Arch with its tiny police station.

The man retrieves his pistol and starts sprinting also, not after Joe's mother, but after Joe and Eddie and Peggy and Wild Bob.

"Run!" Eddie yells.

The rubber ball drops from Peggy's hand and bounces just once on the grass before coming to rest in a pile of leaves.

Peggy is running, Eddie just in front, Joe on their tail, Wild Bob alongside him. A thunderclap sounds behind Joe and an insect buzzes past his head. Bark explodes from a tree just in front of him. It takes him a second to realize that they are being shot at. Another thunderclap and another explosion of bark. A third, and Wild Bob grunts, stumbles, and falls. His arms are flailing and the camera goes flying out in front of Joe.

Instinctively, Joe reaches out and grabs at it . . . It is falling, falling . . . But his fingers close on the strap just before it crunches into the ground. It swings wildly around in his hand and he pulls it close to his body. He slings the strap over his shoulder and runs.

Peggy, Eddie, and Wild Bob were my only
real friends in England. I was always really sad
about what happened to them.

—from the memoirs of Joseph "Katipo" St. George

13

THE CAMERA

Hyde Park, London, March 7, 1941

The boy should stop to see if Wild Bob is all right. To help him if he's not. He knows this but doesn't stop. He runs like the coward he knows himself to be.

The camera swings wildly around at the end of its strap.

They are in among the trees now, jumping over roots, pushing through bushes, ducking under branches. Behind him he can hear their pursuer, beating his own path through the brush.

They come to a gravel path, and Eddie leads them along it, dodging around horse droppings. Joe doesn't like it. There is no cover and the man behind them will have a clear shot. Eddie must know this because almost immediately he turns onto another pathway, crossing a bridge and heading into a thick grove of trees.

"We should split up," Joe pants.

"No!" Eddie calls back. "Follow me!" He darts out of the trees across a small clearing past a fountain. On the other side he dives into a thick clump of bushes, Peggy bursts in after him, and Joe follows her.

Behind the bushes, Eddie is bent over a storm drain in a dip in the ground, trying to lift a heavy metal grate, although he can barely budge it. Peggy grabs hold and strains too, but still the grate hardly moves. Joe skids to a halt alongside them, puts the camera on the ground, and grabs one of the bars of the grate with both hands, heaving. The grate lifts up an inch, but then stops, rusty hinges refusing to budge.

"Where's Bob?" Peggy asks.

"I don't know," Joe grunts. He is afraid that he does know but doesn't want to say.

Tendons stand out on his arms as he strains. A groan comes from the hinges. Joe heaves again and the metal grate rises.

Eddie is first in, as soon as the gap is wide enough, disappearing down a series of rungs in the dark brick wall of the storm drain. Peggy follows.

Joe scrambles down after the other two. Already he can hear footsteps and the sound of someone bashing through nearby bushes. Halfway down, Joe remembers the camera. He reaches up and grabs it, clutching it to his chest with one hand as he grasps the bars of the grate with the other, lowering it as quickly and quietly as he can. The grate has just settled into place when sounds come from right above him—running footsteps clanging on the metal. If the man just glanced down he would see a face staring back up at him. The footsteps pass by.

It is dark in the drain, the only light coming in bright strips from the grate as Joe descends. Peggy grasps Joe's arm and moves him into the shadows, a finger to her lips.

Joe is panting. His chest is heaving, and his heart is pounding so loudly he feels sure their pursuer will be able to hear it.

They wait in the darkness, unmoving, terrified of making the slightest noise.

The footsteps return. Branches and leaves rustle above them, the sound of someone poking around in the bushes. Joe holds his breath, despite lungs that are burning.

The man drops to one knee above them, his shadow blocking the light. His fingers curl through the heavy bars of the grate. It rises with a screech of rusted hinges.

Joe dares not move. He is but a shadow among shadows, a ghost in the gloom, but he knows that movement will attract the eye. He learned that lesson staring out of a bedroom window in Berlin in 1938. He hugs the camera tightly to his chest so that its lens will not reflect the light.

The glow from above casts the man's shadow onto the brick wall of the storm drain. His arm is extended, the shape of his pistol a deadly barb at the end of it, the sting of a scorpion.

Joe waits. Eddie and Peggy also wait—motionless, soundless.

The drain is not as quiet. Into the void of their silence falls the smaller sounds of creatures for whom this is home. The scurrying of tiny paws on old dry leaves. The whine of mosquitos. The scuttling of cockroaches.

Joe hears these sounds, but they do not concern him. Some of the inhabitants of this place may bite, but none will bite as hard as the object in the hand of the man above them.

A large spider descends in front of Joe, a silhouette only, the thread of its web invisible in the darkness. It lands on Joe's nose. He blinks but does not move. It crawls toward his forehead and he shuts his eyes, feeling its tiny feet on his eyelid as it climbs up, farther now, into his hair.

The man above them moves, shifting his position, perhaps to see deeper into the drain. Perhaps his eyes are adjusting to the darkness. Perhaps he has seen them. Perhaps not. The gun has not yet spoken.

That is not quite true. The gun did speak, a few moments ago. Wild Bob went down, arms flailing. Wounded? Dead? There is no way to know.

A mosquito lands on his arm; he feels its bite and winces but does not move to slap at it. He can still feel the spider in his hair and now there is a tugging on his trouser leg. Something is climbing the cloth, perhaps a rat. It is far too heavy for a cockroach or a spider. Unless there are darker, more sinister creatures in this foul burrow. He dares not think of such things. It must be a rat, nothing more.

It reaches his knee, pauses for a moment, then continues to crawl along his thigh. He glances down and can see its eyes reflecting the shadow of the man. It is a rat. Nothing more.

It reaches his waist and scrambles up to his shoulder. Its fur is coarse and prickly against his ear. Its tail flicks around the back of his neck. Tiny paws reach up to his face. Rats carry diseases, don't they? What's it doing? Will it bite? Will he catch the plague?

Another set of tiny claws on his trousers now, another rat. But this one is climbing up the *inside* of his trouser leg. He shudders and tries to stay still. It is nearly impossible.

The rat on his shoulder stands on its hind legs, he can feel its front paws on his ear, its nose sniffing inside his ear. He shudders again and the rat wobbles. The second rat is almost at his knee, still climbing up inside his trousers.

But finally, the man above them has given up. The grate drops into place with a loud clang. Rust drifts down in the shaft of light. The man's shadow moves away.

The rat inside Joe's trousers reaches his knee and Joe cannot help it, he shakes his leg. The rat falls, hitting the ground with a shriek that immediately spreads to dozens of other rats around them. The clamor is deafening inside the narrow passageway, and Joe adds to it by brushing the other rat from his shoulder. He flicks the spider from his hair.

The shadow is back on the wall and the grate again screeches open. The man's legs appear, climbing down the ladder.

"Come on!" Eddie shouts in a hoarse whisper.

He leads the way deeper into the tunnel. He and Peggy, being smaller, are able to duck their heads and run. Joe has to crouch, scampering along with bowed head and bended knees, one hand clutching the camera to stop it swinging around. He glances back to see the man snatch off his hat and toss it behind him. His head is mostly bald and there is a jagged scar across his scalp. He is even taller than Joe so has to run on all fours. He looks like a giant bald spider scuttling through the narrow channel after them.

The drain twists and turns. At one point they enter a wide, tall, circular chamber with a large central standpipe. The chamber is full of water and the only way across is to wade through it. It is waist deep on Joe and chest deep on the others. Wading takes time and they have just reached the other side when the man appears behind them. He launches himself into the water, his long legs wading much faster than Eddie's or Peggy's.

But they are out now, running as fast as they can. The passageway is not as dark here, and Joe can feel the brush of fresh air against his cheeks.

Around a sharp bend . . . and the way ahead of them is blocked by a rockfall, but light is coming from above and he sees Peggy's shoes disappear upward.

They scramble up and emerge into chaos. Or perhaps some surrealist painter's nightmare. It is a vast area filled with everyday objects but jumbled together, contorted, shattered. An ornate wooden wardrobe sits upside down, its doors open, a mahogany table protruding through them as though bursting from its chest. A set of dining chairs, legs cracked or broken, are piled together with half a dozen umbrellas, one of which has sprung open and sits on top of the pile like some bizarre crown. More smashed furniture is strewn with men's and women's clothing, electrical appliances, children's toys, all in a chaotic tangle, in among crushed wooden crates, broken timbers, and stone slabs.

The most disturbing thing is the faces. Demonic faces, some fractured, some blackened and burnt, eyes staring at Joe as he emerges from the storm drain. Some are reflected in shards of fractured mirrors. They stare at Joe, eyes rigid, faces unmoving, lips pursed as if to call his name or curse him, and it takes him a long moment to realize they are mannequins. Some are fully clothed, others have clothing burnt away.

It must be a department store. At least it used to be. But there is a massive hole in the floor above and the floor above that. The sky is visible five floors up. The sales goods from all those floors have cascaded down into the basement. This building was hit, and hit hard. Not by one bomb, or two, but by a string of them.

"Split up," Eddie says. "Find somewhere to hide."

Joe takes the camera from around his neck and scans around for somewhere to put it. He spies a chest of drawers, mostly intact, lying on its back on a pile of rubble. He pulls a drawer open and stashes the camera inside, then covers the whole thing with a pile of rags that used to be fashionable dresses.

Sounds come from the hole in the floor behind them, and he clambers off the pile of rubble just before the balding head of their pursuer appears.

For an instant their eyes meet, then Joe runs. He clambers over piles of toys, crawls under broken beams, runs down a kind of aisle between piles of wooden crates, then crawls into a jumble of broken bodies. He finds a fractured plaster face, that of a man with wavy brown hair and a thin mustache. He puts the face over his own as a mask and lies motionless in among the strange, stiff bodies. Just another mannequin among many.

The mask is cracked, and he can see a narrow sliver through it, of the other side of the aisle. He is staring at a baby in a pink bonnet. A doll of course. Half her face is missing, and her one eye stares accusingly back at him as if he were responsible for the bombs that made such a mess of her and her home.

A dark figure cuts in front of the doll. Joe can't see the gun in his hand but doesn't need to. If this is a surrealistic netherworld, then surely this is the devil.

The man stops in front of Joe and examines the debris on both sides of the aisle. For a long moment he seems to be staring directly at Joe. Joe holds his breath, not even daring to breathe, then the man turns and hurries on.

Joe can no longer see him but can hear his footsteps, and the occasional crash, which he assumes is the man pushing over piles of wreckage. Then silence. Should he move? Or is the man just waiting? Is he like the Gestapo agent who followed silently behind the searchers in Berlin, to catch those who let their guard down, thinking they were safe?

Time passes, and Joe is just about to sit up, when the man steps back into view. There were no warning footsteps this time. The man has moved as quietly as a cat. He again glances to the left and right, then stops and stares at the pile of mannequins in which Joe is hiding. Is he thinking this would be a good place to hide? It is what Joe thought after all.

The man begins to move in Joe's direction and is standing right over him when there is a sharp sound from the other side of the basement. In a flash the man is gone, racing silently away.

There are more crashes, then the sounds of a struggle. Then silence.

Joe waits. He is afraid.

A voice sounds loudly, echoing around the space. "Where is the camera? Bring me the camera. I have your friend." The man has a slight German accent.

"Don't give—" Eddie's voice cuts off into a gasp of pain.

"It's just a camera. Is it worth your friend's life?" the man says.

More silence. Another gasp of pain.

Joe still waits. He is still afraid.

Peggy's voice comes. "Leave him alone."

Only now does Joe move, shifting the stiff arms and legs off him and clambering quietly out from the pile. He does not take the path the man took but scrambles on all fours over mounds of rubble and debris, hoping to circle around behind him.

He rounds a pile of broken stone slabs until he can see the man's back. One hand holds the pistol. In the other, held high, is a man's leather belt. It is looped around the neck of Eddie, who is standing on his tiptoes just to be able to breathe, his fingers scrabbling at his throat.

In front of the man Peggy is crouched behind the chest of drawers where Joe hid the camera. He cannot see her but can see the camera in her hand, raised above her head. He picks up a length of broken copper pipe, then takes one silent step after another.

"You are children. This is not your war. Not yet anyway," the man says.

Breathlessly Eddie manages to gasp out, "Don't do it, Peg."

The man raises the belt higher, lifting Eddie off the ground, his feet kicking wildly.

"All right!" Peggy cries.

The man relaxes his arm, lowering Eddie back to the ground.

"Let 'im go first, then I'll give you the camera," Peggy says.

The devil shakes his head. Droplets of sweat make zigzag patterns across his bald scalp. "I will let him go when I have the camera."

Peggy considers this for a moment, then slowly places the camera on top of the chest of drawers.

"Don't! He'll just shoot us all anyway!" Eddie cries.

Joe can hear Peggy scrabbling backward, out of sight.

The man strides forward, dragging Eddie with him, still clutching at the belt, struggling to breathe. The man is no longer trying to be silent. Joe is though. He creeps up behind the man as quietly as he can, then quickly ducks behind the upended wardrobe as the man climbs the pile of rubble and glances around. He pockets his pistol for a moment to retrieve the camera, slinging its strap around his neck. Now the pistol comes out again.

"Come out where I can see you," the man says.

"If you do, he'll shoot you," Eddie cries.

Peggy does it anyway, stepping into the aisle perhaps twenty meters away.

"Come closer," says the devil.

Joe knows what he is doing. Peggy is too far away for an accurate shot. He intends to kill her. Which means he intends to kill all of them.

Peggy steps forward, and for a moment Joe wonders why. Surely she must realize what the man is doing. Then he understands. He can see Peggy. Peggy can see him. She does not look at him but must be able to see him out of the corner of her eye. She is distracting the man, keeping his focus on her.

She walks forward slowly, very slowly, giving Joe time to move. He moves, choosing each footstep carefully. One wrong step, one cracked timber, one shifting brick and the man will hear him. But if he is not quick enough . . .

He takes another step. Barely a meter or so away from the devil now, he holds his breath again.

Peggy edges steadily closer, showing no fear.

The man's arm moves, raising the pistol, taking aim.

Joe is still too far away. He lunges forward, stretching out, sweeping the copper pipe down at the full extent of his arms. He misses. But the man hears the movement and turns, bringing the gun up. Joe is well within striking range now, and his second blow does not miss. He brings the pipe down hard on the hand holding the pistol. There is a crack and a spurt of blood. The man yelps with pain. He raises the pistol again toward Joe, but his wrist is bent at a strange angle and his fingers do not seem to be working properly. He starts to swap the pistol to his other hand, but a police whistle sounds from the direction of the storm drain. Another. Again and again the shrill sound echoes off the battered walls of the basement.

The man barges into Joe, knocking him over, then turns and runs, disappearing off into the maze of rubble and debris, cradling his hand to his chest.

Eddie has collapsed to the ground, heaving in deep breaths of air. Peggy runs to him, throwing her arms around him, hugging him, desperately. She is crying, snot bubbling from her nose.

Running footsteps come from the direction of the drain

now, and Joe looks up expecting to see the dark blue uniforms of the police.

It is not the police.

It is Wild Bob, one arm dripping with blood, his other hand holding his ARP whistle. He also appears to have been crying. His eyes are red and tears smudge his dusty cheeks.

Despite everything, Joe begins to laugh.

14

THERE'LL ALWAYS BE AN ENGLAND

Camden Town, London, March 7, 1941

The boy's heart is still hammering as they arrive at a rest center.

Over and over again he sees the bullet punching a hole through the tan suit and emerging in a spray of blood on the other side. He hears the metal insect whining past his ear. He imagines the bullet flying a few centimeters to the right, straight through the back of his head, and emerging in a spray of blood out through his eye.

The others don't seem to have been affected in the same way. Peggy, in particular, seems vibrant and excited, full of energy. She seems to relish the idea that she had nearly been killed. She even starts dancing on the way to the rest center. Eddie too is practically skipping along the road. Wild Bob is just hungry.

The rest center is in a local school, closed because the children have been evacuated to the countryside.

They follow the signs for the rest center, with arrows added in crayon, pointing the way to the school lunchroom. The room is long, with three rows of narrow wooden tables. Every seat seems to be already taken. It is warm and muggy with a smell of cooked sausage. Around the walls, paintings of past headmasters stare down at them sternly.

A volunteer, a matronly woman in her forties with her hair in a turban scarf, starts tutting as soon as she sees Wild Bob.

"Over here, luvvie," she says, and makes Wild Bob sit while she cleans and bandages his arm. She doesn't ask any questions, and the efficient way in which she wraps the bandage makes Joe think she has had a lot of practice at this.

After that, she finds Wild Bob a seat by making a row of men in Home Guard uniforms shuffle along to make room. A young couple stands up to leave from the opposite side of the same table. Eddie and Peggy quickly slide in. Joe is left standing for a moment until Peggy shifts half off her chair.

"Park yourself," she says, patting the empty half.

Joe sits. One bum cheek on the chair, one off, rubbing thighs with Peggy, which is not totally unpleasant.

Another volunteer brings them plates of food and collects their coins as Joe looks around.

The meal is fourpence for an adult, but only tuppence for a child. Joe doesn't spend the extra penny for dessert. He doesn't have the stomach for it after what had just happened.

There are a mixture of people. Old and young, men and women. Next to them the Home Guard soldiers are singing "There'll Always Be an England" in surprisingly good harmony. Joe knows the song, but they have changed the lyrics.

It seems unpatriotic to Joe, until he sees that the people around them are laughing and clapping. In the face of such devastation and tragedy, it is their way of thumbing their noses at the Nazis. Elsewhere, gentlemen in bowler hats mix freely with East End hawkers. Socialites chat with cleaning ladies. German bombs are a great leveler, indiscriminate as to whose houses they destroy. Normal social barriers are breaking down. At least here. At least for now.

An air-raid warden, one of the senior ones with a white helmet instead of black, is quietly weeping at the next table, his face in his hands, his food untouched.

Joe stares at his plate for a moment. Two thin wedges of fried American Spam with a slice of fried bread and a spoonful of gravy the consistency of river mud. He pushes the food around his plate with a fork.

"So what happened to you, Wild Bob?" he asks. "I saw you fall down."

"Just a cut," Wild Bob says, and adds proudly, "I never got shot before."

"Didn't he find you?" Peggy asks.

"He just ran straight past," Wild Bob says. "He was after you lot."

"Then what did you do?" Eddie asks.

"I followed him. He couldn't see me, see, coz I was behind him. But when he went into the drain, I lost my nerve. I don't like going in holes in the ground."

"So what did you do?" Joe asks.

"Well," Wild Bob says apologetically, "it took me a bit. But finally I worked up enough courage to go in after you. Didn't like it much."

"But you kept going," Peggy says softly.

Wild Bob nods. "Then I seen him trying to shoot Joe and all, so I blew my whistle."

He pulls the ARP whistle out of a pocket to illustrate.

"Smashing!" Peggy says.

Joe is staring at Wild Bob, open-mouthed, wondering what it must have taken for the big boy to overcome his claustrophobia, to follow them through the storm drain. Now he understands the reason for Wild Bob's tears earlier. It wasn't because of the pain. It was his terror as he stumbled, footstep by footstep, through that dark and dreadful tunnel.

"Thank you, Milton," Joe says.

Wild Bob smiles, not even noticing the use of his real name.

"Your mum is definitely mixed up in summat," Eddie says, pointing at Joe with his knife.

"Thank you, Captain State-the-Bleedin'-Obvious," Peggy says. She finishes her plate and starts eyeing Joe's.

Eddie continues, unruffled, "Who's the geezer what got shot?"

"I dunno," Joe says, although he is sure he had seen the man before. It was the man who exchanged gas mask bags with his mother on Blackfriars Bridge.

He tries to eat but his fingers are trembling and he has no stomach for the food.

"So your mum met this bloke, then another bloke shot him and tried to shoot your mum, then forgot all about her and chased us instead," Peggy says. "Why did he want the camera so bad?"

"Coz I took his picture," Wild Bob says. "I knew he was after the camera, so I chucked it at Joe when I fell down."

That might well have saved Wild Bob's life, Joe thinks.

Peggy pushes her empty plate away and looks again at Joe's untouched food. Joe slides his plate to her. She smiles happily and stabs a slice of Spam with a fork.

"You got his face an' all?" Eddie asks.

Wild Bob nods, his mouth full.

"We gotta give those photos to the coppers," Peggy says.

"I'll develop them tonight and bring them tomorrow," Wild Bob says with a mouthful, spitting breadcrumbs across the table.

"Meet at the church," Peggy says.

Joe nods, but he is thinking about his mother. Is she okay? He saw her run away from the killer. Did she get somewhere safe? Who was trying to kill her and why? These thoughts are tumbling over and over in his brain when there is a murmuring from near the entrance to the room, followed by a rush of movement as the crowd tries to see what is going on. Eddie stands on a chair to see, despite a warning glance from one of the volunteers.

A tall, hard-faced man that Joe has seen before at the War Rooms enters, ushering people away from the entrance and making space around the doorway.

A moment later a shorter, rounder man in a homburg hat steps in.

"Bleedin' 'eck. That's Winston Churchill himself, that is," Eddie says breathlessly.

The great man shakes some hands and quietly chats with a few people before turning to address the crowd. A few hangers-on and press photographers crowd in behind him.

The room goes completely silent.

Churchill flashes his famous "V for Victory" sign, and says, "It's been tough, these last few weeks. Maybe the toughest weeks so far. And it will get tougher yet, before it gets easier. But it will get easier, that I promise you. Hitler can throw whatever he likes at us. We can take it."

Cameras flash.

The crowd remains silent, so he repeats it, louder. "We can take it!"

"I'll tell ya where you can take it," someone yells, and the crowd begins to shift and surge, and cameras flash again.

"We don't see *you* suffering, guv'nor," another voice yells. "Plenty safe in your nice deep bunker."

"We're the ones shivering and dying."

A young woman in a black dress steps out of the crowd, right in front of Churchill, prompting the bodyguard to step in between them.

"I'm not a soldier," she says quietly. "My little Jenny—my wee girl—she weren't a soldier neither, but she died for England just the same."

Churchill looks somber but flashes his *V* sign a few more times for the camera as he, and the rest of his entourage make their way to the exit. The singing Cockney home guardsmen serenade them out of the door.

Joe sleeps little that night. Grable paces endlessly, unwell and uncomfortable. He hopes she will be okay.

Every now and then it occurs to him to hope that *he* will be okay too.

15

LOOTER

London, March 8, 1941

The boy is first to the meeting place in the old church so he is first to see that the church has been the recipient of another German bomb.

"Bleedin' 'eck," Peggy says, arriving behind him. Joe does not turn around.

"I don't think God likes this church," Eddie says.

"It's the Nazis what don't like this church," Peggy says.

"What did this church ever do to the Nazis?" Eddie asks.

The outer walls of the church, previously left standing, are now crumbled piles of brick.

"Where's Wild Bob?" Joe asks.

"He'll be here," Peggy says.

"Unless he got blowed up during the night," Eddie says, and winces as his sister kicks him in the ankle. "What?"

"Don't be horrible," Peggy says.

"Just being realistic," Eddie grumbles, but the point is rendered moot as Wild Bob appears at the end of a side road.

"Blimey," he says, looking at the damage. Joe knows he is wondering about his treasure chest.

"Have you got the photos?" Joe asks.

Wild Bob nods and taps the side of the bag he carries the camera in.

"Come on, then, let's have a gander," Eddie says.

Wild Bob shakes his head and glances around at people hurrying past. "Inside." He nods toward the church.

"There's not much inside left," Joe says.

"Wait up," Eddie says. "Shh. Someone's already here."

Sounds of movement are coming from within the piles of brick.

"Stay here," Peggy says, and skips quickly and lightly to the top of one of the mounds to have a look.

"Come on, quick," she calls down to the others.

The boys struggle up a haphazard pile of bricks that constantly threatens to slip and skate from under their feet.

A weaselly looking man with a peaked cap is working among the ruins, tossing bricks to the left and right.

"I think he's after your treasure." Eddie chuckles.

"I don't think so," Wild Bob says.

A few more bricks are moved, and now they can see what the man is digging for.

"Blimey, he's found a survivor!" Eddie says. "Let's help. We'll be blimmin' heroes."

"It's not a survivor," Wild Bob says.

Wild Bob is right. It is the body of a young woman. She is covered in dust and is clearly dead, although there are no obvious signs of blood or injury. The legs that emerge as the man works are slim and shapely, the dress short and fashionable.

She lies facedown, and as the man drags the body out of a

pile of bricks, Joe looks away, not wanting to intrude on her dignity, or lack of it.

"The dirty beggar," Peggy says quietly.

Joe looks back. The man is wrestling rings off the woman's fingers. One is clearly stuck, the fingers perhaps swollen, and he pulls a pair of pruning shears from the pocket of his jacket.

"Oi!" Peggy yells. "Get away with yer."

Joe joins in. "Hey! Leave her alone."

The man looks around, makes a rude gesture, and settles the shears on the woman's finger.

The first stone misses him but lands just past him, kicking up dust and dislodging a couple of bricks, startling him so that he drops the shears. He scrabbles around for them among the rubble.

It is Wild Bob who has thrown the stone—actually a broken piece of brick—but now Joe, Peggy, and Eddie join in. A hail of brick fragments rains down around the man, one catching him on the side of his arm. To Joe's surprise, he doesn't back away.

"Bloody kids," he yells up at them. "You can't have 'er; she's mine." He picks up a broken length of copper pipe and starts to climb up toward them, despite the rain of rubble.

"Run," Eddie says, starting to turn.

Wild Bob says simply, "No." He reaches inside his bag, and his hand emerges with the camera, telephoto lens still attached. He aims it at the man, who stops in his tracks.

Wild Bob doesn't take a picture, Joe sees. There might not even be film in the camera. But the threat is enough.

The man hesitates.

"Got yer picture now, ya weasel," Peggy calls. "Now get off with yer."

"Gonna give it to the police if you don't beat it," Eddie says.

Joe launches another piece of brick, which catches the man on his cheek, spinning his head around and drawing blood. He starts to back away. More afraid of the camera, Joe thinks, than the missiles.

"Leave 'er alone," the man shouts. "I found her first." He beats a hasty retreat, blood streaming from one cheek, hands up to protect his head as more rubble whizzes past him.

"Someone go get the warden," Wild Bob says. "Or that dirty beggar will be back."

"I'll go," Peggy says, and scurries away across the broken building.

"He weren't doing nothing wrong," Eddie says as they wait for her return. "Not really. Just trying to survive."

"Don't make it right," Wild Bob says.

"She weren't using those rings no more," Eddie protests.

"Ain't right if she were alive, ain't right if she's dead," Wild Bob says. "How'd you like it if it were your Peggy down there?"

"Peggy don't wear no rings," Eddie says, but after a moment he scrambles down from the mound and makes his way over to the woman's body, finding the pair of shears the man dropped.

He climbs back up, grinning. "Spoils of war," he says.

Joe grins back, although he doesn't feel much like grinning. He doesn't have a sister. But he does have a mum. How would he feel if that were her?

"How'd she get there?" Wild Bob wonders out loud. "An' how'd she get dead?"

"Maybe she got caught in a huge explosion," Eddie says. "One of those Hermanns, you know, the two-thousand pounders. Could've blown her 'alfway across the city and she ended up here."

"She doesn't look like she's been in an explosion. Maybe she'd come here with her man for some private time and got killed by some flying debris," Joe says.

"Then where's her bloke?" Eddie asks.

"Under the rubble," Joe surmises. "Or maybe he just scarpered."

"Maybe she was murdered and her body dumped in the church," Wild Bob says.

Anything is possible. Blitz-torn London is a harsh and unforgiving place.

With their HQ no longer available, Joe leads the others to his cellar as soon as Peggy returns, warden in tow.

Peggy descends the steps warily.

"I like what you've done with the place," Eddie says. "Very bomb-site chic."

"You didn't tell us you had a dog" is Peggy's comment.

Grable seems better. She has eaten a little food. Not enough, but a little. The milk yesterday seems to have given her a little strength. Either that or she is just excited to meet some new people.

Peggy fusses over her endlessly, more interested in the dog

than the photographs, it seems. Wild Bob too seems very taken with the little dog. Joe has to prod him a couple of times to get him to bring out the photos, but eventually he does.

The photography is good. The camera is high quality, as is the lens, and Wild Bob clearly has an eye for a good shot.

The first one is of the squirrel, twig in hand, staring right at the camera as if posing for the picture.

The next photo is of Joe's mother leaving the War Rooms. It could have been a professional picture. His mother is perfectly framed, her hair ruffled by a breeze, her face relaxed but determined.

He knows that look. He saw it so many times growing up in Berlin.

Next is his mother on the park bench. The telephoto lens brings her so close. God, how he misses her.

The next photo catches the moment of the murder, even down to the puff of smoke from the pistol. The man in the tan suit is staggering forward, a ragged hole in the back of his jacket, the fedora flying from his head.

The fourth is of the man with the gun, turned toward them, unaware of the gas mask bag that is swinging at his head from behind. His face is perfectly captured: haggard, with vertical jowl lines. The picture is clear enough to see the drooping left eyelid. His mouth is open in a snarl.

"Bloody 'eck," Eddie says. "He's a monster."

Joe can't take his eyes from the man's face. He knows this face. He will never forget it. This is the man from the old cobblestone alley.

"Whatever your mum is mixed up in," Peggy is saying, "she's in way over her head."

Joe just nods, unwilling to trust his tongue to speak.

"What you gonna do now?" Eddie asks. "Take the photos to the coppers?"

"Talk to her," Wild Bob says, handing him the photos. "Then decide what to do."

Joe nods again. Wild Bob, as always, had the best advice.

Joe's mother emerges from the War Rooms at five o'clock on the dot, looking as fresh and unworried as if she hadn't nearly been murdered the previous day.

He follows her, carefully, waiting and wondering when the right moment will be to confront her. He wonders how she will react when she sees him. When she sees the photographs that are tucked inside his gas mask bag. Wondering how he will react.

All he has to do is walk up to her and say hello. The simplest thing in the world. But still he hesitates. He hesitates because he is afraid. He is afraid because he is a coward. There is no easy cure for that.

She meets the tall, thin man with the wire-framed glasses. The man she met on the first day Joe saw her. That seems such a long time ago.

The couple (*are* they a couple?) dine at a fashionable pub in the West End. Joe isn't able to follow them in there; he is not old enough. He waits outside for hours, watching all the comings and goings, until they eventually emerge sometime after nine.

They say goodbye, and the man kisses her, but it's a chaste

peck on the cheek, which pleases Joe. Silly, he knows, in light of everything else that is going on.

Wailing Winnie starts up as his mother, with Joe on her tail, hurries through the darkened streets of central London.

She leads him back to the Café de Paris. Her favorite haunt, he thinks. Or is she meeting another man here? Another spy?

Now he watches her disappear through the doors behind an impeccably dressed couple: he in top hat and tails, she in a fur coat. Joe can hear the music floating up the stairs and across the street to him. He can imagine Snakehips leading the band through a cheerful version of the "Washington Squabble."

A fire engine roars past, heading toward a growing conflagration to the south. There are other fires too, towers of flames licking at the night sky.

How can the Londoners bear this? Every night an orchestra of terror, broken sleep, and the chance of injury or death. This was wrong. This wasn't war. War was between armies. The screaming woman on his first night in London, the little girl in the gutter, the bus driver in the wreck of his double-decker, they weren't soldiers. Just people.

The unfairness, the insanity of it all, threatens to overwhelm him.

He hears a whistle, then an explosion just a few streets away. He crouches low in the meager protection offered by the doorway. The next blast is closer, shattering the windows up and down the street. He knows the pattern of the bombs, he knows it far too well. Bombs drop in a group of five. These are coming in his direction.

He has to get to cover. He jumps up and sprints toward the other side of the road and is in the middle of the street when the next bomb strikes a building just a street away. He ducks, crying out in shock and terror, shielding his face with an arm against a storm of shattered wood and glass and a shock wave that almost knocks him from his feet. He runs. The next bomb has his name on it. He knows it. Beyond doubt.

He makes it to the Café de Paris, bursting through one of the heavy doors, desperate to get to safety before the next blast. He hears the door begin to swing shut behind him as he bounds across the foyer toward the long staircase that leads down into the nightclub. He has left it too late, he knows that. The explosions are always evenly spaced and the next one is already due.

He makes it only to the top of the stairs before the roar blasts open the doors behind him.

Something is wrong. The tempest of smoke, dust, and hot air is outward, not inward, bursting up the staircase in a stark rush of light that lifts him and carries him back out of the club, through the doors, blasted from their hinges.

He lands in the street outside, in a whirlwind of plaster and glass and shattered, crumbled wood. Winded, gasping, he is numb to the pain, for now. Injured? *Maybe.* Dead? *Not yet.* Dying? *Very possibly.*

He lies in the street where he fell, dazed, blood trickling into his eyes and from his nose, staring at the shattered ragged hole where the doors had been.

There is an eerie silence for a moment. Then the screaming starts, welling up the staircase, a chorus of terror and pain, muffled by the thick cotton wool that seems to have grown in his ears.

Screaming! That means there are survivors. Against every instinct to stay where he is, he pushes himself upright, wiping away blood from his eyes so he can see. He staggers to his feet, lurching left and right like a drunkard, then stumbling awkwardly toward the broken doors. His breath comes in harsh sobs, his chest aches, his eyes burn with tears and grit and smoke and blood.

The black car is upon him before he realizes it, screeching to a halt amid the rubble-strewn street, the doors swinging open.

The two men in dark coats run to him, ignoring the devastation. Ignoring the screams. His arms are seized, and he has no strength with which to fight the men as they drag his numb, battered body to the rear of the car.

He may have screamed for his mother; he may not have. He cannot be sure.

He is thrown into the back seat, one of the men climbing in beside him. The other man drives.

Joe stares at the man next to him, his lips framing a question that his voice seems unable to ask.

Who?

The man somehow understands. He fumbles an identity card out of a pocket and flashes it in front of Joe's unfocused eyes.

"MI5," the man says. "You need to come with us."

BOOK THREE

PARIS

At least thirty-four people were killed in the Café de Paris. Many more were injured. People thought it was safe, as they were well below ground level, but a bomb somehow found a ventilation shaft and exploded on the dance floor.

Ken Johnson, the bandleader I'd met that day, was decapitated. To this day I have nightmares of his severed head rolling across the floor toward me, smiling and saying "call me Snakehips" every time his face comes around.

—from the memoirs of Joseph "Katipo" St. George

16

TAR

London, March 8, 1941

The car accelerates away from the smoking wreck of the Café de Paris, veering around a cordoned-off crater in the road. How the driver even sees it, driving in the dark with no headlights on, is a mystery.

Joe glances occasionally at the big man sitting next to him. He can see little except for a strong jaw and a pencil-thin mustache that twitches occasionally at the sound of nearby bomb blasts. Of the driver he can see nothing.

They dodge around cars, taxis, and even a double-decker bus, all abandoned in the street by drivers who are less game than these MI5 men to drive through an air raid.

They are near the Thames, he knows, because he occasionally catches glimpses of bridges, including the famous Tower Bridge. They seem to be heading toward the Tower of London for a while and his befuddled brain considers the possibility that he is being taken there to be hanged.

The driver swears suddenly under his breath and jerks the wheel around to the right, swerving wildly, tires screeching as he struggles to control the vehicle and get it back on course. A flash in the sky lights the road for a moment, and Joe sees the obstacle that has caused the sudden evasive action, a horse lying in the middle of the road . . . dead or dying, Joe can't tell. The tires hit the curb on the other side and Joe thinks for a moment that the car is going to tip over; two wheels come off the ground, but it crashes back down with a jolt that shakes the car and sends Joe flying across into the lap of the man next to him. He pulls himself away and, without thinking, apologizes.

The car regains control, fishtailing down the street, then spins around a corner into . . . Joe has no idea where they are. Somewhere near the heart of London, that is all he knows, because that was where they started and they haven't gone far. Not yet anyway. They bounce over huge hoses snaking across the road. The firemen are kneeling, two to a hose, spraying huge jets of water at a burning office block.

A huge sheet of flame erupts above them as if a giant, fire-breathing dragon has climbed to the top of one of the tall buildings and is raging down at them from above. Bricks shower the car, crashing into the roof, denting it, smashing the car window next to Joe. He is still visualizing the dragon when its head crashes down onto the road in front of them, lit in flickering intensity by the fierce fire in a shop front.

The dragon has exploded.

Joe's numbed, uncomprehending mind struggles to grasp the reality of it, until he sees that the dragon's face and partial torso is also made of stone. It is the remains of a gargoyle blasted from the turrets of one of London's tall buildings.

The car swerves again, careering around the ugly, leering stone face of the creature, bouncing through a minefield of crushed stone. The driver instinctively turns to look at the furiously burning shop front, his face illuminated for half a second before he turns away.

It is long enough. Joe would know that face anywhere. A long, craggy face, mean, with one drooping eyelid.

Instantly, Joe leaps for the door, snatching at the handle, but although it moves, the door does not open. The man in the back seat grabs for his arm, and when Joe wrenches that free, grabs him by the collar instead, slamming his face forward into the seat in front. With blood streaming from his nose, and even more dazed than before, Joe can make no sense of what happens next.

A loud retort sounds from beside the left front wheel. A tire blowout, is Joe's first thought—they must have run over some broken glass or sharp debris—but the sound is accompanied by a flash of light. A bomb? No, the explosion was too small. A landmine? A grenade? How can that be? This is London, not the battlefields of North Africa. Nothing makes any sense. He is calmly thinking all this as the car flips onto its side and slides along the road in a shower of sparks, the large man next to Joe now on top of him in a jumble of arms and legs.

Joe is still trying to make sense of what is happening as the car grinds to a halt against a wrought-iron fence. He pushes at the man, unable to breathe with the weight on top of him, then strong hands reach in through the smashed rear window of the car, dragging the man out. More hands reach for Joe, pulling him out by the same route as flames flicker across the underside of the car from a leaking fuel tank.

When he is hauled to his feet a good distance from the now-burning car, the two men who took him from the Café de Paris are lying facedown on the ground, their hands shackled behind their backs. Dark-suited men with pistols surround them.

Joe is unceremoniously lifted and thrown into the back of a black van. He recognizes this as a police van, the one they called the Black Maria. Has he been arrested? The only window, a small one at the rear of the van, is barred.

This is all happening too fast. He can't cope. Especially with a brain still foggy from the explosion. Especially for someone whose mother has just died.

The next journey is longer, but he sees nothing of it inside the windowless van.

He sees nothing, but he hears something.

Something that buoys his shattered and confused spirits. The all-clear siren. Whatever is going to happen from here, at least it won't end with the shriek of a Nazi bomb.

When the van finally stops and the rear door opens, a large, taciturn man in a dark suit politely invites Joe to step out. When he does, he sees they are on an airfield. The runway is outlined by electric lights, which seems dangerous in the blackout, until he remembers that the all clear has been given. From the noise overhead, a squad of night fighters is coming in to land.

Joe peers at the sky through the dim glow of the landing lights. A plane is coming in low and fast, smoke trailing from its engine. It touches down hard, bouncing high before coming in a second time, bouncing again, and eventually sticking to the grassy landing strip. Ground crew race to the plane as it stops, climbing up on ladders to assist the pilots, clearly injured, from the cockpit.

That plane is followed by another, then another.

The man guides Joe toward a larger aircraft. A twin-engine, twin-tailed plane of a kind that Joe does not recognize. Perhaps a bomber.

The fact that they have come to this airfield bodes well. If it was German agents that had him, it is unlikely that they would bring him here.

Why is he being taken to an airplane? The thought occurs to him that they might be going to take him high over the English Channel somewhere, then push him out, but even if that is the case, there is little he can do about it.

The man leads Joe to a short ladder up to a door in the side of the plane, then steps aside, motioning for Joe to go up. Joe does and finds himself in a cabin fitted out with a few seats and a small table fitted to one wall. The man follows him up.

The pilot, to Joe's surprise, is a young woman. She glances around as he enters but does not speak to him or acknowledge his presence in any other way.

A man is seated at the table looking at photographs. Wild Bob's photographs.

He is handsome, with eyes that twinkle as though he is in on a joke that you know nothing about. His hair is black and slicked to one side, though graying a little at the temples and he wears wire-framed glasses. He smiles an easy smile, probably designed to put Joe at ease. This man is debonair and charming . . . and, Joe decides, not to be trusted. He knows this man. He has seen him before. Twice. Most recently having dinner with his mother in a West End pub.

"Thank you, Sergeant," the man says in a mild Scottish accent. The large man nods and disappears.

The man holds up the photo of the squirrel, smiles briefly, and puts it at the bottom of the pile. He shuffles through the others as Joe waits, spending a lot of time on the photo of the murder. Eventually he looks up.

"Nice to meet you at last, Joseph," he says, extending a hand. "My name is Thomas, but my friends—and I think we are going to be friends, so that includes you—call me Tar."

Joe wonders if any of that is true. He shakes Tar's hand politely.

"How do you know my name?" Joe asks, and adds pointedly, "Thomas."

Tar smiles again. "Well, we wouldn't be very good at our job if we couldn't keep track of a fourteen-year-old boy, now would we, laddie?"

Joe considers that for a moment and notes that Tar avoids saying exactly what his job is.

"Who were those men?" he asks. "The ones who were"—he hesitates, searching for the right word—"arrested."

"Who did they say they were?" Tar asks.

"MI5."

"Let me give you a tip, Joe," Tar says. "Anyone who tells you they are working for MI5 is almost certainly *not* working for MI5."

He looks up as the pilot pops her head back into the cabin. "Field is clear, sir," she says. "We have clearance for takeoff."

Joe's eyes are fixed on Tar. "So who do *you* work for?"

"MI5." Tar chuckles and adds, "You'd better buckle in."

"Where are we going?" Joe asks, pulling the canvas harness over his shoulders. Tar shows him how to clip it together.

"You're not going anywhere," Tar says. "As for where I'm going, that's not your business."

"I don't understand," Joe says.

"Your understanding, or lack of it, is not my problem. I need to talk to you and I don't have much time," Tar says. "Also, I wanted to meet you somewhere we won't be overheard and where nobody will see you."

"Somebody has seen me," Joe says, with a nod at the cockpit.

They begin taxiing out onto the field. The rumble of the engines grows to a roar, and the plane vibrates as they begin to move, faster and faster, until the bumps of the grassy runway soften, then disappear altogether.

"She sees nothing," Tar says. "Nothing she is not told to see. I'd trust her with my life. In fact, I suppose I do, every time she takes the controls. Can I trust you with my life, Joe?"

"I don't know," Joe says honestly. "All I know about you so far is that you don't work for MI5."

Tar smiles. "Well, this is a chance for us to get to know each other a little better. I'll be dropped off somewhere you don't need to know about, and you'll return here. Then Sergeant Smith or Sergeant Jones will take you home. Those are the two large gentlemen who rescued you from the German agents a little while ago."

Joe suspects that Smith and Jones are not their real names.

"That is, if we have reached an agreement," Tar continues.

Joe is about to ask what will happen if they don't reach an agreement, but then remembers his thought about being pushed out of the plane in midair and decides not to ask.

"So you know my name," he says instead. "What else do you know about me?"

"Oh, I know a lot of things," Tar says.

"Such as?"

Tar taps the pile of photographs. "I know that you have been spying on your mother for the last few days."

Joe draws in his breath. "Is my mother alive?" he asks.

"That I honestly don't know," Tar said.

"She went into the Café de Paris just before . . ."

"She did," Tar nods. "I am waiting for a report. But let's come back to you for a moment."

"There was screaming," Joe says. "There had to be survivors."

"I'm afraid I really don't know, Joe," Tar says.

"I thought she might be a Nazi spy," Joe says. "I still do."

"Why is that, Joe?" Tar asks.

"Why would I tell you?" Joe asks. "I don't know who you are and I don't know who you work for. You could also be a Nazi spy for all I know."

"Do you think a Nazi spy would be able to commandeer an RAF airplane and be flown around by the ATA?" Tar asks.

Joe shakes his head.

"Then for now, let us assume that I am one of the good guys," Tar says. "Why did you think your mother was a spy?"

"I was suspicious at first when I saw her with you," Joe says. "She seemed affectionate, which didn't seem right. But she loved . . . *loves* my father."

"You are very observant," Tar says. "And yes, she was quite affectionate. We are old friends—but nothing more. Let me say that you did a good job of tailing her. It was very impressive."

"Clearly not good enough," Joe mutters.

"Well, you knew to keep people in between you when you were following, and to use the other side of the road when possible. When the gas mask bag was exchanged you knew to follow the bag not the carrier. Enlisting the local lads and lasses to assist was just as clever. Turning your coats inside out and changing hats was a nice touch too. It was enough to make us wonder if you had been properly trained. Perhaps by the Abwehr."

Joe had thought he was being careful. But all the time these people had been watching his every move. The murdered man in the tan suit. Had he been one of Tar's people?

"If you know so much about me, then you'd know I don't work for the Nazis," he says. "How could I? I've been living in New Zealand since I was twelve, and before that I barely escaped Berlin with my life."

"Yes." Tar temples his fingers and stares intently at Joe. "I said we *wondered* if you had been trained. We quickly discounted that theory."

"What was happening at the Café de Paris?" Joe asks. "Was that one of your meeting places?"

"Actions have consequences, Joe" is Tar's enigmatic response.

The pilot has been talking quietly on the radio during this conversation. Now she turns and hands Tar a folded note. Tar reads it. His eyes close for a moment, concealing some kind of emotion.

"Is that your report?" Joe demands. "Is Mum alive?"

"Your mother was not among the survivors."

Joe bends his head, hiding his face. Memories of his mother flooding his brain. Is that all he has left—memories? How is that possible! He will never see her, never hear her voice, never hug her, ever again. It is as though a giant void has suddenly opened up in his life.

He fights back tears. He does not want to seem weak in front of this man. But he doesn't want to seem callous and cold either.

He looks out of the window instead—and gasps. They are high above London now and it is a sea of fire! Not one, but a hundred blazes, leaping pillars of flame spouting from the windows of buildings. In the glow of the fires he can see the damage, as if some terrible god has marched across the city, leaving a trail of broken and crumbled buildings.

Tiny dots, silhouetted by the fires, are the firemen on their ladders, clutching hoses, doing their best to quell the inferno.

Joe watches in silent shock and awful understanding of the scale of the devastation. On the ground, when you were in the middle of it, you thought only about the bombs that screamed overhead as you waited for the one that would end your life. From up here, it seems that the whole of London is taking such punishment it is impossible for it to survive.

He drags his eyes back to the man who has been watching him.

"There's a kind of fierce poetic beauty to it all, isn't there," Tar mused.

"Beauty! It's awful," Joe explodes.

"Don't misunderstand me," Tar says, and his voice goes cold. "This is an orchestrated campaign of terror, designed to terrify and demoralize the British people. And it's working."

Joe looks back at the wide swathes of devastation, the crushed buildings and fiercely burning fires and says nothing for a moment. He wipes away tears and stares at Tar through bleary eyes.

"Why have you kidnapped me?" he asks.

"Kidnapped? Aye, there's an emotive word," Tar said. "Rescue is the word I'd use. Kidnapping"—he rolled the word around in his mouth—"that's what the enemy does. That's what they did to you. Rescuing is what we did to get you back. There is an important distinction, although it may not be all that obvious when you're on the receiving end."

"Why am I here?" Joe asked.

"All in good time, Joe. How much do you know about the work your mother and father did?"

"In Berlin? They were diplomats of some kind."

Tar raises an eyebrow. "Really?"

This is a test, Joe realizes.

"They never talked to me about their real work, and why would they? I was very young, but it was pretty clear to me that they were secret agents."

"And now?"

"Now my mother is dead," Joe says bitterly, "and my father is being held by the Gestapo . . . if he's not dead too."

They are passing over the outer suburbs of London now, where the damage is less intense, although Joe can see smoke rising from the Liverpool docks.

"By the SD, not the Gestapo," Tar says. "The Gestapo arrested him, but they passed him almost immediately onto the SD."

"SD?" Joe asks.

"Sicherheitsdienst. German counterintelligence," Tar says. "Part of the SS, as is the Gestapo. If the SD knew who you were, they might threaten to hurt your father if you didn't become a double agent and work for them."

"Never!" Joe says, with vehemence that surprises him.

"That's easy to say," Tar says. "But when a person you love is in danger, it may not be so easy to do."

"I'd never become a double agent," Joe says.

"Your mother did," Tar says.

Joe is silent. He suspected that. He just doesn't like having it confirmed.

"So she was passing secrets to the Germans," he says bitterly.

"Well, yes, but only secrets that we wanted her to pass," Tar says.

Joe raises his eyes slowly off the floor, his brain working overtime. He says nothing.

"The SD recruited her here in London," Tar goes on, "under threat of torture or death to your father. How they must have rubbed their hands with glee, turning one of our top agents into a double agent, with an ear right inside Churchill's War Rooms. But of course your mother told us everything, and we arranged for her to go through with it all. By my rudimentary calculations, that would make her a triple agent."

Joe's heart leaps. The death of his mother is fresh and raw but is somehow made easier knowing that she wasn't a traitor.

"So who was the man who tried to kill her?"

Tar sighs. "It's a complicated game, Joe. Are you sure you want to know all this?"

"I'm sure."

"Her handler, her contact. A German agent posing as a Swiss businessman. We've been onto him for months."

"Why would her own handler want her dead?" Joe asks.

"Not her, the man she was meeting," Tar says. "The man who was killed was a Russian double agent. He had infiltrated German intelligence. Unfortunately he was compromised, and the SD decided he had to be terminated. Your mother was in the wrong place at the wrong time."

Joe takes a moment to try and get his head around all this. It is so much more complicated than the stories in his adventure magazines.

"Why didn't you arrest him?" Joe asks.

"Oh, we would have, if we'd had the chance," Tar says. "A

real treasure trove of secrets he would've turned out to be. But the Germans beat us to it."

Tar taps his fingers on the table and watches Joe for a while. "Actions have consequences," he says eventually.

"So you keep saying," Joe says. "But I still don't understand."

"The Café de Paris was an escape route for us," Tar says. "A way of ditching a tail if someone felt they were being followed."

Joe's heart starts pounding in his chest.

"So my mother knew that I was following her?" he says.

"She knew someone was following her," Tar says.

The cabin is swimming, and it is not from the movement of the plane.

"She went there to escape from me . . ." Joe says.

Tar shrugs. "We don't really know her thoughts, now do we?"

Joe heart is hammering now. Had he been responsible for the death of his own mother? He gulps in air, feeling nauseated.

"The question is, what do I do with you?" Tar says. "Lock you away in a dark place where you can't cause any more damage? Or should I toss you out that door with a faulty parachute . . ."

"It might be what I deserve," Joe says, with a glance at the door.

Tar sighs. "I was joking," he says. "And there is another option . . . I could offer you a job."

"I'll take it," Joe says immediately.

"You haven't heard what it is yet," Tar says.

"What is it?"

"I'm afraid I can't tell you that."

"I'll take it."

"Ah, the impetuousness of youth," Tar says. "This is war. Be careful what you volunteer for."

"Too late," Joe says. "I already volunteered."

"So you did," Tar says. "Well, we need someone to undertake a very important, very secretive mission. But it has to be someone young. A child, like yourself. You will understand that we don't have all that many options."

Joe breathed in deeply, steadying himself. Trying to forget what he had just learned.

"Why a child?" he asks.

"That will be made clear to you at the appropriate time," Tar says. "If you volunteer, you will first undergo a number of tests and some very special training. We'll find you somewhere to live. Somewhere a little nicer than that broken-down cellar of yours."

"I have a dog," Joe says, surprising himself that he should mention such a thing at that moment. "I'm not leaving her on her own."

"Yes," Tar says, tapping his fingers again. "Grable. She'll be able to come and live with you if you like. Her owners are deceased. Her real name is Dot, in case you're interested."

Joe stares at him. He really does know more about Joe than Joe knows himself. *Dot.* He turns the name over in his mind. No, it doesn't stick. Grable will always be Grable to him, and she answers to it now too.

"Grable's sick," he says.

"Is that so?" Tar says in a manner that made Joe think he

already knows this fact. "As it happens, one of the best vets in London is a personal friend of mine, and he hasn't had much to do since the cull."

"The cull?"

"You hadn't heard about that?" Tar shrugs. "Most of the pets in London were put down in the first week of the war. People were worried about a shortage of food and so on. They weren't wrong either. Dot must've been one of the exceptions."

"That's awful!" Joe cries, remembering the milkman's Labrador.

"Quite," Tar says.

Joe is silent for a moment, then says, "Thank you, sir. About Grable I mean."

Tar nods, then asks, "Any other questions?"

Joe looks out of the window at the inferno that is London, now slipping away behind them. His mind is racing. Images of his mother disappearing down the stairs of the Café de Paris collided with memories of the explosion flipping the car onto its side, and Grable alone and frightened in the ruined cellar. The men who claimed to be MI5 but were not. This man, Tar, who seems to be some kind of puppet master, sitting in the shadows, pulling strings. Is he for real? Can he be trusted? Joe's instincts say yes, but he still has the strong feeling that Tar is keeping something from him.

"Just one," Joe says.

"Go ahead."

"What is it that you are not telling me?"

"You think I'm hiding something?" Tar says.

“I do,” Joe says.

“Your mother was right about you,” Tar says. “You have good instincts.”

“My mother talked about me?” Joe asks.

“Incessantly,” Tar says, but his face grows serious. He now seems gaunt and hard. “There are many things that I am keeping from you, Joseph.”

“Why?”

Tar gives up on his pipe now and tucks it away. “Information is given on a need-to-know basis. If I don’t think you need to know something, then you won’t get to know it. Not now, not ever.”

“You may be underestimating my detective skills.” Joe smiles and tries to put a little menace into it.

Tar was not fazed. “I hope so. We’ll find out when you start your training.”

I knew about MI5 and the SOE. I didn't find out until long after the war that I was really working for a different department entirely. In those days it was known as Section Six of Military Intelligence and it was very hush-hush. Nowadays, of course, it is much better known, and usually by its abbreviation: MI6.

—from the memoirs of Joseph "Katipo" St. George

17

WANBOROUGH MANOR

Guildford, March 10, 1941

A staff car picks the boy up from the street corner in London where he stands with all his worldly belongings in a borrowed duffel bag and with a pregnant beagle at his side. The driver seems to have been cut from the same cloth as Tar's pilot. She says nothing throughout the entire trip and barely acknowledges his presence beyond a simple hello and confirmation of his identity. She takes Joe and Grable right to the gate of their new home in Guildford, Surrey—a vast improvement on his most recent lodgings.

The sad-eyed little beagle is full of pups. That was the first news Tar's vet friend gave Joe. Her illness is apparently due to complications with the pregnancy, some kind of infection, but fortunately it is treatable. The vet gave Joe a jar of antibiotic tablets for her.

Tar's real name turned out to be Thomas Argyle Robertson and he really does work for MI5. However, it is not MI5 that Joe will be working for, but the SOE—Special Operations Executive.

The house is old—perhaps hundreds of years old, Joe thinks—one of a number of similar houses in a small village clustered around a large Elizabethan manor house. The walls of the house are wooden weatherboards painted black, and the roof is steeply pitched.

Grable begins to sniff and paw at the window as the car crunches to a halt on the gravel road. Somehow she knows that this is their destination. She jumps down as soon as the door opens and bounds over to greet the woman who is walking up the path toward the car.

Rosemary Bedford is wearing corduroy trousers, riding boots, and just a checkered blouse, despite the chill March breeze. She holds a pair of riding gloves in one hand and kneels down as Grable runs up to her. The woman scratches the dog under her chin, then rubs under her belly before looking up in surprise. "She's pregnant. They didn't tell me we were getting an instant family."

Joe waves away the driver's offer of help with his bag, thanks her, and walks over to the woman.

"She is. I only just found out. I hope that's all right," he says.

"She's beautiful," the woman says. "She and her pups are welcome here." She stands and sticks out a hand abruptly. "Hello, I'm Rosie."

"Hello. I'm Joe." Unsure what to do when a lady offers you her hand, Joe takes it, bends forward, and kisses it, which makes Rosie laugh.

"How very gallant," she says, still clasping his hand.

She is a little taller than him, with dark brown hair pulled back into a ponytail. Very practical, if not very fashionable. Her cheekbones are high, her jawline firm, and her nose turned up just a little at the end. She looks quite aristocratic, but her accent, although Surrey-posh, is not that of the gentry. She is in her mid-twenties, he judges, and attractive in a sensible, common sense kind of way. He likes her immediately.

"You're older than they told me," she says, finally letting go of his hand.

"I'm fourteen," he says.

"Then you're taller than I expected," she says. "Big lad for your age, but I bet you get that a lot."

Joe smiles and nods.

"Handsome lad too. The local lasses will be all a-skitter . . ."

Joe feels his cheeks redden.

"Oh, and he blushes! How delightful."

The staff car backs away out of the driveway and takes off, no doubt to somewhere important and probably top secret.

"Well, come on in and wash off the dust," she says, which Joe takes to be a reference to the trip from London, although the car windows were closed and he did not get dusty.

"There's rabbit for dinner," Rosie is saying as they crunch back down the path. "I shot it myself. You might have to spit out a few shotgun pellets. And there's eggs for breakfast if you like."

"Like? I'd love," Joe manages, surprised. "Fresh eggs?"

"You can't get any fresher," Rosie says. "We send in our allocation to the food depot, but there are a few secret hens in the back of the barn that nobody knows about. A bit like your lot."

Joe stops mid-stride but continues as Rosie laughs. "If you think the village doesn't know what goes on up at the big house, you're mistaken."

By "big house" he knows she means the manor, but her own house seems big to him, especially after the poky terraced houses of London.

"How many people live here?" he asks, admiring the house.

"Just me at the minute," she says. "My husband, Jamie, is in the Hussars." When Joe looks blank, she elaborates, "King's Own Hussars."

"He rides a horse?" Joe asks. He read somewhere that a hussar was a cavalryman.

Rosie laughs, prettily. "In his dreams. He drives a tank. Part of the Third Armored Brigade. They're over in Africa just now waiting for Rommel to attack so they can kick his jolly backside back to Berlin."

"You must worry about him," Joe says.

Rosie abruptly changes subject. "It'll be nice to have a man around the house," she says, making Joe feel very grown up. "Someone to help with the chores, someone to prattle on to."

"Whatever I can do to help," Joe says. "I really appreciate your kindness in billeting me."

"No kindness involved," she says. "I'm being paid handsomely to give you a bed and feed. A little extra for your dog too."

"Grable," Joe says.

"After the American actress?" Rosie asked.

Joe nods.

"Lovely," Rosie says. "Nice choice. I loved her in *Million Dollar Legs.* Did you see that one?"

Joe hadn't. There hadn't been a cinema near the farm in

New Zealand. He opens his mouth to say as much but does not get the chance as Rosie barges on.

"They say Betty Grable's legs really are insured for a million dollars. I wonder how much I could insure my pins for."

Joe suspects she has perfectly nice "pins," but he can't see them due to the boots and trousers and suspects it might be impertinent if he comments, so he says nothing.

He shoulders his duffel bag and his gas mask bag, which seems a little unnecessary out here in the country, and follows Rosie up the driveway to the house.

She shows him to a large room with a narrow bed, a wardrobe in one corner, and floral curtains over a bay window. Dinner is rabbit stew, and it is excellent. Joe is pleased to discover that her mention of the shotgun pellets was a joke. Consequently, he makes a point of pretending to find one and choking on it, which earns him a gale of appreciative laughter when he splutters out the truth as she is pounding him on the back.

If not for the forthcoming training, which scares him, and the thought of what he will have to do at the end of that training, which terrifies him, this could be a very pleasant holiday in the country.

Training starts the following morning at eight, at the manor house. He is surprised to see quite a number of women among the recruits. They seem every bit as serious and deadly as the men.

Everybody is known by a code name, which they use all the time. Joe's code name for some reason is simply Joe, but he has been warned on pain of death not to reveal his last name, or any personal details, to anyone.

"Joe's common enough," Tar had said. "And at least you'll remember to answer to it. You'll have a new code name for the mission."

"What is it?" Joe had asked.

"In due course" had been the reply.

The female agents have code names like Thérèse, Gabrielle, and Véronique. The men are Gustav, Pierre, or Henri.

If the others are surprised to see a fourteen-year-old boy among the recruits, they do not show it. All greet him with a handshake, even the women, and he knows now not to kiss their hands when offered.

The others are in various stages of their training, Joe gathers. This being his first day, he is the newest, as well as the youngest. There are other differences too. The others all live at the manor. He is the only one who lives off-site. Presumably because they feel he needs a parental figure. A surrogate mother. He finds that a little odd. Rosie is so different from his own mother that he can't think of her in that way.

Major Flannery is in charge of Joe's training. He is a hearty Irishman with florid cheeks and a large belly.

"Welcome to the Special Operations Executive. The Ministry of Ungentlemanly Warfare," Flannery says as he gives him a quick tour of the Elizabethan manor house with its high ceilings and wood-paneled walls. "Or, as we like to call it, Churchill's Secret Army."

"Secret Army," Joe repeats the words, liking them.

"Aye, there's more ways to fight a war than cowering in trenches on a battlefield," Flannery says.

"Were you in the Great War?" Joe asked.

"A nasty piece of business, so it was," Flannery replies. "I've seen enough mud and blood and body parts to last a lifetime."

Joe glances sideways at him.

He has met veterans of that war, from both sides of the conflict. Most of those who spent time in the trenches have the same look: a haunted, troubled look as though they are living in a nightmare from which they cannot wake up. Flannery does not have that look, but that does not mean he is lying. People cope in different ways, he knows.

"It must've been terrible," Joe says.

"Don't get me wrong," Flannery says. "This secret war can get quite nasty too, but it's a different kind of nasty. You'll learn. And on that subject . . ." He stops outside a small room with a stretcher and a desk. A plump, middle-aged woman is sitting at the desk, wearing a white-and-blue uniform. "Meet Nurse Agnes."

Nurse Agnes practically leaps out of her chair and greets Joe with a hug, just about squeezing the air out of him.

"I've so been looking forward to meeting you," she says.

Joe mumbles something in reply.

"Nurse Agnes looks after anyone who gets injured," Flannery says. "And she also teaches our first aid course. I'd listen especially carefully to that, it might save your life. Or someone else's."

Nurse Agnes fusses over Joe a little more before she lets them move on.

The various rooms are fitted out for different kinds of training. There are rooms for learning French and German, rooms for studying Morse code. There are classrooms for map reading and others for studying the theory of high explosives.

The actual high explosives are kept well away from the house, but from his first day Joe has to get used to the sharp cracks coming from the rear gardens of the house as agents practice blowing things up. Or as Flannery puts it, "making a pretty mess."

After lunch in the manor's sumptuous dining hall (a nutritionally balanced meal of roast beef and vegetables with Yorkshire puddings, and simply the best meal he has had since coming to England), Joe settles in for his first lesson.

The class is entitled Secret Messages. He spends an hour learning how to send messages by hanging wash on a clothesline. Not quite what he expected from spy school. But certain items of clothing, hung in a certain way and in a certain order, can spell out a message to an observer who is in on the code.

The next hour is spent on documents. He learns what a German identity card looks like, what French papers look like, what he will be expected to produce, to whom, and when.

He is given false identity papers that clearly identify him as one Herr Adolf Hitler, occupation: painter, age: fifty-one. The papers look genuine to him, and the forger who issued them assures him they would pass the closest scrutiny. Except for one minor detail. He is clearly not a fifty-one-year-old man.

After afternoon tea, there is an hour and a half of a self-defense course called Defendu. It consists of a lot of grips, locks, and strikes, often with the edge of the hand, along with kicks and knees to the groin or face.

By the time they finish at five o'clock, Joe aches in places he didn't even know he had. He wonders if he should go to see Nurse Agnes, but none of the others are and he doesn't want to seem soft. In any case, he isn't sure he's ready for her outpouring of fuss. He just wants to get home and lie down.

Rosie seems to be anticipating this because she has a bowl of water and a sponge waiting for him when he gets back. "Come on, let's see what they did to you, then," she says.

He sighs and turns turns away from her, removing his shirt.

"It's criminal what they put you through," she tuts. She gently cleans his battered shoulders and back with the sponge and an oil that smells like eucalyptus. It seems to take away some of the sting.

"Would you post a letter for me next time you go into Guildford?" Joe asks. He winces as the warm sponge passes over a particularly sensitive bruise.

"Leave it with me and I'll give it to the postman," Rose says. "He'll take care of it for you."

"I was just a bit worried that if I did that, the army might intercept it—censor it or something," Joe says.

Rosie laughs. "They'll do that anyway, whether you post it in Guildford or Timbuktu. Nothing gets out of here without a team of people analyzing every word. They'll probably test it for invisible ink as well."

"Oh." Joe is disappointed. He wants to let Eddie, Peggy, and Wild Bob know that he is okay. He hasn't had a chance to see them since being abducted by both German and British secret agents on the same day. He thought of writing to Wild Bob at his father's photographic studio in Camden, but he can't think of how to tell them anything without breaching some sort of Official Secrets Act.

"I'll help you write your letter," Rosie says. "I know what they're likely to cut out. Put in too much and the letter will just disappear, so just say the bare minimum. Let them read between the lines a little."

"You'll help me?" Joe says, relieved. He has never been much of a letter writer, even in New Zealand when it was the only form of communication he had with his mother.

"I will," Rosie says. "Now let's put iodine on some of these cuts so they don't get infected."

They sit together at the dining table after dinner. Rosie offers him some pink, scented writing paper. Joe raises an eyebrow at that.

"My great-aunt gave it me for Christmas," Rosie says. "It's all I have at the minute. Your friends will have to put up with it."

After several drafts of a letter, each one rejected by Rosie as giving too much information, Joe ends up with:

Dear Eddie, Peggy, and Milton—

I am just writing to let you know that I am okay. I decided to get out of London to get away from all the bombing. I have found work on a small farm near Guildford. Please write back to me if you can. I would love to hear from you.

"I haven't really told them anything," Joe says, staring at the few lines on the light pink paper that smells ever so faintly of roses.

"You've told them you're alive," Rosie says. "Sometimes that's all they need to know."

Joe's training is different from the other recruits, he discovers. He still learns most of the basics, such as how to blow up a railway line, how to disable a tank, and the best way to slash a car tire. He learns how to disable a train by tossing an explosive-filled dead rat into the coal bunker. He learns how to operate a radio set and how to conceal the same from Gestapo investigators.

But the others seem to spend more time learning explosives and weaponry. They learn how to disable factory machinery in a way that will be hardest and costliest to repair. They practice Morse code until they dream in it.

Joe's time is spent learning the art of silent killing. He is taught poisons and pressure points and different ways to garotte a man, or how to stab someone in the heart while avoiding the ribs. He is trained in the use of umbrellas with poison tips and stiletto knives disguised as fountain pens.

It seems clear to Joe that, unlike the others, he isn't being trained as a spy or a saboteur. He is being trained as an assassin.

If that is the case, then clearly the "job" that Tar has recruited him for is not a spy or sabotage mission. It is to kill someone.

Exactly whom he will have to assassinate Joe does not know, and he knows not to ask. But there is one person who seems an obvious target.

As for why they need someone Joe's age, he has an idea about that too, which is confirmed when he is taken into a private room in the manor, well out of earshot of any of the other recruits, and made to learn the words of the Horst Wessel song. The anthem of the Hitler Youth.

Each day now, Hitler Youth training becomes part of his day. He learns the ranks, the salutes, the greetings, and the customs. He is fitted out for the uniform.

The irony of this is not lost on Joe. As a young boy, he had dreamed of joining the Hitler Youth. Finally it looks as though he will become a member.

Physical training, known as PT, is compulsory for everyone. Each day they march many kilometers, lift heavy objects, climb ropes, run through obstacle courses, compete against one another in games of tug-of-war, and generally run themselves into the ground.

If you want to blow up trains or telephone lines, apparently you have to be fit. Perhaps so you can run away quickly afterward.

Defendu, the self-defense program, is another daily part of training. Joe hates it. He hates the humiliation of being thrown and punched and kicked to the ground, as much as the pain from the cuts and bruises.

There is only one way to avoid the pain, and that is to get better at it. So he trains hard and practices in quiet moments and at home in front of the mirror. Slowly he improves. Soon he is holding his own, even beating the other recruits.

If a German soldier decides to attack Joe with his bare hands, he is fairly confident he can get the better of him. Of course if the soldier decides to attack Joe with a pistol or a submachine gun, Defendu will be of little use.

Rosie's house is always a welcome respite from the stress and toil of the training. But Rosie, Joe has discovered, is not as tough and confident as the image she projects. By day she is resourceful, strong, and resolute, tending the animals and the vegetable garden, volunteering at the Royal Surrey County Hospital, and "keeping the home fires burning." But at night, when the bombers drone overhead on their way to attack Southampton and Portsmouth, she stops talking and starts to shake, wrapping her arms around herself and rocking back and forth on the settee.

Feeling awkward and not knowing what to say, Joe says nothing.

When there is a good moon, he sometimes goes outside and stands, neck craned at the sky, watching the weaving aircraft and the long lines of tracer as the RAF night fighters engage the Luftwaffe in an increasingly desperate air war. Then his gaze always turns toward the southeast. It is when the moon is full that the secret planes fly, he knows, transporting agents into German-occupied France. He imagines he can see them, flying low over the Channel to darkened fields where men and women from the Resistance wait with flashlights. Soon he will be on one of those planes. From France it is just a small step to Germany. To Berlin, where surely his target is waiting for him.

One night, in the middle of March, Rosie comes to stand beside Joe as he gazes at the distant orange glow, a fiery dome over London.

"They're taking a pounding tonight," Joe says.

"I don't think we can take much more of this," Rosie says, her hand trembling next to his, and he knows it isn't England she is talking about.

The next day she receives a letter from her husband, postmarked from North Africa. Words, and even whole sentences, have been heavily censored with blocks of thick black ink. She smiles as she reads it and afterward holds it to her face as if it is her husband's cheek.

Joe does not get to read the letter, but from her reaction he deduces that Rommel has not yet attacked, and that the situation in Libya is looking more and more positive.

Grable is improving every day, thanks to the pills the vet has prescribed. Rosie has taken over administering the medication and seems to be developing a mutually affectionate relationship with the little dog. Joe is pleased. When he leaves on his mission, it will be nice to know that Grable is in good hands.

The beagle sleeps in the scullery in a large wicker dog basket lined with cushions and towels. She isn't allowed in the bedrooms but spends her days in the garden, or following Rosie on her walks, or just resting in the parlor on a soft bed of blankets that Rosie keeps there for her.

Somewhere along the way, Joe mentions to Rosie that he doesn't know how to drive.

She seems surprised at that. Not that a fourteen-year-old can't drive, but that the SOE hasn't included it as part of Joe's training.

"Well, we'll have to do something about that," she says. "Follow me."

She leads him around to a large barn on the manor grounds where she keeps her car. The car is black with bright green mudflaps and tire spokes. For some reason the green makes Joe think of a frog, and the two chrome headlights attached to the mudguards look remarkably like eyes.

"Beautiful, isn't it," she says. "Riley Nine Monaco. 1932 model. It was my father's, but he bought a brand-new model a couple of years ago, and this was our Christmas present."

She closes her eyes for a moment, then takes a deep breath and continues, "We only drove it once . . . Jamie and me, I mean. Took it up to the lake. Had a lovely picnic. Next day he mobilized. Now I just use it to run into town for supplies. A bit of a shame really. She's a beautiful machine."

"Are you sure you'd trust me behind the wheel?" Joe says. "I wouldn't want to crash it or anything."

"Come on, hop in," Rosie says, ignoring him. "I'll show you how to start her up."

When Joe said he couldn't drive, that was not entirely true. He had driven his uncle's tractor on the farm back in New

Zealand. But that simple system of levers and pedals seems a world away from the complicated controls of the Riley.

"Magneto on," Rosie says, showing him what to do. "Check the engine is not in gear . . . good. Now press the starter button."

The engine growls a couple of times, then catches, roaring for a moment, before settling down into a steady but slow grumble.

Driving isn't hard, Joe decides. At least with Rosie's patient tutelage. Push in the clutch to disengage the engine, put the gear stick into first gear, then slowly release the clutch while pressing on the accelerator. The car starts to roll forward.

"Try not to hit anything," Rosie says, at which point Joe realizes there is another aspect to driving, which is the steering.

There are four gears, each a higher ratio than the one before. Low gear is for slow driving and high gear for faster driving. To change gear, he simply pushes in the clutch, moves the gear lever to neutral, releases the clutch, presses it in again, and moves the gear lever to the new gear, before releasing the clutch a second time.

Nothing much to it.

He avoids some chickens clucking obliviously around the yard in front of the barn, a man on a horse on the long driveway that leads to the road, and even manages not to hit a large black car parked on the side of the road not far from the manor.

There is a small mirror attached to the outside of the car, which lets him see behind, and it is in this mirror that he notices the black car move smoothly out from the side of the road and start to follow them.

He tries not to read too much into it, and by the time they get to Guildford he can no longer see the car. Just a coincidence, he thinks, although he wonders if he should mention it to Major Flannery as a precaution.

He is watching out for the black car and doesn't notice the elderly lady with the shopping bag until Rosie says, "Also, try not to kill anyone. I hate wiping blood off the mudflaps."

Joe looks up to see the woman crossing in front of him. He jams the brake pedal to the floor, forgetting all about the clutch. The car shudders to a halt and stalls in the middle of the road. The old woman gives him a filthy look as she walks in front of them.

"Sorry," Joe says as he restarts the engine. "That was really embarrassing."

"Embarrassing? That wasn't embarrassing," Rosie says. "Embarrassing was the time I farted in church just as the organist stopped playing." She put a hand to her mouth. "Ooh, did I really just tell you that?"

"Did that really happen?" Joe laughs.

Rosie grins. "Worse than you can imagine. Everybody looked at me. I was only twelve. Now, fair's fair, what's your most embarrassing moment?"

"They happen all the time," Joe says, driving slowly forward and looking for a place to turn the car around. "But I can never remember them later. I think my mind blocks them out."

"God, I wish mine did," Rosie says. "I relive them over and over."

"Although there was that time I was the soloist in the school choir," Joe says. "I was eleven and my voice broke in the middle of the performance."

"Ouch," Rosie said.

It had been a German song, in a German school, in a world that seemed so far away, so foreign now. It makes Joe think of his old school friends. Of Klaus.

"Another time," Rosie says, "we went to Blackpool and my father bought me an ice cream cone. I was quite little and he was holding me in his arms. Anyway I went to lick the ice cream and it toppled off the cone and landed on the hat of a man sitting on a bench seat we were passing. I don't think he noticed and we walked on and I could see the ice cream melting all over the brim. I was mortified!"

She doesn't stop giggling until they get home.

That night, the bombs are closer. Much closer. Whether the bombers were lost or whether there was some kind of valuable target nearby, Joe does not know. Perhaps they are bombing the Vickers aircraft factory at Brooklands again. Apparently, many people died there in a raid the previous year.

Joe is used to the sound of the bombs after his time in London, but it's still disconcerting to hear them falling so close to the house.

The night is clear so he goes outside to watch, taking a seat on a wide wicker chair on the porch, pulling a blanket around himself against the chill night air.

A few moments later he hears the door behind him open.

"Shuffle over," Rosie says, and he does. The seat is just wide enough for two.

She is shivering, as she does, and he knows it is not just from the cold, but he offers her the blanket. She takes it and drapes it around both of their shoulders.

It is nice, being so close to someone. It reminds him of when he had been much younger, climbing into bed between his mother and father during a thunderstorm.

The movement of her breathing and the warmth of her skin comforts him and he suspects she feels the same, and so they sit together, wrapped tightly in the blanket as they watch the world explode.

18

ZOPYRUS

Guildford, March 23, 1941

"Her name is Welrod, but you will call her ma'am," Flannery says. "Other, less couth people, call her the assassin's gun."

"Yes, sir," Joe says.

"Now ask your lovely new lady friend if you may pick her up."

Joe looks at the major for a moment to make sure he is being serious. Flannery's face is expressionless.

"Excuse me, may I pick you up?" Joe asks.

"Ma'am," says Flannery.

"Ma'am," Joe says, feeling foolish.

The Welrod is the least feminine gun Joe has ever seen. It consists of a long black metal tube, not unlike a bicycle pump, with a handle stuck awkwardly on one end.

"Ma'am takes a .32 ACP round," Flannery says. "She is difficult to aim, not particularly accurate, and each time you fire you must manually reload and cock her."

Joe raises an eyebrow and looks at Flannery, waiting. There has to be more to *ma'am* than that.

Flannery nods toward the target at the end of the small firing range. Joe raises the pistol in that direction.

"The rear knob is the safety catch. Give it half a turn, pull the knob backward, then let it go. This will load and cock the weapon," Flannery informs him.

Joe does as instructed.

"You may fire her when you are ready," Flannery says.

Joe aims at the center of the target and squeezes the trigger. The sound is no louder than a strong cough. A hole appears in the paper target, about four centimeters from where he was aiming.

"It is certainly quiet," he says.

"Ma'am is very discreet," Flannery said, "as a good woman should be."

Those words are oddly reassuring. One thing that has been on Joe's mind is if this mission is a suicide mission—whether he is supposed to escape after the assassination or be captured or killed. If he is killed, he can't reveal any details of who he is or who had sent him, so he rather suspects this will be the most likely outcome. But giving him a silent assassin's pistol means at least there will be a chance to escape.

After weapons training is lunch, and Flannery and Joe take it together, as has become their custom. Joe really likes the gruff old Irishman, and he seems to have taken Joe under his wing.

"What are you prepared to do for your country?" Flannery asks over a corned beef sandwich on thick rye bread.

"Anything," Joe says. "I'd give my life if I had to."

"A lot of people have," Flannery says. "And a lot of people will."

"Of course, my country is on the far side of the world," Joe says.

Flannery laughs. "You're as much a part of this show as we are."

"I know," Joe says.

"Let me tell you the story of Zopyrus," Flannery says.

"Who?"

"Just listen," Flannery says. "Zopyrus was a nobleman in Persia a long time ago. Before the birth of Christ. It was the time of Darius the First, the king of kings. There was a city called Babylon—you'll have heard of that, no doubt."

Joe nods.

"They revolted against Darius. But the problem was that they had high, thick walls and many well-armed defenders. So our friend Zopyrus cuts off his own nose and ears."

"What?" Joe exclaims. "Why?"

"Then he goes to Babylon and is taken in front of the princes. He tells them that it was Darius who mutilated him, and says he wants to join the Babylonians' revolt. They believe him, see, on account of his missing nose and ears. They even put him in charge of their army . . . And he promptly leads them into an ambush. Revolt over, Darius wins."

"What happened to Zopyrus?" Joe asks.

"How should I know?" Flannery says. "They probably chopped his head off. Now, what's the point to this story?"

"Don't get sucked in by a noseless man?" Joe suggests.

Flannery shakes his head. "There are two morals. The first is, if you want someone to believe something, give them a reason to believe it. The second is that you have to do whatever it takes to win. There'll come a point in your life, on this mission or the next, where you'll have to make that kind of a call."

"I hope I don't end up cutting off my own ears and nose," Joe says.

"Would you, if you had to?"

"I'm not sure. Maybe."

"It may not be you that's getting mutilated," Flannery says. "Think about that. What if it was someone you loved? Would you still do whatever it takes?"

"I don't know," Joe admits.

"Well, you'd better decide. Because when the time comes you'll need to have your answer ready."

That afternoon is Joe's first parachute training, or, as their trainer liked to call it, falling-off-a-perfectly-good-truck training. Collins is a hard-faced paratrooper from the south of England, and it was a fair enough description of what the training would be all about.

Joe and the others stand at the rear of a truck driving across an open, grassy field. One by one, on command from the trainer, they move to the tailgate of the truck, facing forward. Then, traveling at fifty kilometers an hour, they step backward . . .

That has Rosie tutting and dabbing his bruises with the eucalyptus oil and iodine again that night.

After the truck, they graduate to jumping from a

three-meter high tower, which Joe achieves almost flawlessly; only once does he manage a mild sprain of his left ankle.

The next stage involves an airplane. Joe is not looking forward to that, but he shuts his eyes at the door of the plane when it is his turn and just jumps. Apart from being a little windier, and a longer drop, it isn't that much different from jumping off the truck.

The night after Joe's first actual parachute drop, he and Rosie sit on the porch again, under the blanket, watching the sky, although there is no raid, or if there is, it is against targets too far away for them to hear. After a while her head slips down to his shoulder and he can tell by the soft rhythm of her breathing that she is asleep. He does not want to wake her, so they stay there until it is nearly midnight, and the blanket can no longer fight off the cold air.

The following night he sits on the porch again and she joins him. From then on, this is the pattern of their nights, even when he comes home bruised and bloodied from training. The agreement between them is unspoken, the contract binding. It is a connection of comfort and, he would like to think, caring, helping each other through the dark days as the Nazis pummel England and Joe's instructors pummel him.

19
THE MISSION

Guildford, March 27, 1941

A staff car is parked on the road alongside the barn as the boy walks to the manor the next morning. As he approaches, one of the rear doors opens.

"Hello, Joe," a voice says. "Get in."

The man Joe knows as Tar slides across to the other side of the seat to make room for him and shakes Joe's hand. "Close the door," he instructs.

The car moves off.

"It's nice to see you, Joe," Tar says, and sounds like he means it. "How's the training going?"

"Painful," Joe says.

"I won't keep you long," Tar says. "I wouldn't want you to be late for training this morning—people might ask questions."

Why should his trainers be kept in the dark about his purpose? Joe wonders. What is so secret that it has to be kept secret from Churchill's Secret Army?

Tar turns over a photograph that has been lying on the seat between them. Joe holds out a hand for it, but Tar pulls it back out of his reach.

"General Reinhard Heydrich," he says, and Joe notices his

face grow cold as he speaks the name. "Known as the Hangman, and the Butcher of Prague. Head of the Gestapo from '34 to '36. Currently head of Nazi intelligence, including the SD. He was also the architect of Kristallnacht."

Joe draws in a long breath. Kristallnacht. The Night of Broken Glass. He remembers it vividly—and why wouldn't he? It was the night his father was arrested.

"A truly evil man," Tar says.

"I know," Joe agreed.

"No, Joe. No, you don't," Tar says quietly. "Heydrich is also responsible for the systematic murder of at least a million Jews. Civilians—men, women, and children. And not only Jews. Romani as well. Possibly others."

"How . . . why . . ." Joe can barely speak. He has seen one murder firsthand. And the Blitz is kind of murder in a way, killing innocent civilians. But even wide-scale bombing has not caused anything like a million deaths.

"The how does not matter. And the why is not something that someone like you or I will ever understand," Tar says.

Joe thinks back to Berlin. He knows about the persecution of Jewish people. But there is a world of difference between treating people badly and *murdering* them. And the number is staggering. "Is this true?" he asks. "I mean, has this information been confirmed?"

"It may in fact be much worse than we know," Tar says.

Joe swears under his breath, scarcely able to believe what he was hearing. Over a million people? Civilians . . . women . . . and children?

"You may have realized that you are being trained as a killer," Tar says. "I am told your training is going very well."

Joe shrugs noncommittally.

"No doubt you wondered why," Tar says. "Perhaps you wondered who. Well, now you know."

Joe stares at the face of a mass murderer. Blond hair. A long, lean face. A thin, aquiline nose. Hooded eyes, set too closely together. Thin, hard lips.

A million innocent civilians. Plus one who mattered more to Joe than all the others.

"Not quite who you were expecting, perhaps," Tar says.

Joe thinks about that question for a moment or two before answering. Tar does not hurry him.

"Would his death end the war?" Joe says finally.

Tar shakes his head. "Does that matter?"

"Of course it matters," Joe says. "How many lives could you save if you could end the whole war with a single bullet?"

Now Tar hands Joe the photograph. "You'd like to assassinate Hitler instead."

"Wouldn't anyone?" Joe asks. He thinks of Eddie, who wants to cut Hitler into pieces and put him in a trash bin. And Wild Bob who wanted to punch him in the face, then the guts, then the face again.

Tar says, "Hitler is very well protected. Don't think we haven't looked into that. Hitler is not your target. Heydrich is. He will be visiting Paris next month, where he will meet with Marshal Pétain."

"The French president," Joe says.

"The French puppet," Tar corrects. "With Hitler's hand up his rear end."

"Why would Heydrich meet with Pétain?" Joe asks, afraid that he already knows the answer.

"We think the meeting is to discuss the deportation of French Jews and Romani to concentration camps in Poland," Tar says. "But the reason for the meeting should not concern you. At the same time a large congregation of Hitler Youth will be visiting Paris as a reward for exemplary service. Young men will be coming from all over Germany. You will join them."

Joe nods. The reason for his Hitler Youth training has become clear.

"Heydrich will attend a May Day parade on the Champs-Élysées," Tar says. "As will the Hitler Youth."

Joe is silent. This is what he has trained for. It is what he has wished for. But now that it is laid out in such clinical terms, he wonders at his own ability to carry it out.

"This mission is currently being evaluated by Winston Churchill himself," Tar says. "If we get approval to proceed, you will be at that parade."

Joe realizes that Tar is watching him, assessing him.

"We don't need heroes," Tar says finally. "I don't need an excitable boy on this mission. I need a cool, calm professional. You will slay a monster, quietly, without fuss or attention. And then you will escape."

He looks at Joe very carefully. "Escaping is very important."

Joe couldn't agree more.

Tar continues. "If the Nazis capture you, they will make you talk. If you talk, there will be consequences. It is essential that the Nazis believe one of their own committed this act, a member of the Hitlerjugend, the pride and future of the German nation."

"And if I can't escape?" Joe asks.

"I think you know the answer to that question, Joe," Tar says evenly. "And I won't lie to you—that is a possibility."

He turns and speaks to the driver. "Cath, would you mind leaving us alone for a moment."

Cath, one of Tar's women who sees and hears nothing, pulls the car over to the side of the road, crunching lightly on the gravel. She turns off the car, opens her door, and gets out, walking down the road well out of earshot.

"I thought you trusted your people with your life," Joe says.

"This is far more important than my life," Tar replies. "Listen very carefully. I have your code name. It is Katipo. You know this word?"

"It's a spider," Joe says, nodding. "The only venomous spider in New Zealand, as far as I know."

"And a perfect code name for you." Tar smiles, but then his face grows serious. "You will tell nobody about your code name. Absolutely nobody. Not even Rosemary."

"Is she one of yours?" Joe asks. "Has Rosie been spying on me?" Another even more horrifying possibility strikes him. "Is she a Nazi spy?"

That possibility fills him with dread. If she is, then surely she will be hanged. Was it real, those nights they sat together on the porch? Or was it all an act, to build a relationship, to tease information out of him? He tries to think back to everything he has said to her. Has he given away anything?

Tar shakes his head. "I have no reason to think that she is anything more than just a lonely soldier's wife. But we keep close tabs on all our agents. A small matter of national security. I am sure you will understand."

"The black car that followed us," Joe says.

Tar nods. "One of mine. Now, back to my question. You do not mention your code name to anyone. Is that clear?"

"Crystal clear, sir," Joe answers.

"Good. Now repeat it back to me," Tar says.

"Katipo," Joe says immediately.

Tar's eyes glitter coldly. "You just committed treason," he says.

"But—"

"You were given a clear order to say that code name to nobody."

"But, sir, you—"

"Nobody means *nobody*," Tar says. "Is it clear this time?"

"Yes, sir. It is clear, sir," Joe says.

"I'll be in touch if and when the mission is confirmed," Tar says.

20

THE LETTER

Guildford, April 1, 1941

On the evening of April 1, April Fools' Day, there is a letter waiting for the boy in a clean white envelope on the mantelpiece in the dining room.

The letter is from Wild Bob. It is short, functional, and to the point, much like the way Wild Bob speaks. He thanks Joe for his letter, then says that Peggy is in the hospital and it would make her happy if Joe were to visit her. The letter makes no mention of Eddie.

Only those who lived through the Blitz will ever
understand what it was like to live through the Blitz.

—from the memoirs of Joseph "Katipo" St. George

21

BLESS 'EM ALL

London, April 3, 1941

Thursday is the boy's one day of leave, so he catches the early train into London.

It is still dark when he leaves Guildford and the carriages are gloomy, the only light coming from dim blue bulbs, just enough to let him read the large notice taped to the wall, warning passengers to *Lie down on the floor in the event of an air raid.*

Joe pats the cork in his pocket. He carries it with him everywhere, even outside London where the danger from air raids is greatly reduced.

For most of the trip, he goes over in his mind every conversation he has ever had with Rosie, as best as he can remember them. Tar said he has no reason to suspect Rosie, but he did not say that Rosie was innocent, or even that he did *not* suspect her. He merely said he had *no reason* to suspect her, which was not the same thing.

Rosie seems to know a lot about the activities at the manor house. More than she should, Joe thinks. He cannot remember telling her anything that would compromise his mission, and he doesn't know the details of anyone else's operation. But he has implicitly confirmed, by not denying it, that secret training is going on at the manor house. Perhaps that in itself is too much information.

He changes trains at Victoria Station and takes the Tube to Brixton, where he buys a small posy of pansies from a flower seller in the concourse. He walks the rest of the way to King's College Hospital. It is guarded by two police officers and surrounded by a protective wall of sandbags, taller than Joe.

Because of his early start, he arrives before morning visiting hours and so has to wait outside. He watches nurses, doctors, and orderlies coming and going through the gap in the sandbag wall for about half an hour before he is able to enter.

Inside, a nurse in a blue uniform with a starched white apron, who looks disconcertingly like Rosie, directs him to the children's ward. An orderly at the nurses' station points down a long aisle of beds with crisp linen sheets.

A gramophone on a small table near the door is playing cheery tunes, currently "Kiss Me Goodnight, Sergeant Major." The ward has the antiseptic smell he associates with hospitals, but it is tinged with the smell of unwashed bodies, a vaguely unpleasant odor that comes from those whose only bathing consisted of a daily sponge and sheets that are changed only when necessary. There is also an underlying smell of urine and feces from the many bedpans. The ward is quiet, with the soft, rustling sounds of nurses going about their business, except for a low moaning that comes from a bed at the end of the room. That bed is screened by curtains.

Joe walks through the ward, checking faces to left and right, afraid that he won't recognize Peggy for some reason, but the mop of red hair is unmistakable, as is the cheerful smile that lights up her face the moment she sees him.

It is only as he reaches her bed that Joe realizes the bedsheets are flat. There is no lump under the covers where her long legs should be. The smile freezes a little on his face, although he tries to pretend he hasn't noticed.

Perhaps Peggy should have insured her legs for a million dollars.

That thought comes unbidden, and it horrifies him that he could think such a thing. He blinks his eyes a couple of times in an effort to wipe the thought from his mind.

Peggy has bandages covering one ear and wrapped around her throat. One arm is in a cast, but she does not seem to be in any pain. Perhaps they have her on drugs.

"Torpedo Joe," she exclaims, and holds up her good arm for a hug. Joe moves around the side of the bed and embraces her awkwardly.

A nurse comes then with some pillows and helps Peggy sit up. She takes the flowers from Joe, bringing them back a moment later in a jam jar filled with water.

"You're looking good," Joe lies.

"What's left of me," Peggy says with a small giggle, then covers her hand with her mouth as though she has said something naughty.

"What happened?" Joe asks. There is a wooden chair by the side of the bed, and he takes it, lowering himself so she doesn't have to crane her neck to look up at him.

"Landmine," she says, as if it were an everyday occurrence. "Delayed reaction or unexploded bomb or something. We were in the shelter at Camden Town."

"You were in a bomb shelter?" Joe asks, surprised.

"Yeah, I know. Eddie didn't want to, but I talked him into it. The bombing was getting so bad. Horrible place it was. Smelly and crowded and full of mosquitoes. I didn't half get bit. But that's not where it happened. They had sounded the all clear so we were heading home, and that's when it went off. A lot of people were killed, so I was one of the lucky ones."

"You were lucky," Joe agrees, avoiding looking at the flat bedsheets. "What about Eddie?"

The smile fades and she lowers her eyes. "Bob didn't tell you?"

"He didn't tell me anything. Just that you were in the hospital," Joe says.

"He was in front of me," Peggy says. "Typical Eddie. Always had to go first. But they reckon his body shielded me from the worst of the blast. So he was kind of a hero, I think."

"He'd like that," Joe says gently, trying to bring Eddie's face to mind. His messy red hair and cleft chin stretched into his trademark cheeky smile. The image won't come. Instead all he can see is their mother, her hair—undoubtedly also red and tied up in a turban scarf—screaming for her children from the cold hole of the Anderson shelter in their backyard.

"How are you doing?" he asks. He means dealing with the death of her brother, but she misunderstands.

"Well, the bad news was that my legs got all smashed up,"

she says. "But the good news is that there was a warden nearby, so he managed to stop the bleeding."

Joe nods silently.

"Then the bad news was that my legs had to be cut off," she says brightly, "but the good news is that it was below the knee, which means I can get artificial legs—so I'll be able to walk again."

"You're very brave," Joe says, because it is all he can think to say.

"I guess the really good news is that it was my legs they had to cut off and not my arms," Peggy says. "I don't know how I'd cope without . . ." She stops and glances guiltily over at a boy in a bed on the other side of the ward. Joe doesn't need to look.

"What did you find out about your mum?" she asks. "I been dying to know."

Joe hesitates. He has been trying not to think about his mother for weeks, but there is no way of avoiding this question.

The song on the gramophone finished and another starts. "Bless 'em all," a man with a thin, reedy voice is singing. Joe glances around the ward at the young frightened faces, some contorted in pain. Bless them all indeed. They need it.

"I went to confront her," he says. "To give her a chance to explain, before I took the photos to the police."

"What did she say?" Peggy asks.

"I never got to talk to her," Joe says. He pauses and she waits patiently. "Did you hear about the bombing at the Café de Paris?"

"Oh my god," Peggy says. "That was terrible! She wasn't in—" She stops again and clamps a hand over her mouth.

Joe nods. "I only just missed the blast myself. I was following her inside when it went off."

Peggy reaches out her good hand and takes his. "Life is pain," she whispers. If she has intended those words to help, they don't, but Joe nods anyway.

"I'm sorry about Eddie," he says. "I'm glad he was a hero, but I'm sad that he died."

"Everybody dies," Peggy says matter-of-factly. "It's just a question of when."

"I know," Joe says, "but it still must be very painful for you."

"Of course," Peggy says. "But life is pain, remember."

Joe wonders again about what drugs she may be on.

"Suffering is the only path to happiness," Peggy says, and continues without pause. "Have you been to see Wild Bob? He'd think it were smashing if you went to see him."

Joe shakes his head. "Not yet."

Peggy slides her palm around and intertwines her fingers with his. "I thought we might have been summat, you and me," she says. "But you wouldn't want half a girl, would yer? Nobody would."

Joe reaches across with his other hand and brushes away a strand of hair that has fallen across her face.

"Anyone in their right mind would want you to be their girl, legs or no legs," he says. "And you aren't half a girl. Nobody will even know after you get your prosthetics."

"But I won't be doing no more dancing, will I?" she says, and for the first time there is real heartbreak in her voice.

"My aunt June lost her legs in a farming accident back in New Zealand," Joe says, "and she dances better than anybody."

"Truly?" Peggy smiles at that and says, "Anyone in their right mind . . . including you?"

"Especially me," Joe says.

After several more awkward hugs and promises to visit again soon—promises that he is not sure he can keep—Joe departs. With directions from the front desk nurse he takes the Tube from the Morden to Camden Town station, where he finds himself barely a five-minute walk from the only photography studio in the town.

Peggy is very much on his mind as he walks. He curses Adolf Hitler for what he has done to her.

And he curses himself a little as well. He doesn't have an aunt June.

—

The shop, like most, has windows crisscrossed with gauze tape to prevent flying glass from bomb blasts. However, unlike the others, which are usually diagonal, these strips are vertical and horizontal, creating rectangular panels into which photographs have been taped, creating a large montage of faces, presumably all photos taken by the studio.

There are pictures ranging from babies to elderly folk, individually and in groups or families. All are looking fixedly at the camera lens, most smiling, some rigidly so. There are many photos of soldiers in uniform, and Joe can't help wondering how many of them are still alive. The thought makes him uncomfortable.

He pushes open the door and enters a dimly lit world of cameras and framed photographs. To one side is a wooden chair in front of a wide cloth hanging down one wall. In front of the chair, a large camera sits on a heavy wooden tripod.

A large framed portrait of King George VI dominates the other wall. The king is wearing an ornate military uniform, his chest covered with medals, and Joe wonders if the studio took the photo or just displays it out of patriotism. He also wonders what the king has done to earn so many medals.

The man behind the counter is a dead ringer for Wild Bob, just older. He too is quite stout and has the same thick eyebrows. He is examining some photographs with a magnifying glass, apparently looking for imperfections.

When Joe asks after his son, he shakes his head and says, "Milton's working. He's busy."

He even has Wild Bob's slow manner of speaking.

"I'm a friend of his," Joe says.

Again the man shakes his head.

"I was a friend of Eddie's," Joe tries.

The man stops what he is doing and puts down the glass.

"Milton only ever had one real friend, and that was Eddie," he says. "What makes you his friend?"

"I hadn't known him long," Joe says. "I only arrived in London a few months ago. But we liked each other well enough. He wrote to me."

The man raises his head in understanding. "You're the stowaway."

"It was the only way I could get to London to find my mum," Joe says.

Now the man allows himself a smile and lifts a section of the counter to allow Joe through. "He'd want to see you. He's in the back. Don't keep him too long; he's on the clock today."

Wild Bob is cleaning camera lenses using a fine brush and a small rubber air blower. He looks up when Joe pushes through the heavy cloth curtain that separates the rear of the shop from the front, and his face lights up.

"Joe!" he says putting down his tools. "You came! It's good to see you."

"You too, Wild Bob," Joe replies, then does something he has not done before. He walks up to the big boy and embraces him. Wild Bob hugs him back without embarrassment.

"You should call me Milton," Wild Bob says. "It were Eddie what called me Wild Bob. Seems wrong now."

"Seems to me like a good way of remembering him," Joe suggests.

Wild Bob grins happily. "Okay," he says. "He were my best mate."

"I'd like to think I was your friend too," Joe says.

"I'd like that too," Wild Bob says.

"And Peggy. Don't forget Peggy," Joe says.

"I ain't forgot Peggy," Wild Bob says. He picked up the blower and squeezes it, blowing some invisible dust off a lens. "I'm glad we're friends."

"Me too," Joe says.

"How's your new job on the farm?"

Joe shrugs. "It's good. Hard work though."

Wild Bob smiles without looking at Joe. "You don't really work on a farm, do you?"

Joe is suddenly cautious. "What do you mean?"

"I speak slow, so a lot of people think I'm stupid," Wild Bob says. "But I ain't stupid. You're a spy now or summat, ain't ya?"

"Don't be silly," Joe says.

"Only 'cause you're a spy, you ain't allowed to talk about it," Wild Bob says. "But that's okay. I know. And I know you're doing summat to beat them Jerries."

Not for the first time, Joe reflects that Wild Bob reminds him of Klaus. Not because he is tall and strong, or that he needs to shave, but because he is wise and his heart is good.

"I saw your mum," Wild Bob says.

"What do you mean?" Joe asks. "When did you see her?"

"Yesterday," Wild Bob says. "She was on the Tube to Highgate."

Joe lowers his eyes. "That wasn't my mum," he says softly.

"It sure looked like her—that woman what we followed," Wild Bob insists. "I was delivering some photos for my dad."

"Mum died in the bomb at the Café de Paris," Joe says.

"Ohhh. That were a bad one." He adds as an afterthought, "I'm sorry for your loss."

He says the words by rote, automatically, and Joe wonders how many times Wild Bob has said those words since the start of the Blitz.

"Will you do me a favor?" Joe asks.

"Anything."

"Try to help out Peggy in any way you can? It won't be easy for her now that Eddie's gone. Especially without her legs."

Wild Bob nods. "I already asked me dad and mum if Peggy could come and live with us—when she gets out of the hospital, I mean."

Joe smiles to hide a surge of emotion. "You're a good man, Wild Bob," he says.

"So are you, Joe," Wild Bob says.

Joe doesn't try to correct him.

I never saw Milton Foster, aka Wild Bob, again. His eighteenth birthday was in January 1944. Just in time for D-Day. He joined the Royal Engineers and died at Sword Beach, clearing mines and obstacles to help pave the way for the infantry.

—from the memoirs of Joseph "Katipo" St. George

22

GUILDFORD

Guildford, April 3, 1941

It starts raining, and the boy is sopping wet before he reaches the Tube station. He has a damp train ride back to Guildford. There the rain has eased to a drizzle, but he is still soaked to the skin by the time he reaches Rosie's house.

Something is wrong.

Grable is tied up outside, looking pregnant and thoroughly miserable. Her leash is looped over a fencepost at the gate. Joe's first thought is that she has been sick or has made a mess inside the house, so Rosie decided to put her outside.

Then he sees his duffel bag, also soaked through, lying on the gravel path next to the bedraggled beagle, who is staring up at Joe with accusing eyes.

He leaves both the bag and the dog where they are by the gate and sprints to the front door. It's locked. He knocks, and when there is no answer, he hammers on it with the flat of his hand. Still no response.

He tries the back door, but that too is locked.

Where can she be? Why has she put his things on the path?

He spies a small manila telegram envelope, torn open, lying on the front step. It is addressed to Rosemary Bedford. He nudges it with his toe, but the torn flap just flutters in the breeze. The envelope is empty. But he knows what was in it. It has the seal of the British army on it. These are the telegrams that widows receive when their husbands have been killed in action.

He knocks again, and when there is still no answer, he walks back to the gate and unhooks Grable. He picks up his bag and trudges through the rain toward the manor house, the only place he can think of to go.

23

ARISAIG HOUSE

Scotland, April 4, 1941

If the boy thought the SOE training at Wanborough Manor would prepare him for commando training in Scotland, he was woefully mistaken. Within the first week he crossed a river on a two-rope bridge while being drenched and almost knocked off by explosions in the water to simulate artillery fire; he came ashore on a boat as part of a beach assault while live ammunition blasted over their heads; he scaled cliffs and then descended them; and he undertook a fitness regime that made the Wanborough Manor seem like kindergarten.

He was placed with a group of wild Scotsmen from the No. 11 Commando unit, under the command of a mad captain named MacDonald—Mac for short. Mac had the broad accent of the Highlands, so thick that Joe struggled to understand most of what he said. He also had a wicked sense of humor; at least Joe thought he did, when he could understand what the man was actually saying.

Mac was large and strong, totally bald, but with bushy red eyebrows and a constant five o'clock shadow. He was the toughest, smartest, most competent man Joe had ever met.

• • • •

Right now, Mac is staring at him across the barrel of a pistol. For all Joe knows, it's loaded. The man is wearing a black overcoat with a band of red cloth tied around one arm. A Gestapo uniform, close enough. Two more commandos stand by the door, a wiry Glaswegian named Gordon and a solid Edinburgher named Kinnock, both armed with Schmeisser machine pistols, and wearing similar costumes to Mac.

In between Joe and Mac is a trestle table on which is arrayed a set of carpenter's tools, to represent instruments of torture. A claw hammer sits next to a pipe wrench. A screwdriver, a chisel, and a set of pliers are lined up neatly with a coping saw and a mallet.

"I'm an evil Gestapo man, black to ma villainous core," Mac is saying. "All I want tae do is to turn ye guts inside oot and fry them up for ma breakfast while ye watch. Noo what are ye going to do about that?"

"Not much I can do while you're holding that gun and your two armed goons are watching," Joe says.

"D'ye hear that, Gordon?" Mac says. "He called ye a goon."

"I'd be insulted if I knew what a goon was," Gordon says.

"It's an English word," Mac says. "It means a silly, foolish person."

"That's not how I meant it," Joe says.

"So the wee whippersnapper thinks I'm a bit of a numpty, is that it?" Gordon says. "When do we start the torture? I'll go find my pliers."

"Put me and him in a room with a pair of pliers and see who starts screaming," Joe says. He has quickly learned with these hard men that offense is better than defense.

All three laugh.

"He thinks he can take me," Gordon says.

"'Course he can," Mac scoffs. "Ma little sister could take you, blindfolded."

"Is that a boast or a promise?" asks Gordon.

They are in a cottage on the extensive grounds of Arisaig House, the Scottish version of an English manor house. The cottage has been repurposed as a training area, where the commandos practice clearing buildings, demolition, and rescue missions.

For this exercise Joe is playing the part of a high-ranking British officer who has been captured by the Gestapo.

"Any second now," Mac says with a glance at his watch.

"So what do I do?" Joe asks.

"Ye're the tough guy," Mac says. "Do whatever ye like. Make sure ye have a plan A, a plan B, and a C. But this pistol isnae leaving yer face." To Kinnock he says, "Better move away from the door a wee bit. It's about to pop."

Kinnock takes a quick step to the right, just in time, as a second or two later the door explodes from its hinges, shattered pieces flying into the room.

Had it been a real door or a real explosion there might have been real casualties, but the door is lightweight balsa and the explosives that demolish it nothing more than detonators encased in a mixture of flour and sawdust. Mac's own concoction.

The effect seems real enough.

Two commandos are in the room before the cloud has dispersed, Thompson machine guns raised.

"Bang, bang, bang," one of the commandos yells, his gun pointed at Gordon. Another is yelling the same at Kinnock who has been "knocked over" by the simulated blast.

The shouting seems a bit silly to Joe, although he knows it's not safe even to use blanks in such a confined space. He's been waiting for the attack, preparing himself mentally and physically, tensing his muscles.

The room is filled with smoke and dust and commandos shouting at one another. In the haze and confusion, Joe is moving, diving to the floor in front of the table, a screwdriver in his hand. There is little else he can do but to get out of the line of Mac's fire and hope the other commandos can get to Mac before Mac gets to him.

"Bang! Bang!" Mac is yelling, and the first two commandos drop but others are pouring through the door. Joe rolls onto his back, clutching the screwdriver, thinking to slide underneath the table and surprise Mac from below, but he looks up to see the muzzle of Mac's pistol about a centimeter from his face, and behind it, Mac's bushy eyebrows and wild Scottish eyes.

"Bang," Mac says.

Their quarters are in tents in a field at the rear of the house. There are empty rooms at the house, but tough commandos are not supposed to sleep in warm, comfortable bedrooms, so they don't. Joe has a tent to himself, while the men share. He likes the privacy but doesn't like the feeling that he is not really part of the team.

He wears the same khaki uniform as the other men but is given a green beret as his headgear. The others wear Scottish tam-o'-shanter bonnets, with a feathered black hackle on one side.

It is a minor detail, but an important one. Joe is an outsider, tolerated but not accepted.

They don't always sleep in tents. Some nights they trek into the forest and build bivouacs out of branches and heather. Joe feels lucky it's April, and the weather is beginning to warm up. He can't imagine sleeping rough in the middle of a Scottish winter.

On a table in front of the cookhouse each morning is a large metal pot filled with what appears to be pig swill. On his first morning Joe saw men with bowls lined up and quickly found out that the pot contained a mixture of oatmeal, water, and salt. He soon found out that it tastes terrible but gives the men the energy they need for the arduous day of physical exertion ahead.

The training isn't all physical. Joe especially enjoys Weapons Skills. He is rapidly becoming an expert in all kinds of guns, both British and German, from pistols to machine guns.

"If ye run outa ammo, ye grab any bloody thing tae hand," Mac told him. "Kraut or no. And ye'd better bloody know how tae use it."

Joe can hit the target on the firing range as well as any of the commandos with most of the guns except the Thompson submachine gun. That bucks and kicks and lifts in his hands no matter how much he tries to hold it steady, spraying bullets in a wild pattern around the grassy bank behind the target but seldom actually hitting it.

After training one evening, Kinnock approaches Joe. "I'm told you speak German," he says in German.

"I do," Joe confirms.

"I wondered if you would help with my pronunciation," Kinnock asks. "Seems to me that if I'm ever caught behind enemy lines, it might be a useful skill to have."

From then on, Joe spends an hour each evening coaching Kinnock. His accent is good, but he has a tendency to add a Scottish burr to the *r*'s. His German is also quite formal and old-fashioned, with none of the modern idiom. He gives Joe a sheet of phrases that he particularly wants to learn:

Good evening.
Everything is good.
Wait a moment.
Here are my papers.
I'm sorry, I have lost my way.
I don't know.

Other phrases seem oddly specific:

I'm going to the weapons recycling depot.
I must deliver my consignment before morning.

I'm dropping him back to his billet.

We came through Clichy.

The gearbox has seized.

After two weeks of commando training, Joe is physically and mentally exhausted. But he also knows he is better prepared for whatever might come than at any other time of his life.

He actually finds himself enjoying the challenges, despite the hardship, and is almost disappointed the day he is called away from training in the middle of the day.

He has a visitor. Major Flannery. Approval has come down from the top echelons of Whitehall. His mission is a go.

The table is covered in a thin white cloth. Flannery moves to the door, closes and locks it, then returns to the table, pulling off the cloth.

It reveals a map of Paris, spread out and weighted down with wooden blocks. From a folder Flannery extracts a number of photos of Reinhard Heydrich, scattering them across the map. One is an official-looking portrait, the same photo Tar showed him at Wanborough. Others are candid shots, some taken from behind potted plants or pillars. Joe studies the photos carefully, committing the face to memory.

"Welcome to your first mission briefing," Flannery says. "Hopefully not your last."

"If I survive, you mean," Joe says.

"I actually mean that if your mission is successful, we will undoubtedly find more work for you," Flannery says. "Perhaps next time the target will be even more . . . shall we say . . . tantalizing."

"Der Führer," Joe says, imagining Hitler in his sights.

"Anything is possible, providing you are not compromised, or identified by the Gestapo," Flannery says. "That would limit your usefulness severely. Do you know anyone in Paris? Anyone who would be able to identify you?"

"No."

"Good," Flannery says. "Depending on the weather conditions, we will either fly you in on a Lizzie or toss you out of a converted Whitley bomber."

"I'll swim across if I have to," Joe says.

Flannery smiles. "I think you'll find the aerial route a little less . . . damp. Once we've got you on the ground, you'll be met by members of the Resistance. The leader of the group is called Albert. He will know your code name. If anyone approaches you without using your code name, or with an incorrect one, you should assume they are a German agent or a traitor. That's why we have been so careful to protect it. To make sure it doesn't find its way into enemy hands."

Joe nods his understanding.

"You haven't forgotten it, have you?" Flannery asks.

"No, of course not, sir," Joe says.

"And it is . . ."

Joe laughs. "I don't fall for the same trick twice, sir."

"Good lad. Here are your identification papers," Flannery hands him an ID card and a travel permit.

"Josef Eichmann?" Joe interrupts. "Like Adolf Eichmann?"

Eichmann is one of Heydrich's deputies.

"It is a common enough surname, but people will wonder if you are related," Flannery says. "They will not want to question you too closely."

He takes the papers and puts them back in the folder.

"There is a biography in the folder also," he says. "Where you went to school, who your parents are, and so on. Memorize it until you start to believe it yourself. You must stick to your cover story under all circumstances. Even if arrested. Especially if arrested."

"When do I leave?" Joe asks.

"As soon as possible. It all depends on the conditions," Flannery says. "We need a good strong moon or the pilot won't be able to navigate. There aren't many nights between now and May that will meet the criteria. Then we need good weather. That strong moon is of little use if it's covered by clouds and no use at all if there's a thunderstorm. You need to be ready to go from now on." He smiles briefly. "With luck you'll have time for a Continental holiday before your assignment. Now, let's skip forward to May first."

He stabs a finger at the map.

"This is the Champs-Élysées, where the parade will take place. This is the Arc de Triomphe. The parade will start here, travel through the Arc, continue past the VIP grandstand here, and finish at the Place de la Concorde, here, where they will disperse. Prior to the parade, the Hitler Youth will assemble here, then move to this location adjacent to the grandstand."

Joe examined the map, memorizing the locations.

"How do you know all this?" he asks.

"You don't need to know that," Flannery says. "Heydrich will arrive by car. Probably an open-top car as that is his preference. Do not try to assassinate him while the car is moving—you will most likely miss."

"All right." Joe nods.

"Heydrich's visit to France has been shrouded in the utmost secrecy," Flannery says. "This is his only public event, and he flies out immediately afterward, back to Czechoslovakia."

"Why all the secrecy?" Joe wonders aloud.

"In case someone decides to take a shot at him," Flannery says. "Funny that."

"Hilarious," Joe says.

"You will have to decide when is the best opportunity to take your shot," Flannery says. "One possibility is as he walks from the car to the grandstand. Another might be when he is seated in the grandstand. That part will be up to you. I'd suggest not leaving it until he leaves. You might miss your opportunity."

"Yes, sir," Joe says.

"Once Heydrich is dead, Albert's people will detonate a bomb somewhere near the Arc de Triomphe. They're not trying to kill anyone, they just want people to scatter. You will escape in the confusion."

"Why aren't they trying to kill anyone?" Joe asks a little cynically.

"The area will be full of French people," Flannery says. "A lot of children too. German or not, dead kids make bad headlines." He bends over the map and runs a finger down the line of a main road. "You'll take Avenue Foch, this street here. Try to keep away from number eighty-four. It's the headquarters of the SS, both the Gestapo and the SD."

Joe grimaces.

"Nothing to worry about there, unless you let yourself get captured."

"I'll try to avoid that, sir," Joe says. He notes the location and makes a mental note to keep well away from it.

Flannery points to a large green area on the map. "Avenue Foch leads directly to this large forested park, the Bois de Boulogne. It's huge and there are many places to hide out."

"Won't they track me with dogs?"

Flannery shakes his head. "Track what? They'd need your scent. There will be hundreds of people at the parade, hundreds of different scents all on top of one another, and unless you drop your handkerchief, or give them some other obvious clue, they'll have no way of tracking you."

"I'll be sure not to drop my handkerchief," Joe says.

"Albert will rendezvous with you somewhere in the park as soon as it's safe to do so. I don't know where and I don't want to know. Nobody on our side will know. Albert will tell you when he meets you. It will be up to him to spirit you out of the city. Any questions?"

"Not right now, sir."

"Good. All the other details are in this folder. Study it carefully, but take nothing from this room. Is that clear?"

"Absolutely, sir."

Flannery smiles and nods. "One last thing." He holds up a small metal tin about the size of a matchbox. He flicks the lid with his thumb and it snaps open. Inside, on a bed of cotton wool, is a tooth. A molar, from the look of it.

"Expecting the tooth fairy, sir?" Joe asks.

"Tomorrow you will visit our dentist," Flannery says, with no trace of a smile.

Joe is startled despite himself. "The murder house, sir?"

Flannery raises an eyebrow. "If anywhere is a house of murder, you're standing in it."

"Sorry, sir," Joe says. "That's what we called it in New Zealand. The dental clinic, I mean."

"I am amused, I truly am," Flannery says. "Tell me why. Did people die?"

"No, sir, nothing like that," Joe says. "It was run by this woman, a dental nurse, with a foot-powered drill. It's torture, sir."

He falls silent, thinking about what he has just said.

"The Gestapo call their torture chambers 'kitchens,'" Flannery says. "I think you would find them a little more unpleasant than your dental clinic."

"Yes, sir."

"So tomorrow the dentist will remove one of your teeth and replace it with this one."

Flannery takes the tooth from the tin and holds it up for Joe to examine. At the rear of the tooth is a small cavity, into which a small glass pill is nestled.

"This is your L-pill. It contains a dose of potassium cyanide. Do I need to tell you what that is?"

Joe shakes his head. Tar has already warned him that he must not be captured. He was expecting something like this.

"L stands for lethal. It's quite safe until you crack the pill open," Flannery tells him. "A good hard bite will do it. After that you will have a minute or two to say your last words, or prayers."

"It won't crack open just through eating?" Joe asks.

"It shouldn't," Flannery says. "Hasn't happened to anyone yet. Of course you might be the first." He smiles. "You can press the pill out from the tooth with your tongue, like so." He demonstrates with his little finger. "Bite down on it and think up some famous last words. That's all there is to it."

24

FRANCE

France, April 19, 1941

There is a hole in the floor of the aircraft. It is covered, but it is there, and the boy knows it is there. He knows it is there because he will soon be dropping through it. He will soon be dropping through it because they have just crossed the French coast.

The aircraft is an Armstrong Whitworth Whitley bomber that has been converted to transport paratroopers. The gun turret in the stomach of the plane has been removed to create the hole that Joe is now staring at.

This is a world away from training. Stepping off the back of a truck traveling at fifty kilometers per hour in the daylight does not come close to falling out of a converted bomber above enemy-occupied territory in the dark!

They had practiced night drops of course, but always with the knowledge that if something went wrong, like if he sprained or broke an ankle, there would be a cup of tea and sympathy, along with the best medical treatment, immediately available. If he hurts himself on this drop, he is on his own, in a hostile land.

He wishes the no-nonsense paratrooper who trained him

was here. Collins had a way of instilling confidence in people.

This whole mission seems much too real, much too soon. Even if he lands successfully and uneventfully, that will be just the start of it.

It is April 19. That means Joe will have to hide out in France for nearly two weeks before the May Day parade. A "Continental holiday" Flannery called it. Yeah, right. Some holiday, Joe thinks.

The moon is up and the skies are clear. Not that Joe can see any of that. The body of the aircraft is windowless. There are no seats, nor room for any. Nor is there room to stand up. He stretches his legs by lying lengthways down the aircraft, feeling the vibration of the two Rolls-Royce Merlin engines along the length of his body. The noise the engines make is terrific. He tries sticking his fingers in his ears, but that doesn't seem to help.

"Five minutes, hook up."

It is the voice of Sergeant Twigge, the jumpmaster, shouting over the roar of those engines. Joe flashes a thumbs-up signal and sits up, clipping his static line to a wire that runs the length of the fuselage.

A red light above the hole in the floor begins to flash.

Sergeant Twigge comes scrambling back to check the static line a moment later. He picks up a cord from a metal equipment canister and snaps that onto the same wire. The bullet-shaped canister is about the size of a small suitcase.

After satisfying himself that Joe has managed to attach his

line correctly, the sergeant hooks a safety line to his own webbing harness, then winds a handle to raise the two half circles that form the cover of the hole.

Joe finds himself looking down at France through a metal tube that is nearly a meter long and about as wide. The landscape is dark, but lit by flashes of moonlight, glinting off ponds and streams. They pass over a river, a silvery scar slashed across the countryside. He is amazed at how low they are, but knows why—to avoid enemy radar. As he is watching, the dark countryside begins to recede. They are climbing to a safe height for parachuting.

Twigge shouts, "One minute! Remember to keep your body straight and rigid. I don't want you damaging my plane with your head!"

Joe gives him another thumbs-up, too nervous to try to speak. He moves to the edge of the hole and swings his feet over the edge, letting them dangle, buffeted by the airflow.

Twigge is looking at him. "Why ain't you in school?" he says, shaking his head. "You should be playing soccer with your mates and showing off to the young ladies. What are you doing jumping out of an airplane over occupied France?"

Even if Joe wanted to answer, there is no time. A light on a bulkhead begins to flash red.

"Thirty seconds," Twigge calls, hand raised. "Stand by!"

Below Joe now is all darkness, vague shapes of trees and fences, ghostly shadows in the moonlight. Joe is amazed that the pilot knows where they are. The red light snaps off, and a green light comes on.

"Green on," Twigge shouts, tossing the equipment canister down through the hole. The static line snaps tight for an instant, then slackens. "Go!"

Joe pushes off the edge and falls through the center of the hole in the floor, holding his body rigid and upright as he has been told.

The slipstream smashes into him, a solid wall of wind, tearing him away from the aircraft overhead, tumbling him, so that his feet are facing the sky, but only for the briefest of moments before the static line snatches the parachute out of its bag. There is a jerk, dragging him back upright as though he is a marionette in the hands of a deranged puppeteer. Now he is swinging in the grip of the wind and the fully open chute above him. Below, caught in the moonlight, is the silken circle of his equipment chute. Looking up he realizes his is just as bright. An easy target for any German soldier.

If there are any, he will soon find out.

Parachuting at night is much harder than during the day. You cannot judge distances in the dark. You cannot see the ground to estimate your height. It is like parachuting blindfolded.

The wind buffets him, rippling his canopy. It's so cold at this height. He begins to sway from side to side and pulls on the risers to try and stop it.

He can see a small stand of trees below, just visible in the moonlight. He tries to steer away from them, but the wind seems to be carrying him toward them. They are rushing at him now . . . faster and faster . . . No matter how much he pulls on the risers and suspension lines, he doesn't seem able to avoid them . . .

Then he is in among them, falling through the canopy, branches snapping under his weight, somehow missing any large branches that would have broken an ankle, a leg—or worse if he had come down astride one.

He prepares himself for his roll, then comes to a shuddering stop as the parachute snags in the trees . . . tears free . . . snags again . . . and ends up dangling him a meter off the ground.

Dark figures are running across the fields toward him, and there is absolutely nothing he can do about it. If they are members of the Resistance, he is exactly where he is supposed to be. If they are German soldiers, he is about to be captured or killed. His only weapon is his Welrod pistol, and that is packed in a padded bag inside the equipment canister.

A young man reaches him first. He wears dark clothing and has an ancient rifle slung across one shoulder.

"Albert?" Joe asks hopefully.

The man shakes his head. "Non, je suis Antoine," he says, and gestures toward two more people, a man and a woman, dark shapes running toward them.

The man is older, his back as straight as a ramrod, a former soldier for certain. He carries a revolver. The middle-aged woman at his side is shorter with a sharply lined jaw and thick eyebrows that meet in the middle. She is unarmed.

Joe undoes the parachute release and drops to the ground, landing lightly.

"Bonjour, Albert," he says, extending a hand.

It is not the old soldier who takes it, but the woman. "C'est moi," she says.

His surprise must show on his face, even in the dark, because she asks in heavily accented English, "Not who you were expecting?"

That makes Joe realize that she has not yet given him his code name, so he says nothing and waits. She moves closer to him, grips him by the arms, and kisses him lightly on one cheek after the other in the French style. As she does so, she whispers, "Hello, Katipo."

She releases him and remarks, "Three trees in the entire field. Yet you managed to find them."

Joe smiles. "Just a good shot I guess."

She doesn't return the smile but speaks rapidly in French to the younger of the two men, Antoine, who nods, produces a pocketknife from a holster on his belt, then begins to climb the tree.

"My equipment?" Joe asks.

"In the next field," she says. "Antoine will bring it to the farm after he has dealt with your parachute."

It is clear that landing in the tree has complicated things, and she is less than impressed.

"We must leave," she says. "Vite. Hurry."

That first night is spent in a farmhouse, in a large wooden box in the middle of a hay pile in the barn. It is the size of a large closet. There is food, water, and a bucket for a toilet, and Joe is instructed to remain there and remain silent. If any German observers have heard the plane, or seen the parachutes, there will be searches. Albert is not going to risk moving Joe out of the area until she knows it is safe to travel. This is a country in the iron grip of its oppressors.

After two days hiding in the hay, itching constantly at insect bites, the Resistance fighters move Joe to another farmhouse, to a cellar full of wine bottles and rat droppings, the entrance to which is disguised by a dog kennel. The next move is to an old stone cottage in a small village on the outskirts of the city.

In all that time he does not see Albert even once. It is Antoine or his father, Jacques, the old soldier, who comes to move him, once on bicycles and once in a farm truck converted to run on coal gas. It smells like a smithy.

The cottage is uninhabited. A window by the door at the rear of the cottage has been broken and the glass left lying on the floor. That is safer for the owners as it makes it look like a break-in. If he is discovered living there, they can deny all knowledge.

Water comes from a well, with a hand pump in the front yard. The handle is rusty, but it works and the water looks clean enough.

There is a kitchen stove, but Joe is forbidden to use it, in case anyone notices smoke from the chimney. For the same reason there are no warm baths, and he has to content himself with a daily wipe down with a cold rag. The toilet is a small shed out the back, full of spiders and snails.

Jacques or Antoine visit every second day with a basket of

food. Always at night when they are less likely to be seen, although that means breaking curfew, and risking searches by German patrols.

Joe has been there almost a week when Albert shows up unannounced one morning. Joe is playing chess with himself, using a chessboard and pieces he'd made by tearing pages from a book he found in the bedroom and marking them with a piece of coal. The book was in French, and he didn't understand it anyway.

He is winning, on the verge of checkmating himself, when he sees Albert and the young man, Antoine, cycling along the road that leads past the cottage. They dismount and walk up the narrow path to the front door.

They lean their bicycles against the posts of the fence near the water pump, then Albert comes to the door while Antoine turns and trudges away back down the path.

"Welcome to my humble abode," Joe says.

She pushes past him. "Shut the door." Then, "All plans are in place. This afternoon we will enter Paris and stay there until the operation."

"So soon?" Joe asks, secretly glad to be away from this rustic but primitive cottage.

"The closer we get to the day of the parade, the tighter the security will be," Albert says. "Better to enter the city early. We'll be staying with a woman in Grenelle, in the southwest of the city. Beatrice. She's my aunt."

"Really?" Joe asks.

Albert gives him a withering look. "Of course not. And

she is not a part of the Resistance either, but does whatever she can to help. If you are easily embarrassed, please look away."

Joe does not look away as she reaches rather indecorously up under her skirt and produces a tight roll of paper that must have been strapped to her thigh. She unrolls it and spreads it out on the small wooden kitchen table, raising a small cloud of dust. It is a hand-drawn map of Paris.

"When the beast is slain, I will meet you in the Bois de Boulogne . . . here," she says, pointing. "There's a restaurant, Le Pré Catelan. It will be closed, but there may be staff around, preparing for the evening. So do not approach the building. I will meet you in the stand of trees to the east of the building, here. Once you reach the park, avoid the roads. Avoid footpaths where possible. Stay in the trees. Avoid contact with anyone. If you cannot avoid that, you are looking for a lost dog."

"Perhaps I should carry a leash," Joe suggests.

She glances at him, apparently impressed. "I will organize one," she says. "How good is your French?"

"Basic," Joe answers honestly.

"That is what they told me," she says. "Repeat this after me. 'Avez-vous vu un petit chien noir?'"

Joe's basic French is good enough to understand that. *Have you seen a small black dog?* He tries to imitate her.

"Non," Albert says. "Chien. Try it again."

"Avez-vous vu un petit *chien* noir?"

"Better," she says. "No matter what they say to you, no

matter whether you understand it or not, say 'merci' and walk away calling the dog's name."

"What name?" Joe asks.

"Whatever you want," Albert says.

"Grable?" Joe asks.

"If you like, it means nothing," Albert says.

She is wrong. It means something to him.

"Now let me hear you say 'merci,'" she says.

He repeats it, copying her intonation.

"Très bien," she says. "And the first phrase?"

"Avez-vous vu un petit chien noir?"

"Good," she says. "Keep practicing it."

Joe does so, feeling the shape of the words in his mouth.

That isn't all he can feel in his mouth. His tongue keeps being drawn to the slightly odd shape of the second-to-last molar on his lower left jaw. If he presses on the glass capsule it wobbles a little in its cavity. He hopes it won't come loose.

"How do we get to Paris?" he asks.

"By train. It is a short walk to the station at L'Étang-la-Ville. If anyone asks, you are my nephew, visiting from Germany. May I see your papers?"

His papers are in a small suitcase that also contains his weapon, the Welrod, in a concealed compartment. He extracts the papers and hands them to her.

"Josef Eichmann." She says the surname with some distaste. "These papers say that you are from Berlin. Can you pass as a native of Berlin?"

"Absolutely," Joe says.

She studies him for a moment, her thick eyebrows knitting together. "Overconfidence is dangerous," she says.

"My German is perfect and idiomatic," Joe says. "Both high German and the Berlin dialect. I spent many years there when I was a child."

"You are still a child," she says softly.

Joe looks at her for a moment. She stares back without blinking.

"I feel that you don't like me very much," Joe says.

Only then does she look away. She hands him back his papers and tucks the map back under her skirt.

"I do not feel strongly about you one way or the other," she says. "I have barely met you. I hope you are competent, that is all. It is the operation that I dislike."

"Why?" Joe asks.

"Get your things," she says. She picks up a bellows from the fireplace and pumps it rapidly around the room, raising clouds of dust which settle slowly, disguising any evidence of Joe's stay. She backs toward the doorway erasing their footprints in the same way, then leaves the bellows by the doorway.

"I have spent almost a year building my network, my maquis," she says as they walk toward the bicycles. "The slightest stumble could send it crashing down and send people I care about to the Gestapo kitchens. This operation is foolish and dangerous."

"But important," Joe says.

She shrugs. "Who can say? But even if it is successful and we are not compromised, there will be consequences. Reprisals. Many innocent Français will lose their lives. Already the Germans hold prisoners, hostages, against just this kind of event. The assassination of such a high-ranking Nazi will be repaid with terrible interest."

Actions have consequences. It was one of Tar's
favorite sayings and it was never more true
than in France during the occupation.

For any German killed, the Gestapo would execute fifty to a
hundred innocent French civilians. For that reason, and others,
I ended up being responsible for a great number of deaths.

—from the memoirs of Joseph "Katipo" St. George

25

AN OLD FRIEND

Paris, April 25, 1941

Albert's "aunt" Beatrice turns out to be an elderly woman who dresses in long black gowns, sparkling jewelry, and Chanel No. 5 perfume no matter what the time of day.

Joe knows it is Chanel No. 5 because her apartment is decorated with the empty bottles.

Beatrice was an artist and a life model in her youth. There are a number of paintings of her hung in prominent places in the apartment. Joe knows they are of her, because she takes great delight in telling him, on numerous occasions.

Beatrice hates the Germans, calling them "les Boches" in private, yet is impeccably polite to any she meets in public. She is elegant, charming, and nutty as a fruitcake in Joe's opinion, but she cooks beautiful meals and her home is airy and spacious.

The apartment is sumptuously furnished with antiques and paintings, some of which Joe suspects are worth more than the actual building they hang in. A balcony on the east side even has a view of the Eiffel Tower, although you have to stand on the very end of the balcony and lean dangerously forward to see it.

Albert sleeps in the spare room, and Joe has a foldout sofa bed in the drawing room. Albert goes out only when she has to, and Joe goes out not at all.

Not until April 30. The day before the parade.

Aunt Beatrice comes with them to "show them the way," although Joe is quite sure they would have found their way to the Arc de Triomphe without her. Perhaps she just wants some air, an outing.

Despite her age, she walks quickly, striding ahead of them in her long black gown, pearl necklaces swinging, rings sparkling, her hair elegantly coiffured into elaborate rolls and braids.

She leads them to a checkpoint, a barricade of sandbags stretching right across the road, with only a narrow gap wide enough for one vehicle to pass, and another even narrower for pedestrians. It is manned by German soldiers in the gray-green uniforms of the Wehrmacht, carrying Mauser Karabiner 98k rifles that Joe recognizes from his training. He can load, fire, and fieldstrip one of these rifles as well as any of these soldiers.

Beatrice marches straight to the front of a short line of people waiting to pass through the checkpoint. People move aside to let her to the front, and the German soldiers wave her through without a glance at her papers. When Joe tries to follow Beatrice, Albert takes his arm and draws him to the rear of the line.

"We do not want to be noticed," she murmurs, softly so that only he can hear.

Joe glances quizzically after Beatrice, who is now chatting

with the owner of a fruit and vegetable stand at the side of the road, complaining loudly about his produce.

"She is not noticed, because she is so noticeable," Albert says. "We do not have that luxury. Make sure you do not appear nervous. The French are used to these checkpoints, they pass through them every day. It is routine. If you appear nervous, the guards will think you have something to hide. Especially as your papers show you to be German. Why would a German be nervous?"

Joe nods. Not appearing nervous is easier said than done, but he tries to adopt a nonchalant air. Just a boy from Berlin enjoying a Parisian holiday.

The line shuffles forward until it is Albert and Joe's turn.

The soldier checks Albert's papers first, comparing her face to her photograph, then extends a hand for Joe's.

Joe hands over his ID card and his travel permit. The soldier scans them then, to Joe's surprise, smiles at him.

"From Berlin," he says, using the Berlinese dialect. "Me too. How are you enjoying Paris?"

Joe feels a chill travel from his spine to his scalp but keeps his voice light and amiable. He replies in the same dialect. "Paris in springtime." He grins. "What's not to like?"

"That Eiffel Tower is something, isn't it?" the soldier asks. "And the Arc de Triomphe."

Joe shrugs. "The Brandenburg Gate is more impressive," he says. "Especially at sunset."

"This is true," the soldier agrees. "Where do you go to school?"

"St. Andreas, in Kreuzberg," Joe says. It is better to stick as much to the truth as possible, according to his training.

"St. Andreas. I had a cousin who went there," the soldier says. "He told me the headmaster was a real bully. A big, fat man from Hamburg, who liked nothing better than to give a boy the cane."

"The headmaster is a short, thin man from Munich," Joe says. "Herr Schneider. But the part about the cane is true." That was the case the last time Joe was at the school. He hopes the headmaster has not changed since he left.

The soldier laughs and cuffs him on the side of the head as he lets them through.

Albert looks sideways at Joe once they are well clear of the barricade. "That was acceptable," she says, sounding perhaps a little surprised.

Joe nods his thanks. Perhaps he will prove to be competent after all.

Beatrice clearly enjoys being out and about. This is her city and nothing the German occupiers do will change that. She seems to know everybody and everybody knows her, at least around Grenelle.

It is about a half-hour walk from the checkpoint in Grenelle to the Champs-Élysées and the Arc de Triomphe, and Joe is amazed at how Germanified the city has become. Although it has been less than a year since the start of the occupation, swastika flags hang from buildings, street signs have been replaced, or supplemented by German language ones, and whole stores are devoted entirely to the German masters.

There are Soldatenkinos and Soldatenkaffees—cinemas and cafés exclusively for German soldiers.

A Soldatenbäckerei has a window full of bread: baguette, pain d'épi, and brioche. Two blocks farther on, a boulangerie for the French has no bread on its shelves, and a line of people that stretches around the corner.

Beatrice seems to take great delight in being hospitable to her German oppressors. She chats in fluent German to soldiers and flirts with handsome young officers.

"She seems to love the enemy," Joe mutters as Beatrice whirls and blows a kiss to a high-ranking German officer being driven past in the rear of a staff car.

"All part of her act," Albert says. "She will be the first to poison their marmalade when liberation comes."

If liberation comes, Joe thinks. Just as the Vikings once conquered England, and the Spanish conquistadors conquered South America, now the Germans are the masters of the continent. Perhaps they will succeed in bringing all of Europe under their control, as the Romans once did. Perhaps, as Hitler promised, his Third Reich will last for a thousand years.

Their walk takes them past the Eiffel Tower, which is indeed impressive, a huge lattice of wrought iron, soaring up out of a park on the southern bank of the River Seine.

A group of uniformed Hitler Youth are admiring the tower; they mill around, chattering and laughing, overflowing with exuberance and excitement. How long has it been since he felt like that? Joe thinks he never will again. The importance of his mission, of his responsibilities, weigh on him. How wonderful it would be to be so carefree. But that part of his life—his childhood—is gone.

Tomorrow, however, he will have to pretend to be one of these happy young sightseers. He watches how they move, how they talk. Tomorrow he needs to exhibit the same confidence. The same arrogance.

A tall boy, who would be at least seventeen and on the verge of joining the army, has a camera to his face, lining up his friends in front of the tower. He is kneeling down and aiming the camera upward to try and get the people and the tower in the same photograph. That isn't working so he lies on his back, his head toward his friends, and turns the camera upside down.

There are cheers and laughter from his friends when he sits back upright holding up the camera and waving it to show that he has taken the photograph.

It is Klaus. Klaus Bormann. Joe's old school friend. His one-time blood brother.

Joe raises a hand to his face to hide it and turns away, trying to make the movement as natural as possible.

Albert sees it. "What is it?" she asks.

"Nothing," Joe says.

"It's not nothing . . . What is it?"

"Someone I know. I mean someone I knew. A long time ago in Berlin."

Albert quickens her pace, without appearing to hurry. Joe has to lengthen his stride to keep up with her.

"Did he see you?" she hisses.

"I don't think so."

"You don't *think* so," Albert says. "Could he identify you? Did they not tell you in England that if anyone identifies you, this mission and your career as an SOE agent are over?"

"He didn't see me," Joe says.

It happened too quickly. He was too far away, just a face in a crowd of passersby. He wouldn't even have recognized Klaus if his attention had not been drawn to the antics with the camera.

"You're sure."

"I'm sure," Joe lies. He is *almost* sure. He is sure enough not to want to end his career before it starts. To abort the mission. A waste of time and resources. A squandered opportunity. All because a boy he knew years before might have noticed him in a crowd.

Albert seems satisfied. They stop for coffee and breakfast pastries in a Soldatenkaffee on the Avenue Marceau. Every table is taken and the café is reserved for German soldiers, but Beatrice waltzes in and a German officer waves a hand at a waiter, who disappears and returns with an extra table and chairs.

Beatrice blows a kiss to the officer as they sit, and the officer catches it and clasps it to his heart with a broad smile.

Joe thinks about the man choking on his marmalade on liberation day and smiles with the others.

Although reserved for soldiers, the Soldatenkaffee is not populated exclusively by them. Many of the soldiers are sitting at tables with stylish young Parisian ladies, deep in earnest conversation. Joe can't help but wonder whether the young women genuinely enjoy the attention of the handsome young soldiers, endure it, or are spies, chatting up the soldiers for details of their units, their locations, and their troop numbers.

After breakfast, Beatrice leaves them, heading off to visit an old friend, she says.

Joe keeps a careful eye out for bands of Hitler Youth as he and Albert make their way to the Arc de Triomphe. He sees many of the brown uniforms but not the group of friends that includes Klaus.

The Champs-Élysées is being prepared for the big parade. Metal barriers have been put up to hold back the crowds. A small grandstand has been erected in the shadow of the great arch from lengths of tubular steel, which has created tiered rows. Padded chairs are being set out along each row as Albert and Joe draw near.

"Stop and tie your shoe," Albert suggests.

Joe kneels down, untying his shoelace, then retying it. His eyes are on the scaffolding that creates the grandstand. There are gaps between each tier. If he could get behind the grandstand, under the seats, he would be able to move right up behind Heydrich and put a bullet in his spine. A second bullet in his head, as he falls, if there is time. The silent pistol will ensure that nobody knows what is happening. Not until it is too late.

That will be his plan A, as MacDonald drummed into him.

But that depends on the security. If they block off the rear of the grandstand, that option will be taken away.

He gauges the distance from the road, where Heydrich's car

will arrive, to the grandstand. That is another option. If he is right at the edge of the crowd, he will be within a meter or so of the man. That would be close enough. Plan B.

He cannot think of a plan C.

He finishes tying his shoe and stands. Together they walk casually past the grandstand and carry on along the Champs-Élysées.

"Well?" Albert asks when they were well away from any listening ears.

"It's possible," Joe says. "It depends on the security on the day how close I'll be able to get."

"But you're confident?"

"As much as I can be," Joe says.

"You had better be" is her response.

Joe keeps a careful eye out for Klaus all the way home, but his mind is elsewhere. How did he get to this? It seems only yesterday that he was reading adventure stories and playing with tin soldiers. And now he has just spent the last hour planning the best way to kill another human being.

26

MAY DAY

Paris, May 1, 1941

The next day is warm, a perfect summer's day for the parade. Overhead the boy can see Messerschmitt fighters circling, waiting for their flyover.

He and Albert have joined the crowd lining the street. The old soldier, Jacques, is there too. He wears his military uniform and medals from the Great War. At first Joe wonders how the Germans will treat an old soldier in uniform, but they seem to regard him with respect, and one or two even salute. Jacques does not return the salutes.

He is near Joe and Albert but does not acknowledge them in any way. Fifteen minutes before the parade is due to start, he slips away.

Joe doesn't need to ask Albert where Jacques is going; there is a bomb to be set off.

Joe is wearing the coat of a butcher's boy to cover his Hitler Youth uniform. An overcoat would have looked out of place on such a warm afternoon, but the white cotton coat conceals the uniform adequately until he can join the throng of real Hitler Youths. In the pocket of his pants he has a thin leather dog leash.

They work their way to the front of the crowd, where Albert stands behind to shield Joe as he slips off the white coat.

"Bonne chance," she whispers as he passes it back to her. He shuffles his way forward into the throng of excited young men in their brown shirts, short pants, and tall socks.

Many of them hold swastika flags for waving at the tanks or artillerymen or the aircraft doing their flyover. Joe has one too. Except his flag is attached to the long barrel of a Welrod assassin's pistol. For now he has wrapped the flag around the gun, concealing it from all but the closest inspection.

Without glancing back at Albert, he works his way into the center of the Hitler Youth, smiling and nodding at people as if he knows them. They smile and nod back, perhaps thinking they have met him already, on the train or in the mess hall or at a rally in Berlin.

Joe shuffles his way toward the grandstand, which is cordoned off by a ceremonial rope and guarded by black-suited SS soldiers. There is no chance of getting behind or under the grandstand. Plan A is out of the question. He moves to plan B.

He judges the distances. The Welrod is not particularly accurate. He will have to get as close as he can to Heydrich before pulling the trigger.

Nor are there any guarantees that he will have time for a second shot. Perhaps in the confusion, if nobody identifies where the shot has come from, then he might be able to close in for the final blow—the coup de grâce, as the French say. But he cannot be sure of that, so the first shot has to be a good one. To the head, if at all possible. To the heart if not. The neck is also a good target—a well-placed shot there will tear open arteries and major veins and Heydrich will bleed to death before anyone can save him.

He is examining the grandstand, calculating the distance from the ropes to the steps, from the steps to the road, working out the position of the SS guards, when, on the other side of the grandstand, in the middle of a crowd of Hitler Youth, he sees Klaus again.

His heart stops.

Klaus is looking right back at him.

Joe keeps his face impassive and glances away as if he hasn't recognized the boy. Just another face in a crowd. A blond-haired boy in a throng of blond-haired boys. And at a distance. Just a coincidence, that is all. A doppelgänger perhaps, like the nurse at Peggy's hospital who was a dead ringer for Rosie.

He moves to put a few people in between them. After a moment he risks a quick peek.

It is not good news.

He sees Klaus shuffling his way through the throng in his direction. Has he seen Joe? Or is he just jostling for a better position, a better view? Joe ducks his head lower behind two tall boys with Bavarian accents.

The crowd suddenly quiets and heads turn. Heydrich's car is pulling from the Champs-Élysées onto the Place de L'Etoile where the huge Arc de Triomphe is situated. It pulls slowly to a halt in front of the grandstand where a line of German VIPs wait. Behind them is a line of French dignitaries.

Joe risks another glance at Klaus but cannot see him.

He reaches down and unfurls the flag from around his pistol, careful to keep it low, out of sight.

Joe rotates the rear knob and pulls it backward, hearing the faint click as it loads the bullet into the chamber.

The car stops, and an SS guard moves to the rear door to open it.

Still no sign of Klaus.

Joe shuffles forward a little, as if with excitement.

The car door opens.

The man that emerges is tall and thin, dressed in the uniform of an SS general. He salutes the guard who holds his door.

It is not Heydrich. It is not even someone who looks like Heydrich. This face is rounder, softer, the eyebrows fuller, the face more lined. He is older, grayer.

He moves down the line of German officers, returning their salutes, then crosses to the French dignitaries, shaking each hand in turn.

Something is wrong. Their intelligence is wrong. Heydrich must have changed his plans, decided not to attend the parade.

Why would he do that?

Joe can think of only one reason: Heydrich has been tipped off about the assassination attempt. Who would have done that? Who *could* have done that? So very few people knew about the plan. Not Albert, surely. Jacques? He had fought the Germans in the last war. Antoine is his son. Surely not either of them.

Beatrice? Albert seems to trust her, but she *is* overly friendly with the occupying army.

Could it have been Beatrice?

The high-ranking German officer moves to the small grandstand and takes the center place in the stand. Joe remains where he is. Unsure what to do.

If he is right, then German intelligence knows about this operation. They are expecting someone to try and assassinate Heydrich. Which means they are expecting Joe.

With the VIP now in place, the parade begins immediately, row after row of goose-stepping soldiers passing in front of the grandstand. The Hitler Youth throw their hands in the air in the Nazi salute, and Joe joins in with as much enthusiasm as he can fake.

A solo drummer on horseback, with a large drum on each side of the horse, canters in a circle around a mounted brass band. He holds his drumsticks high, bringing them down for a quick military beat, then raising them back above his head.

The brass band trots its way past the grandstand, the drummer wheeling around them.

Row after row of horse-drawn artillery follows. Huge 10-inch field guns, each with a team of four horses.

Then comes the armored cars and half-tracks at first, but in the distance, Joe can hear the tanks.

"What are you doing here, Joe?" Klaus's voice asks quietly behind him, startling him.

Joe turns.

Klaus has to be sixteen now, even taller and broader. His chin is dark with regrowth of a full beard. He undoubtedly has to shave every day.

"I'm sorry? You mistake me," Joe says. "My name is Hans. Hans Schmidt."

He turns away from the boy. It has been more than two years. Joe knows he has changed in that time. Surely Klaus will have some doubts.

However, he is too slow to react when Klaus's strong hand grabs his wrist and twists, exposing his palm and revealing the scarred swastika.

"I saw you on the train platform that day," Klaus says as Joe wrenches his arm away. "And your mother. I didn't tell the Gestapo men."

"My mother is dead," Joe says bitterly.

"I'm sorry to hear that," Klaus says.

"Not as sorry as I am," Joe says.

"I had to give Blondie away," Klaus says after a moment. "My mother was allergic to dogs. You knew that."

Joe *had* known that. "What else could I have done with her?" he asks, wondering where this conversation is going. Why is this important? Here? Now? It is like two old friends catching up over coffee. "Did you expect me to slit her throat? Leave her to starve?"

"My father gave her to his brother. The Führer's personal secretary, you remember," Klaus says. "But my uncle gave her to his boss."

"No," Joe breathes through clenched teeth. Blondie is Adolf Hitler's pet? Now he wishes he *had* slit her throat.

"What are you doing here, Joe?" Klaus asks again.

"I saw the writing on the wall," Joe says feigning a deep sigh.

"Germany is going to win this war. They will conquer the world. I want to be on the winning side."

"No, Joe," Klaus says, moving close to Joe, speaking softly, right by his ear to ensure he cannot be overheard. "I do not believe you. I was with you that day at the bakery, remember? We both saw what happened to Herr and Frau Reinsgart. We both know what the Nazis are capable of. I know you too well. You might act the part, but you will never be a Nazi."

"If you are so sure, then why are you?" Joe whispers.

"I am a German by birth and a Nazi out of necessity," Klaus says stiffly. "I am a patriot. As are you. I have no choice but to fight—and if necessary, die—for my country. As do you. But my country is not your country, and yours is not mine."

"So your beliefs, your morals, your knowledge of right and wrong are less important than the accident of your birthplace," Joe says.

"Would you betray your country?" Klaus asks.

Joe shakes his head.

"And I cannot betray mine," Klaus says. "But I have no wish to see you tortured or killed as you will surely be if the Gestapo get their hands on you. Go now. I will say nothing. I'll give you one hour, blood brother. Get clear of the parade. Leave the city. When the hour is up, I will raise the alarm."

Joe stares at him, surprised, not at Klaus's kindness, his *good*ness, but that those qualities have survived two years of war. Two years of National Socialism. They both look up as a trio of Messerschmitt 109s make a pass down the street, low over the Arc de Triomphe, their shadows fluttering over the crowd, the roar of their engines infusing onlookers with excitement. The planes soar skyward, banking, circling around for another pass.

"This is a great gift, blood brother," Joe says. "How can I thank you?"

"By never returning to France or Germany," Klaus says. "By surviving this war, so that when our countries are no longer enemies, we can again be friends."

"You are a good man," Joe says.

"As are you," Klaus says.

Joe does not bother to correct him.

He holds out a hand to Klaus, who takes it and shakes it.

"Auf wiedersehen," Joe says.

"Auf wiedersehen," Klaus repeats. *Until we meet again.*

Joe grasps Klaus's hand a moment too long, waiting for the shadow of the planes to pass for a second time before he shoots him.

The Welrod kicks in Joe's left hand, the muzzle less than an inch from Klaus's chest. The soft *phut* of the gun is inaudible, lost in the roar of the aircraft engines, the sound of the drummers and the brass band, the rumble of the tank engines.

A small hole appears in Klaus's uniform shirt, above his heart. There is no blood. Not yet. Klaus looks shocked. He glances down at the hole, then back at Joe. He opens his mouth, to scream, or shout, but then seems to change his mind. He shakes his head sadly.

"Get out of here, Joe," he says in a faint voice as a spurt of blood erupts from his chest, splattering down his clean brown shirt and short pants.

Joe backs away, horrified, sliding the Welrod back under the flag, as blood continues to gush, rhythmically, from the hole in Klaus's shirt.

One more step and Klaus is lost from sight, although Joe hears the commotion as Klaus staggers and falls, the gasps then the shouts as other boys crowd around him.

Joe keeps walking backward, sensing without seeing the barrier behind him or the milling crowd behind that. What did he just do?

The click sounds just by his left ear. He turns his head just slightly, swiveling his eyes to the left, seeing the cold hard circle of the muzzle of a pistol. A Luger. The hand that holds it is crisscrossed with scars and old burns. He dares not turn farther. He slowly reaches for the Welrod, knowing that it will take too long to recycle the bolt and reload it but determined to try.

A low voice says, "It is such a beautiful day. Do not choose to die today."

It is good advice, but Joe ignores it.

His orders were clear. He must not be captured.

He chooses to die.

27

INTERROGATION

Paris, May 1, 1941

The boy lives. The boy breathes. Blood flows through his veins. His heart pumps, wildly but steadily.

The opportunity has passed. He had reached for his pistol, even drew back the bolt before it was wrenched from him. His hands were twisted behind his back by a black-coated SS officer.

He was searched and his papers and the dog leash were taken. A moment later the leash was tied tightly and roughly around his wrists.

Now they walk down Avenue Foch in the direction of the Gestapo headquarters. The man with the Luger and the scarred hand walks beside Joe, one arm around his back in a friendly, paternal way, as though he were a father taking a walk with his son . . . except for the firm hand on the leather that binds his wrists. And except for the two armed SS men with them, one walking in front, one behind.

Civilians and soldiers alike make way for the group, with frightened looks and urgent whispers, as they stroll down the center of Avenue Foch, which has been closed to traffic because of the parade.

"My name is Hauptsturmführer Regensburg," the man says. He speaks in German, in a friendly tone.

"Gestapo." Joe spits on the sidewalk in front of them. Regensburg is careful to avoid stepping in it.

"Sicherheitsdienst," he says disdainfully. "The Gestapo are policemen. I am quite a different beast. A spy catcher."

"And yet still a beast," Joe says.

Regensburg chuckles. "Touché. But what is a spy catcher doing, playing policeman? A deluded member of the Hitler Youth decides to kill a high-ranking official. That is surely not a matter for a spy catcher, is it?"

Joe says nothing.

"Unless you are not who you appear to be," Regensburg says. He waves Joe's ID papers casually in the air. "So who are you, Josef Eichmann?"

"I am a proud member of the Hitler Youth," Joe says. "The man I went to shoot is a traitor. I knew it but could not prove it, so I decided to take the law into my own hands."

"Very good." Regensburg laughs. "You think well on your feet. So now explain why it is that you were carrying a British assassin's pistol."

Joe has no ready answer for that.

"You are young, much younger that I expected," Regensburg tuts. "Now they are sending children to fight their battles. So very young, with the beauty and innocence of youth. Yet here you are. In the clutches of the SD. It is a tragedy."

They reach the building at 84 Foch Avenue, a plain building, unremarkable, not even as tall as the buildings around it.

It is unadorned with flags, swastikas, or other Nazi regalia.

Joe is surprised when they walk straight past.

"Let me explain to you how this works," Regensburg says, as they continue to stroll down the avenue. "My job is to catch spies, and then to find out what they know, to help us catch other spies. And I have caught you."

He is sophisticated, erudite, and charming, which make his words no less chilling.

"Lucky for you," Joe says.

"I want . . . No, that is wrong. I *need* you to tell me everything you know," Regensburg says, his hand patting Joe lightly on the shoulder. "You will not want to tell me anything. And so the game begins."

"So it's all a game to you?" Joe mutters. "Schweinehund."

"Manners, please," Regensburg says. "Now I could ask you politely for information, but you would politely refuse to tell me anything. Or you would lie to me. So let us examine my other options. The most obvious one is to cause you physical pain."

"I am sure you'd enjoy that," Joe says.

Regensburg shakes his head. "Far from it. Pain is a tool. It is to the interrogator what a hammer is to a carpenter, what a stethoscope is to a doctor. No more. It is true that there are some people who enjoy causing pain. I assure you I am not one of them. So now my quandary is: Can I persuade you to talk without causing you pain, which would distress both of us?"

"Me more than you," Joe says.

"I suspect so."

They reach a small circular park at the end of the road, cross it, then follow another road into the Bois de Boulogne. Joe wonders if there is any way to make a break for it, to hide in the trees and somehow still make his way to the rendezvous with Albert. With two armed guards and bound wrists, he cannot see how.

Regensburg is silent until they reach a lake. A grassy verge leads to a concrete promenade. Two French boys, about eight or nine years old, are racing model sailboats.

Regensburg stops, and having no choice, Joe stops with him. Regensburg gazes fondly at the boys and their boats.

"I used to do this myself in Germany, in Dresden where I grew up. Such a simple pleasure," he says, and continues without pause, "Let us start with the simple questions. Who are you? Your German is excellent. You speak it like a native. You look like a native. Perhaps you are a native. Perhaps we could begin with your real name."

"Josef Eichmann," Joe says.

"I asked for your real name," Regensburg says. "Not the fake name on your fake ID papers."

By way of a reply Joe makes an anatomically improbable suggestion.

Regensburg laughs. "Such bravado. All I want is your name. Such a simple thing. And I might remind you that under the Geneva Conventions you are required to tell me your name, rank, and serial number."

He is playing with him now, Joe knows. The Geneva Conventions do not apply to spies. He keeps his mouth shut and watches the yachts glide across the water.

After a few moments they move on.

"The Gestapo will want you," Regensburg says. "You are a murderer and dealing with murderers is their job, not mine. The boy you shot, it may interest you to know, was the nephew of Martin Bormann—perhaps you have heard this name? He is the personal secretary of the Führer. When this news gets back to Berlin, it will ignite a firestorm. The Gestapo will not care about getting information from you, it will be all about revenge. It will be extremely unpleasant, in ways you cannot even begin to imagine. I can protect you from that, but only if you cooperate."

There is an island in the middle of the lake. Joe watches a pair of swans take off near it, their feet skimming across the water. If only there were a secret drain, like in Hyde Park. If only Eddie and Peggy were here, to show him where to go. If only Wild Bob were here to punch Regensburg in the face, then in the guts, then in the face again.

"If you talk to me, and tell me what you know, I will make you disappear," Regensburg says. "You can spend the rest of the war sailing toy yachts on some remote lake in Switzerland. That is all we will discuss for now. I want you to think about it. I will give you some time to reflect on your options, and we will reconvene our discussions this evening."

Their route now takes them back to Avenue Foch, number 84. There Regensburg politely bids Joe farewell. The two guards take him to some kind of prisoner processing room where he is photographed and his fingerprints are taken.

After that he is gently but firmly shown to a room in the

basement with no windows and a door made of metal. His wrist restraints are removed. There is no escaping from this room.

A bundle of blankets in one corner of the cell is the only comfort and Joe spreads them out and lies down, his hands beneath his head, as he waits for the evening.

The blankets smell like urine.

He is given a meal at some stage of the afternoon. A bowl of stew, with carrots, potatoes, onions, and some sort of indeterminate meat floating around in thick gravy. It smells good, but Joe can't eat it. His stomach is tied in knots, and he is quite sure that should he take one mouthful of the stew he will vomit.

He lies on the blankets and watches cockroaches crawling up the walls as the hours slowly pass. How many hours, he can't tell. He has no idea of time. There is no clock, nor even a window to gauge the sunlight. The only light comes from an electric bulb hanging on a cord from the ceiling. He is lucky, Joe thinks. At least they left the light on.

He toys with the glass capsule in his false tooth, running his tongue over the smooth round shape, wondering if he has the guts to be a hero and to take it. He decides he will wait. He will hold off until the last minute. Once he bites into that capsule there is no coming back. It is the last resort and he is not yet at that stage. Close, but not yet.

The door opens without warning, and two guards are standing in the harsh light from the corridor. One stands back, Schmeisser machine pistol raised, as the other motions

Joe forward. To his relief they do not restrain his wrists again, and merely march him in front of them, up four flights of stairs.

On one of the stairways, he passes Beatrice in the grip of two Gestapo officers. Her hair is disheveled, her face bloodied, her eyelids swollen, and she appears to have lost some teeth. Still she holds her head high, and although her eyes flick to Joe, she does not acknowledge that she knows him.

The stairs lead to a corridor, and that to a door.

This will be the torture room, Joe thinks, and is surprised to enter into a pleasant, wood-lined drawing room. A library of books covers one wall, and a Nazi flag dominates another. Behind a large, ornate wooden desk, a photo of Adolf Hitler hangs above a fireplace. The dog leash is coiled on the desk in front of Regensburg.

A wooden dining chair has been placed in front of the desk, and Regensburg gestures to it.

"Please sit," he says, with a pleasant smile. One of the two guards leaves, closing the door behind him. The other stands in front of the door.

"I won't talk," Joe says, but he sits anyway. There seems no harm in sitting down.

"Oh, everybody says that." The SD man waved a hand dismissively. "Albert said that too, for the first two hours." He smiles cheerfully. "We'd been after Albert for months, but without success until now. Largely thanks to you."

Joe's heart sinks at the thought of Albert screaming her lungs out in a Gestapo torture kitchen. He stares at the floor.

"Albert told us everything," Regensburg says. "He didn't want to, of course, but I can be quite persuasive."

Joe keeps his eyes fixed on the floor. Regensburg said "he." Which means he still has no idea who Albert is. Perhaps they captured Jacques. Or perhaps the whole thing is a lie.

"If you please," Regensburg says to the guard at the door.

The man shoulders his Schmeisser and moves to the fireplace on the wall behind the desk. He prods with a poker at the stack of wood and paper in the firebox, then lights the fire using a cigarette lighter.

It is already warm in the room, a steamy Paris spring night. There is no need for a fire. No need at all.

Regensburg picks up the dog leash and examines it as the soldier takes the poker and shoves the end into the fire, propping the other end up on a piece of firewood on the hearth. Joe's blood runs cold, remembering stories he has heard of people having their eyes put out by red hot pokers.

Is that what's in store for him, or is Hauptsturmführer Regensburg just trying to frighten him?

The soldier backs away from the fire, now crackling nicely, and moves back to his position by the door, blocking any chance of escape.

If only Mac's men were here to rescue him. "Bang!" they'd shout. "Bang, bang!"

Regensburg stands and opens the window to let in some fresh air. He rubs at his right hand, scarred and burnt. Joe wonders if he has been tortured sometime in the past. Wonders if the boot was once on the other foot.

And does that mean he now delights in inflicting pain on others, despite his protestations?

"A warm evening, isn't it?" Regensburg says. The fire licks up around the firewood in the grate. The end of the poker is starting to smoke slightly. "I am intrigued by the dog leash," he says. "I have been racking my brain trying to work out why you were carrying it, but alas without success."

"Put it around your neck and I will show you," Joe says.

Regensburg laughs. "Against all reason the bravado continues. I enjoy it. But I suspect it will disappear all too soon."

Joe tries to smirk, but his eyes are drawn to the poker, which is now beginning to glow a dull red.

"So barbaric, yet so effective," Regensburg says, without looking behind him. "I hope we won't get to that. Unbutton your shirt."

He places the dog leash neatly back on the desk.

"No," Joe says.

"Please," Regensburg says.

"No."

Regensburg smiles. "I had hoped for more . . . intelligence from you. I could have your shirt ripped from your body. I could do it myself if I was of a mind. Just remove it. Fight me on the big things, if you must, but not the inconsequential things."

Joe does nothing. Regensburg raises a finger to the guard, but before the man can move, Joe reaches up and begins to unbutton his shirt.

Regensburg moves his chair out from behind the desk, placing it right in front of Joe.

He glances behind him at the poker, now glowing redly in

the fire. "But as I said, we may not get to that. Let us start with the simple question again. What is your name, your real name?"

"I will not tell you. Not ever," Joe says.

"Such misplaced confidence." The man smiles. He touches his fingertips gently to Joe's cheek. "My fingers are cool and soft. The poker is not."

Joe looks steadily at him, running his tongue over his L-pill.

"Have you ever felt that kind of pain? Of course not. Can you imagine the smell of burning flesh? I would have to leave the room." Regensburg bursts into laughter. "Oh, you are much too intelligent for that. I have no intention of searing your flesh. It is just something I do to scare people. A little theatrics. Or"—he winks at Joe—"am I lying about that? Perhaps now I am lulling you into a false sense of security. You see the poker is still glowing in the hearth." He laughs again.

Joe thinks he is quite mad.

Regensburg stands and moves back to the desk, opens a drawer, and takes out a revolver.

"Isn't this a thing of beauty?" he says. "A Lebel revolver, Model 1892. Standard issue for French officers in the Great War." He examines the gun, looking over the top of it at Joe. "A war not nearly so great as the one we are currently engaged in, I think."

"No war is great," Joe says.

The man smiles. "So young and idealistic," he says. "Let me educate you. War is the human condition. It is what we are, it is who we are. It is how we keep our populations at a manageable level. It is survival of the strongest. It is natural selection."

"There is nothing natural about Nazi atrocities," Joe says. "You are all insane."

Regensburg seems genuinely surprised that Joe has not agreed with him. "I personally do not approve of war. I do not like the idea of all that death and suffering. But you would be mad to think that human beings can exist without war. Put two men and one woman on a desert island and within a month the weaker of the men will be dead. That is our nature. That is evolution. That brings us back to you . . . *Kiwi.*"

He shoots the last word at Joe like a bullet.

Joe jumps, despite his best efforts to remain still and show no emotion. How did he know Joe was from New Zealand?

Regensburg smiles. "Yes, you see I know more about you than you think."

Joe again runs his tongue over the L-pill concealed in his molar.

"It may interest you to know that Obergruppenführer Heydrich is not in Paris. In fact, he never planned to come to Paris," Regensburg says. "It is curious, is it not, how a small piece of misinformation, carefully placed, can cause such an avalanche of consequences."

Joe tries to process that information. His mind doesn't seem to be working. Heydrich was never in Paris? That was a lie, told to MI5. For what purpose? To flush out a killer? To catch Joe? That doesn't make sense.

"So it was all a trick," he says carefully, finally meeting Regensburg's eyes.

"A trick, as you say," Regensburg says. "A magic trick.

Abracadabra. Come, Kiwi, and see me pull Heydrich out of a hat. And you came. MI5 is a joke. So easily manipulated."

Joe looks down at the floor in what he hopes is a defeated expression. But his mind is racing. Regensburg has twice called Joe "Kiwi." Does he know that Joe is from New Zealand? Does that mean he knows Joe's true identity? If so, why is he so insistent on Joe revealing it?

"Does your mother know what you do for a job?" Joe asks, looking Regensburg squarely in the eye. "Does your wife? Do your children?"

Regensburg smiles easily. "I confess that I am unmarried. A confirmed bachelor, I fear. As for my mother, I killed her myself. I strung her up with piano wire when she refused to join the Nazi party."

The shock must show on Joe's face.

Regensburg bursts into laughter. "You see, you will believe anything you are told. Nazis are butchers, we are evil, we would torture our own mothers. No, my mother is alive and well and living in a comfortable apartment in Dresden. I call her on the telephone every weekend. My father died in the Great War and she gets a little lonely. As for my job, she is proud of my efforts to root out Germany's enemies."

"God might not look on you so favorably," Joe says.

"Oh, I do so enjoy chatting with you," Regensburg says. "This is so much more interesting than that usual name, rank, and serial number nonsense. But alas, we must get to business. Let us start with a little game. One, incidentally, that I read about in an American adventure magazine."

"We can play cards if you like," Joe says. "I'm quite good at gin rummy."

"It's a different sort of game," Regensburg says. He opens the revolver and shakes the bullets out of the cylinder, selecting one, with some thought, and replacing it. He places the other five bullets on the desk, then spins the cylinder like a cowboy in a Western movie before snapping it shut.

He sits back down in the chair facing Joe.

"Six chambers, one bullet," he says. "How do you like your odds?"

Joe looks steadily at him, trying not to show his fear.

Regensburg reaches over and places his free hand on Joe's kneecap. His skin is warm, and Joe thinks he can feel the man's pulse. He grips Joe's knee tightly. "The patella," he says. "A bullet would shatter it as it passed through, also smashing the ends of your femur and tibia, while tearing apart the ligaments that hold them together." He tuts. "Such a mess. You would never walk again. But that will be the least of your worries. I am told that the kneecap is the most painful place in the human body to be shot. People have been known to have a heart attack and die, just from the pain. But you are young and strong. I feel your heart will be able to stand it. So answer me, how do you like those odds?"

Joe stares straight into the man's eyes, keeping all expression from his face. The last thing he wants is for Regensburg to see the terror he is feeling.

At last he understands the real reason for the glass capsule concealed in the false tooth at the back of his lower left jaw. It is not for some heroic sacrifice, some noble act in the name of the greater good. It is a cowardly escape. And he is going to take it. Because he is a coward.

"I don't like those odds at all," he replies.

He is telling the truth. The L-pill has much better odds. One hundred percent guaranteed. A matter of a few minutes, Flannery told him. He casually moves his tongue to the back of his mouth and begins to work the L-pill out of its cavity. It seems stuck.

Regensburg places the revolver against Joe's knee and pulls the trigger. There is a loud metal click.

Joe closes his eyes and tries to stifle his sigh of relief.

"You see how this game works," Regensburg says. "It is very simple really."

He opens the revolver, spins the cylinder around again, then shuts it with a flick of his wrist.

Again he places the muzzle on Joe's knee.

"What is your real name, Kiwi?" he asks.

"Joseph St. George," Joe says. What does it matter anymore? His mother is dead and his father already in Gestapo custody. Joe himself will be dead in a matter of minutes. "I went to the St. Andreas School in Kreuzberg. My parents were diplomats at the British Embassy in Berlin."

"I don't believe you," Regensburg says.

He pulls the trigger and the world explodes.

28

THE L-PILL

Paris, May 1, 1941

The explosion is not the sound of a gun, it is far larger than that. The entire building rocks and the windows shatter, showering glass into the room.

The boy is thrown forward as the floor bucks like a wild horse. The desk rocks, papers fly, the spare bullets roll, scattering across the floor.

The glass pill jolts loose from its cavity. It falls out onto the back of Joe's tongue, and he gags to avoid swallowing it. He coughs it forward in his mouth and turns it over with his tongue.

Regensburg swaps the revolver to his other hand and draws a Luger pistol from the holster under his arm, aiming it directly at Joe's face. "This one is fully loaded," he assures Joe, then turns to the guard. "Go and see what is happening. I want an immediate report."

The guard raises his Schmeisser and runs from the room, slamming the door behind him.

"If I had to hazard a guess, I'd say your people want you back," Regensburg says coolly.

He is wrong. He had to be wrong. There is no way MI5 or

the SOE will have had time to organize a rescue mission. Joe had only been captured a few hours before and has not yet missed any scheduled radio contacts.

Regensburg must be drawing the same conclusion. "Or perhaps it is the French Resistance." He shakes his head dismissively. "Such amateurs. Anyway, it just makes me even more determined to keep you. And if I can't keep you, then I will certainly make sure that they can't have you either."

The pistol is still aimed straight at Joe's head.

Another explosion rocks the building, but the Luger does not waver. Outside someone is screaming, but there is another flurry of shots and the screaming ceases.

More shooting, very close, and a number of splintered holes appear in the wooden door. A vase on the mantelpiece behind Regensburg shatters, spraying water and flowers over the shelves.

Regensburg ducks instinctively, his eyes leaving Joe for a moment.

That is all Joe needs. His hand is closed around two small metal shapes. Bullets that he caught as they rolled off the edge of the desk. With Regensburg momentarily distracted, Joe flicks his wrist.

The sound the bullets make landing in the fireplace is no greater than the popping and crackling of the burning firewood.

There is more shooting from outside the room. He knows these guns. He knows the sound. He recognizes it from his training. These are Thompson submachine guns. British guns. He hears the answering stutter of the Schmeissers.

"You can't win," Regensburg says. "Even if they burst through that door I will put a bullet through your brain before they—"

It is as far as he gets before the first of the bullets in the fire cooks off, followed rapidly by the second.

Regensburg spins around toward the fireplace. Only for a second, but it is enough.

Joe launches himself up out of the chair, one hand reaching for Regensburg's Luger, the other for his neck.

He is lucky. His left hand catches the barrel of the gun as it swings back toward him, forcing it away just before it fires. He hears the shot, feels the jerk of the pistol and the heat of the gases as they explode from the muzzle. The bullet embeds itself in a wall, with a puff of plaster dust.

Regensburg's chair overbalances backward, crashing into the wooden floor with a thud, followed by a crack as Regensburg's head hits the floor. Joe lands on top of him, straddling him, one hand tightly gripping the barrel of the Luger, the other still clenched around Regensburg's neck.

Joe hopes that the man's head hitting the floor has dazed him, or even knocked him out, but it doesn't seem to affect him at all. Regensberg drops the revolver and grabs Joe's wrist with his free hand, wrenching it away from his neck.

Joe is strong, from years of hard farm work and weeks of intense training.

Regensburg is stronger.

He twists the Luger around toward Joe's face, and only a desperate shove from Joe forces it away again, just as Regensburg fires. The gunshot, so close to his ear, is like being struck on the side of the head with a hammer. His ear is ringing, deafened, but Joe barely notices. All he sees is the dark mouth of the gun turning back toward him.

Still straddling the bigger man, his hands trapped, Joe leans forward, bringing his face closer to the other man's face, bringing his lips closer to the other man's lips. Regensburg's eyes widen, and his grip on the pistol wavers momentarily.

Joe lifts his knee from the floor and drives it deeply into Regensburg's midriff. The German gasps for air, and at that precise moment Joe spits a small, round, hard object straight into the man's mouth.

Regensburg knows what it is. He can't not know. He tries to push the capsule out of his mouth with his tongue. He lets go of Joe's hand and reaches up to his mouth. It is a mistake. The moment his hand is free, Joe rams the heel of his palm into Regensburg's jaw, slamming his mouth shut, hearing the crunch as the capsule shatters.

The SD man's eyes open wide and he makes one last effort to bring the gun around, but Joe fights like a wild thing. A few minutes, they told him, that is all it will take. He hopes that is true, but with a surge of dying strength Regensburg wrenches the gun back until it is pointing right at Joe's left eye. He braces himself for the flash of light and the crack of thunder . . .

It never comes.

Regensburg begins convulsing, and when he does finally squeeze the trigger, it is too late because Joe has pushed the gun to the floor and the bullet merely scores a line across the floorboards and embeds itself in the skirting boards.

Regensburg is foaming at the mouth, not yet dead, his face contorted, his chest heaving, dragging in his final breaths. There are boot steps on the landing outside the door, German jackboots. Joe knows that sound too well. He tries to wrestle the pistol from Regensburg's hand, but the fingers are spasming, clenching.

The French revolver has fallen to the floor during the fracas, and Joe snatches it up. One bullet. One chance.

He raises it to the door just as it bursts open. He aims at the center of the familiar gray-green Wehrmacht uniform with the German silver eagle on the chest, a Schmeisser submachine gun already rising toward him. Joe pulls the trigger. There is a click, and nothing more.

"Bang," Joe says.

The soldier's eyes scan the room, settling on the foam around Regensburg's mouth. "Good job, laddie," he says in English. "Noo, let's get outta here before the cavalry arrive."

29

THREE BRIDGES

Paris, May 1, 1941

A distant alarm begins to sound as the boy follows Kinnock downstairs into a scene of utter carnage.

The bodies of SS guards are lying on the stairs or in doorways, some still twitching. Many have been shot. Others show the effects of high explosives or grenades. The building has been extensively damaged by the explosions. All the windows are shattered, walls are peppered with shrapnel, and part of the ceiling has collapsed.

The fighting has clearly been floor to floor, room to room, but concentrated on the stairwell. The stairs are slick with blood. The commandos have got away lightly. Mac is kneeling over one of them feeling for a pulse. He stands and shakes his head. Another, who Joe knew as Lockie, has taken a bullet to the forehead. There is no need to check his pulse.

Joe is surprised to see that, except for Kinnock, Mac's team are all wearing commando uniforms and tam-o'-shanter headwear. How they managed to infiltrate this far into occupied territory in British uniform Joe can't imagine.

In the distance he can hear the clanging of fire bells and the high-pitched warble of an emergency siren.

Gordon, the small, wiry Glaswegian, is seated at a radio in a booth near the main doors. He is wearing headphones, no doubt belonging to the Gestapo radio operator sprawled lifelessly at his feet. He takes off the headphones and tosses them down on top of the body.

"Expect company—lots of it—and very soon," he says.

"Anything from HQ?" Mac asks.

"Couldnae raise them, sir."

"Well, we cannae expect everything to go according to plan," Mac says with a gritty smile. He turned to a man Joe knows as MacLeod. "Charges set?"

"Aye, five-minute timer," MacLeod replies, holding up a small metal box with a red twist handle secured by a safety pin and ring like that of a grenade.

"What are you waiting for, man?" Mac asks.

"Kinnock and the lad, sir," MacLeod says, pulling the pin out and twisting the handle. "Seemed a bit uncharitable to blow them both up."

"To the truck, then," Mac says. "Let's hope MacLeod can actually count to five."

"What about the others?" Joe asks, looking at the two fallen commandos.

"Pryde and Lockie?" Mac says. "They've bought it."

"Aye, but shouldn't we—"

"Risk our lives and yours to take their dead bodies home? Och, their mams would appreciate it, but our mams wouldn't. Besides, it is important that they are seen, and in uniform. The Nazis must know that this was a military operation."

Joe understands. If the Germans were to think the attack was the work of the Resistance, the consequences would be terrible.

He follows Mac out through a rear door into a small courtyard where a German army truck sits, engine idling. The moon is up, offering just enough light for Joe to see that the rear tray of the truck is piled high with wooden crates: damaged and faulty weapons for repair or recycling, according to the thick black letters stenciled on the sides.

"Beatrice!" Joe cries, turning back toward the building. Mac catches him before he has gone two steps, his fingers steely on Joe's arm.

"Who's Beatrice?" he asks.

"The lady I stayed with in Paris," Joe says.

"Tall lady in a black dress?" Mac asks.

"Yes!"

"She didn't make it," Mac says. "Caught in the cross fire."

For some reason that upsets Joe more than it should. He barely knew her. But this was her city. To die, beaten, bloodied, and degraded in the dungeons of the Nazi war machine, was an ignoble death for a noble woman.

Crates are piled up on both sides of the truck to make it appear fully loaded, but with a space in the middle. Canvas is stretched over the top.

At the rear of the truck a Vickers machine gun is mounted to the floor. Joe wonders what a British machine gun is doing mounted to the floor of a German truck. Unless he is very much mistaken, this operation has been planned well in advance.

Kinnock, still in German uniform, goes to the cab and climbs up behind the steering wheel.

"You're in the front with Kinnock," Mac says, jerking his head in that direction, before he and the others clamber over the tailgate into the back of the truck.

"You're planning to just drive out of Paris?" Joe asks.

"Aye," Mac says. "We don't want to get into a firefight. There's four of us against an entire German army."

"Nae," Gordon agrees. "Wouldna be a fair fight . . . poor Nazi dobbers."

Gordon and MacLeod are shifting more crates to the rear of the truck, stacking them up, leaving a gap through which the machine gun can fire.

"Perhaps we should even it up. Let Mac take them on by himself," MacLeod suggests. He pulls up the tailgate with a rope, closing off the back of the truck and concealing the machine gun.

Joe laughs and hurries to the front of the truck, climbing up into the passenger seat. The passenger door is extremely heavy, and he sees a heavy metal plate has been welded to the inside of it. He grunts as he pulls the door closed.

"Right-o, laddie," Kinnock says. "Let's make ourselves scarce."

Joe buttons his shirt as the truck lurches into gear and begins to move around a winding lane that leads out of the courtyard and behind a row of tall buildings.

A narrow panel in the rear of the cab slides open and Mac's face appears. He passes Joe some papers. "New ID papers for you. Same name as the old set," Mac says.

"And you just happened to be carrying them with you . . ." Joe says.

"Aye. Funny coincidence that. Now if shooting starts, you hit the deck, ye ken?"

"I can fight," Joe protests.

"Did you feel that was a suggestion, laddie?" Mac asks. "Was there something in my manner that made you feel I was offering you advice?"

"No, sir," Joe says.

"So tell me, boy, what will you do if there is shooting?"

"Hit the deck and let Captain MacDonald take on the entire German army by himself."

"He learns quick, this one." MacLeod laughs from somewhere behind.

They have just turned from the narrow lane behind the buildings onto Avenue Foch when the building at number 84 explodes, rocking the truck on its suspension. A shroud of dust and smoke envelops them, pouring in through the open windows of the cab, stinging Joe's eyes. It is so thick that he can barely see the road in front of them.

"That was never five minutes," Kinnock says, coughing and waving a hand ineffectually to try and clear the cab.

"Five minutes it was," MacLeod's voice floats through the open panel behind them. "I cannae help it if ye're such a slow driver."

They hurry away from the scene of the explosion, merging onto a large roundabout where cars, troop trucks, and fire engines are converging from all directions, no doubt heading for the SS building. Their truck is just one among many, and they attract no attention as they circumnavigate the roundabout, turning off on a narrow track into the forest of the Bois de Boulogne.

There are no streetlamps here, and the truck's weak headlights show only dark trees rushing past, reaching out with grasping skeletal fingers, tapping and scratching against the sides of the truck.

After a few moments Kinnock turns off the headlights, driving by feel, navigating only by the guiding hands of the forest. The reason for the lack of lights becomes clear as they reach the end of the track and wait, engine idling. The highway in front of them is busy, a constant stream of traffic. Their activities tonight have stirred up a hornets' nest.

Two half-tracks—vehicles with tires at the front and tracks at the back—race by in quick succession, followed by a number of small, open-top cars—Kübelwagens.

Nobody seems to notice the darkened truck, waiting quietly among the trees.

When the road clears for a moment, Kinnock turns on the headlights and they pull out, heading west, away from the center of the city. They are overtaken a couple of times by other vehicles, blaring past in a rush of noise and headlight.

"Can't this thing go any faster?" Joe mutters.

"That depends," Kinnock says.

"On what?"

"On whether we're a band of desperados making a getaway, or just a truck with a load of crates to deliver . . ."

The first crossing of the Seine is at the Pont de Puteaux. The Puteaux bridge. Two soldiers are manning a barrier arm while another keeps watch from a guardhouse.

The panel behind Joe slides shut as the truck slows and stops at the gatepost. One of the sentries strolls around the truck, giving it a cursory inspection before returning to the driver's window.

"Good evening," Kinnock says in fluent German, his accent perfect thanks to Joe's lessons.

"Papers" is the sentry's response.

Kinnock hands over some paperwork.

"Where are you going?" the sentry asks, examining the papers.

"Amiens," Kinnock says. "The weapons recycling depot."

The sentry climbs up onto the running board and scans around inside the cab using an electric torch.

The light settles on Joe's face.

"Who is the boy?" the sentry asks.

"My nephew," Kinnock says. "I'm dropping him back to his billet in Sartrouville."

"At this time?"

"There was some kind of ruckus at the parade," Joe says. "We all got scattered. I got lost."

The sentry nods. "I heard a boy was killed."

"Mein Gott," Joe says. The horror on his face and in his

voice is not feigned. Every time he closes his eyes he sees Klaus, shaking his head sadly as blood pumps from his chest.

"Is that true?" Kinnock asks.

"All just rumor so far," the soldier says. "What is going on in the city? We heard explosions."

"I don't know, we came through Clichy," Kinnock replies.

That seems to satisfy the man. He steps down from the running board and uses his flashlight to wave them through.

It is at the next bridge that things turn sour. Much the same conversation ensues and the barrier arm is being raised when the third sentry runs out of the guardhouse waving his arms. The barrier arm lowers. Kinnock swears under his breath.

"What is it?" Kinnock asks as the sentry comes running over to the window.

"I'm sorry," the sentry says. "We have just been told to lock down the bridge. Nobody in or out. There has been a terrorist attack in the city and all movement is banned until further notice."

"But I have to drop my nephew off to his billet in Sartrouville and deliver my consignment to Amiens before morning," Kinnock protests.

"Nothing I can do. The bridge is closed," the sentry says. "Nobody gets through until we have further orders."

"Of course," Kinnock says. "Have a pleasant evening."

"Get out of here," the sentry says.

Kinnock puts the truck into reverse and begins to back away from the bridge.

After about fifty meters he stops. The engine revs, but the

truck does not move. The engine is in gear, Joe notices, but the clutch is in. Again the engine revs with no result.

"What's happening?" Joe asks.

"Watch and learn," Kinnock says. He leans out of the window and waves to the soldier to come over. When the sentry has just about reached the window, Kinnock says, "The gearbox has seized . . . Oh . . . wait a moment, everything is good."

He releases the clutch, and the truck begins to move. It rolls slowly for few seconds, then Kinnock stamps on the accelerator. The engine roars and the truck surges forward. The other sentries are still watching, as yet unconcerned, but as the truck hurtles toward them, both start to unsling their rifles. They are too late; already the truck is upon them and they throw themselves to the side, out of its path.

The truck smashes through the wooden barrier, demolishing it. A piece of broken wood bounces up over the front of the truck, cracking the windshield right in front of Joe, making him jump. They race over the bridge. Shots ring out behind them and Joe hears the bullets hitting the wooden crates on the back, ricocheting off the piles of old metal inside.

Mac pushes open the rear panel.

"What's the plan?" Kinnock asks.

"Still Chambourcy," Mac says. "One bridge to go. See if you can get us there before they block it off."

The truck rolls through streets lined with leafy trees, some reaching out over the road, so low that they brush the top of the truck.

The road is long and straight and clear of traffic. The citizens of Paris are indoors, obeying curfew. German patrols have headed to Avenue Foch.

Not all of them, it turns out.

The metal plate in Joe's door shudders under machine-gun rounds. The firing stops as suddenly as it started and Joe glances in his side mirror to see a half-track turn out of a side street after them. The heavy machine gun on the top starts to fire again and bullets smash into the wooden crates at the rear of the truck but the makeshift armor seems to be holding. The half-track is joined by a Kübelwagen, a Mercedes staff car, and two soldiers on a motorcycle with a sidecar.

"Here we go, lads," Mac roars in the back of the truck.

Through the rear panel Joe sees MacLeod, commando knife in hand, cut the rope that holds the tailgate closed. It swings out and down, and now he can see the German vehicles through the gap in the crates at the back of the truck.

Gordon is sitting on the floor of the truck behind the Vickers. It starts firing with a thunderous roar, echoing around inside the wooden crates, vibrating the whole truck. Streaks of tracer light up the darkness and sparks come from the armor of the half-track. But the half-track's gun is firing too and the wooden crates at the rear of the truck are shattering.

"Grenades!" Mac shouts.

He and MacLeod pull grenades off their belts, extract the pins and drop the grenades on the ground behind the truck. Joe counts the seconds—three, two, one—before twin explosions light up the night beneath the half-track. The tires disintegrate and the vehicle swings wildly from side to side. A petrol tank must have ruptured because a moment later the half-track is engulfed in flames and runs off the road, crashing into a stone fence.

Gordon is now concentrating his fire on the Mercedes. Its windshield shatters and the car slews sideways into the Kübelwagen. The two vehicles end up in a tangled wreck blocking the street. The motorcycle has wisely decided to stay back, content to follow for now. Gordon aims a couple of bursts at them, but they are well out of range.

"Look out!" Joe shouts.

Kinnock has seen it too. An armored car, eight-wheeled and heavily armed with a powerful autocannon, is barreling along a side street, trying to cut them off. From the other side an amphibious Schwimmwagen is racing to join it, to create a roadblock.

The truck reaches the intersection just before the armored car and swerves around in front of it, ramming the much smaller Schwimmwagen and spinning it around to face the way it had come. But the armored car is turning to chase them, and the autocannon is swiveling around after them. It begins to fire, and shells slam into the crates in rapid succession, exploding, the old guns and gun parts that have been their protection cascading down onto the road behind them. Streaks of tracer from the Vickers lash the armored car, but the bullets simply bounce off its thick hide.

Again Mac and MacLeod hurl grenades out of the back of the truck, but they bounce and explode harmlessly in the road, well in front of the armored car. It is moving now, eating up the distance between them, firing as it comes.

The truck will not withstand this kind of punishment and Kinnock clearly knows that. He veers around a corner, putting an old brick building in between them and the armored car. The corner of the building explodes in a shower of broken brick as the armored car continues its onslaught.

Kinnock swerves around another corner, and another, trying to prevent the armored car getting a clear line of fire. They end up back on the road that leads to the bridge.

The soldiers here are prepared for them, rifles protrude from behind the sandbag wall. They begin to fire as the truck approaches.

"Get down," Kinnock shouts, and Joe ducks down just before the windshield shatters above him. Kinnock too is crouched down, raising his head just enough to see above the dashboard. The side mirror on Joe's side explodes.

More firing and Kinnock shudders and grunts, collapsing forward onto the steering wheel.

"Kinnock!" Joe shouts. He grabs the man by the shoulder and pulls him back.

Kinnock's eyes are shut, his mouth open. Blood is running freely from a head wound, dripping down his face, flowing into and out of his mouth. His foot must be jammed on the accelerator as the truck surges forward, faster and faster, swerving violently to the side, on the verge of toppling over. Joe grabs the steering wheel, hauling the truck back on course.

The armored car is back behind them now. Joe can hear its

cannon and feel its shells pounding what is left of their defenses.

"What's happening?" Mac yells through the open panel.

"Kinnock's hit," Joe shouts back. There is a lot of machine-gun fire coming from behind them in addition to the pounding from the autocannon. In the one remaining side mirror Joe sees motorcycles and half-tracks racing up behind them, firing as they come.

Joe risks a quick glance over the dashboard and ducks back down as bullets fly just above his head. He tries to keep the truck in a straight line by looking out of the side window, gauging his distance from the side of the road. More bullets punch holes in the wall of the cab behind him.

Now there is a new sound, a clanking rumble. He has heard this sound before, and his breath catches in his throat.

He risks another quick glance, confirming his fears. Two Panzer tanks have appeared over the brow of the bridge, one on each side of the road, blocking both lanes.

Mac has seen it too. "Take the side road!"

Joe does not turn. The tanks have not yet fired, and Joe thinks he knows why. If they miss, they'll hit their own vehicles coming up behind the truck.

"Take the side road or we'll all die!" Mac shouts.

Joe shouts back, "If I take the side road, they'll have a clear field of fire! Let me know when the guys behind us drop back. That's when the tanks will start firing."

He risks another quick glance and corrects his steering just in time. The truck bursts through the barrier arm and races out onto the bridge.

"They're pulling back!" Mac yells.

In his mirror Joe can see the armored car has not followed them. It is turning off onto the side road, and the troops are scattering, giving the tanks their clear field of fire.

The big guns on the tanks are tracking the truck. Joe swerves to the right. One tank fires, and the shell passes so close to the side of the truck that the shock wave punches at Joe like a huge fist of air. He flings the steering wheel back in the other direction just as the other tank fires. The stone wall on the side of the bridge explodes.

"It'll take them a few seconds to reload," Mac cries. "Go, laddie, go!"

Joe stops swerving and heads straight for the tanks, for the gap between them, for the raised concrete median barrier that separates the two lanes of the bridge. The gap between the tanks does not look wide enough, but there is nowhere else to go.

They are right under the guns of the tanks now, which are swiveling around toward them. If either fires, the truck will be obliterated. Why they do not, Joe can't imagine, unless they can't fire at a target so close. Or are they still reloading?

Now they are between the two tanks, scraping along the side of one of them, sparks flying. Then they're through and racing over the crest of the bridge, but still the main guns of the two tanks are turning, turning, tracking. Joe swerves wildly, throwing the truck from left to right. The next shot hits the road and explodes, blasting the truck with concrete and cobblestones.

Joe wrenches at the wheel, but with no effect. The truck slews sideways into the wall, grinding along the stonework, but only for a moment before the wall, the bridge—the world—disappears in an all-enveloping cyclone of sound, flame, and confusion. The truck is airborne, spinning. Joe sees the bridge and the river below, then the sky, then the river again, which is racing toward him . . . faster . . . faster.

The river rushes in through the front of the truck tearing away the shattered remains of the windshield. Joe shields his face with his arms, managing to draw in a deep breath before the water overwhelms him.

There is a jolt as the truck hits the bottom of the river and slowly topples over onto its side.

Joe finds himself outside the truck, tumbling and turning through the underwater current. He has no memory of kicking for the surface, but he must have, for he surfaces downstream with enough presence of mind not to attract attention by windmilling his arms.

The current is strong and he is carried quickly away from the bridge. Back on the bridge there are lights, and he can hear shouts. Spotlights converge on the wreck of the truck, but so far no one has thought to shine them farther downstream. Has anyone else escaped the truck? He can see no one else in the water.

He is swept along in darkness, lost in the river, barely above water, just able to breathe.

The current changes as he nears a bend. As if the river is unhappy with this intruder, it rolls him over. He gags, sinks, resurfaces, splutters, and finds himself around the river bend, no longer within sight of the bridge.

Only now does he start to swim, stroking weakly for the riverbank. He pulls himself onto a stony shore, then crawls through long grass toward a road. Halfway up the bank he stops. He can move no more. His reserves of energy are gone. He lies there, sopping wet, shocked and exhausted.

The exhaustion is not just physical. He is overwhelmed, his mind unable to cope with the events of the last few hours. He does not understand what is going on and he has no idea how to get himself out of the situation he now finds himself in. His thoughts go to Mac. And Gordon. And MacLeod. And Kinnock, with the blood flowing freely in and out of his mouth. Did any of them get out of the truck?

Are they all now dead?

And is it all his fault?

A car engine sounds nearby. He sees headlights and a spotlight playing along the bank. As a Kübelwagen passes, he lies still in the grass, hoping it is long enough to cover him. Hoping that the marks of his passage from the water are not visible. The Kübelwagen does not slow.

When it is well past, and after a quick scan of the road, Joe summons reserves of energy he didn't know he had and crawls up the bank, across the roadway, and over a low stone fence into the front yard of a two-story house.

After another minute or two of watching and waiting, Joe skirts around the side of the house. The rear garden is full of flower beds and he is careful not to leave footprints. A back gate opens out onto a narrow lane.

Glancing behind as he sneaks down the lane, Joe sees a long trail of water behind him. He hopes it dries before anyone sees it.

He judges his position by the moon and heads away from the river, moving, turning, moving again—quartering, as his mother taught him to do in Berlin.

It is instinct, not reason, that guides him.

He finds himself on a street of shops and hurries down it. Three shops along, he finds what he needs. A menswear shop. The front door is locked and bolted. He could smash the store window, but that would leave a trail for anyone looking for him.

He backtracks to a narrow lane leading around behind the row of shops and finds the rear of the menswear shop by counting along the back doors. This door is a simple wooden door closed with a latch, but the SOE taught Joe what to do with latches. The door drifts open with a soft creak. Joe strips off his wet clothes so they don't make a puddle of water inside the shop, then creeps inside.

A worktable is covered with rolls of fabric. Another has two sewing machines set on either side of the table. A tray is filled with scissors and measuring tapes.

A set of stairs leads up to a second floor, and the sound of quiet snoring drifts down. Joe pads softly toward another door. It is unlocked and leads to the front of the shop. The barest glimmer of moonlight trickles through the store window and he moves excruciatingly slowly, worried he will trip over something unseen in the dark.

He silently examines the rows of clothing, feeling his way in the almost darkness. He dares not turn on a light. A pair of trousers from a shelf seems to be about the right size. A shirt on a hanger, socks from a drawer.

He leaves the way he came in, re-latching the door and taking the hanger with him. A missing shirt might not be noticed for a few days, but an empty hanger might be. He also takes his sodden Hitler Youth uniform, hiding it along with the hanger under a thick hedge on the other side of the lane.

Parked behind one of the other shops he sees a motorcycle and stares at it for a long time, before shaking his head and walking away. He has never ridden one, and in any case it will be too noisy. It might be heard, but more importantly, it might stop him hearing another vehicle approaching.

The clothes fit well enough. He no longer looks like a bedraggled escapee in a Hitler Youth uniform. If accosted, he at least has a chance to lie his way out of trouble. The dry clothes bring a kind of comfort also. A feeling of normality. He needs that feeling, because he has never felt so lost and alone.

If he is to survive it is up to him, nobody else. There will be no commando rescue team this time.

He is in the middle of occupied territory with no friends, no food, and little chance of evading capture. If he is caught, he will be delivered to the Gestapo and he doesn't even have his L-pill any longer as an escape from the torture they are sure to inflict.

He stays away from the main road, taking only lanes and alleyways. Here there is more cover, more places to hide. Less chance of being seen by a German patrol.

Several times he hears vehicles passing on the main road and catches glimpses of headlights. Only once does a patrol come into his lane, a motorcycle with a sidecar, but he hears it coming and sees its headlight before it turns the corner and he's able to duck behind an outhouse before it gets close.

Behind a block of apartments he finds a bicycle. It's not even chained. He wheels it silently away from the building, and only when he is around the next corner does he put a leg over the bike and begin pedaling.

He stops almost immediately. In front of him is a road sign. One arm points to St. Germaine. The other to Chambourcy.

Chambourcy! That is where the commandos were heading. He remembers Mac telling Kinnock.

He follows the sign, taking the main road now, stopping and hiding at the slightest sound of a car engine.

In the daytime, without having to stop and hide, it is probably no more than a fifteen-minute ride. It takes Joe an hour. He wonders constantly what he will do when he gets to Chambourcy. Where will he go? Is there a rendezvous point? What had Mac and the others planned to do when they got there? He has no answers to those questions, but still the name Chambourcy gives him hope.

The moon is dropping toward the horizon by the time he reaches the outskirts of the village, but it is still large enough, bright enough, and high enough to cast the town in a silvery glow.

A two-story brick house with a high conical tower marks the town boundary. Two wagons are lined up in the front yard, although the horses that pull them are nowhere in sight. For a moment he considers looking for the horses and fantasizes about galloping off into the wilderness and hiding out until he can make contact with the Resistance and get spirited back to England.

Above the wagons, wash hangs on a line strung between two of the upper-story windows. Something about the clothes catches his attention. He stares at it for a moment. There are two shirts on the left of the line.

He thinks back to his training. A white shirt, hung sideways. That is a *C*, in the code he was taught. The second shirt is blue and hung the same way. An *H*, unless this is just a coincidence. The next item is a towel, hung by one peg. Joe struggles to remember. Is that a *U* or a *V*? He is starting to wish he had paid more attention in that lesson. A skirt hung upside down is an *R*. The last two letters are another *C* and *H*.

C-H-U-R-C-H.

He scans around the village. The spire of a church is clearly visible, glinting in the remains of the moonlight, on top of a hill in the center of the village. His hopes buoyed, he cycles in that direction, up narrow, winding roads, past crumbling stone walls.

The churchyard is dark and deserted. He leaves the bike leaning against a tree and walks to the front of the church. The doors are locked.

He considers knocking but decides against it. He does not want to make a noise.

He is about to investigate the back of the church when a dark figure emerges from around a corner of the building. A man, tall, dignified. There is enough light to see he is dressed in priest's robes.

"Suivez-moi," he says. *Follow me.*

30

ENEMY OF MINE ENEMY

London, May 19, 1941

London seems rather dull after Paris, and it is not because of the gray skies or the smoke haze over the city from the bombings that continue unabated.

It is the young man who has changed, although he cannot put his finger on how, or even why. He has been given a flat in the city, close to Whitehall, presumably so MI5 can keep a close eye on him. It comes with its own air-raid shelter—a curtained-off bunk built into the basement—and he spends most nights down there, not even waiting for the air raids to start. When it gets dark, he gathers a few things, perhaps a Coleman lantern and a book to read, and makes his way downstairs.

He catches the train out to Guildford one day, hoping to see Grable, but when he gets to the manor he finds that she is not there. Rosie has claimed her.

He wants to see the dog but is unsure how Rosie will receive him. After numerous cups of tea with Nurse Agnes, and avoiding all requests for information on how his mission had gone, he chickens out and catches a ride back to the train station.

He wouldn't tell anyone about the mission even if he was allowed to.

It was a disaster.

The only part that succeeded was his rescue, and that came at the cost of how many lives?

He still hasn't managed to work out how the commandos came to be in Paris and so well prepared for the raid on the SD headquarters. Or even how they knew he was there. Perhaps Albert had a way to contact them. That was the only likely explanation.

Albert was still alive. Joe was pleased to find that out when the priest led him away from the church to a small shed on the outskirts of Chambourcy where she was waiting.

After that it was back to scratchy hideaways inside haystacks for another two weeks until the next full moon. Then finally, a Lysander flight home.

It wasn't until the following Monday that he was curtly summoned to see Tar.

The burly sergeant whose name is probably not Jones picks him up in a staff car and drives him to an unmarked and unremarkable building somewhere in Whitehall.

The other burly sergeant, not Smith, escorts Joe along unmarked corridors in the deepest basement of said building. They arrive at an unmarked door. Not-Smith softly raps twice before opening the door and ushering Joe inside.

Tar sits at an unremarkable desk with a map of Europe on the wall behind him. In front of the desk stands Major Flannery, hands behind his back. The two men are chatting, but stop as Joe enters. He suspects they have been talking about him.

"Good to see you, lad," Flannery says.

"You too, sir," Joe says. They both sit in the low chairs in front of the desk.

Not-Smith closes the door, but remains in the room, which Joe thinks is a little odd since Tar has not asked him to stay. The sergeant puts his back to the wall, a few feet behind Joe's chair. Not for the first time Joe wonders if he is in big trouble.

Flannery says, "I think we're a bit lucky to have him back. Mission was a bit of a washout, I heard."

"Well, we got this one out all right, so there's that," Tar says. "But you're right. The mission was a complete failure. Heydrich escaped unscathed."

"There's a shame, to be sure," Flannery says.

"Indeed," Tar says. "Now, I'd like to hear your perspective, Joe. Reports of your performance are glowing, I should let you know."

"You've got to be joking, sir," Joe says. "I did nothing."

"I wouldn't say that," Tar says. "You killed your interrogator with your own L-pill. Nice touch of irony there by the way. Word is you handled yourself very well in the escape from Paris too."

"I don't know who could have told you that," Joe says bitterly. "They're all dead."

Tar inclines his head slightly but does not comment further. That gives Joe a smidgeon of hope. Perhaps some of the team survived. He guesses that information is on Tar's need-to-know list.

"So, tell us your version of events," Flannery says. "From the moment you touched down in France."

Joe takes a deep breath. He has rehearsed most of this in his mind, numerous times. "The drop went well, apart from landing in a tree," he says, and continues a detailed account of his abortive mission, leaving out nothing that seems important. It takes nearly an hour, and neither man interrupts him nor takes notes. Joe suspects that a recording device is getting his every word.

"Good work, Joe," Tar says when he has finished. "An excellent memory and eye for detail as well. Do you have anything to add?"

"There was one thing," Joe says. "Hauptsturmführer Regensburg seemed to know a lot about me. He called me 'Kiwi' twice."

"Now that is a worry," Flannery says. "How could he possibly have known your code name? You didn't let it slip, accidentally, early in the interrogation?"

"Certainly not, sir," Joe burst out. "Besides, he had it wrong."

Flannery looks confused.

"He wasn't just testing you?" Tar asks. "Teasing you with wrong information in the hope that you would correct him?"

"I don't know, sir," Joe says. "Perhaps."

"I told you not to repeat your real code name to anyone," Tar says. "Did you?"

Joe shakes his head, more and more confused.

Tar turns to Flannery. "It seems Regensburg knew all about the mission, except for one thing—Joe's code name."

"Then it would appear that we have a viper in our nest," Flannery says.

"Indeed. And there is only one way he could have learned that incorrect code name," Tar says.

"And how is that?" Flannery asks.

"From you," Tar says. "I told you that Kiwi was his code name a month or so ago."

Joe draws in a deep breath. What is Tar saying?

"You told me no such thing, neither you did," Flannery says.

"Ah, well . . ." Tar says, tapping his fingers absentmindedly on the desk, "when I say 'told,' what I mean of course is that I left it in a top-secret folder on my desk while we were having a meeting. You will remember that I had to take an urgent radio call, leaving you alone for a moment. Just long enough to peek inside that folder."

"Anyone could have seen inside that folder," Flannery blusters.

"Quite. And everyone had the same opportunity. But each time the code name inside the folder was different."

There is silence for a few moments.

"Ah," Flannery says finally, and with a deep sigh. "A barium meal test."

"Quite so," Tar agrees.

"Well . . ." Flannery draws a deep breath and lifts his head high and proud. His normally soft Irish brogue seems to coarsen. "Then I sit here unmasked, so I do."

A slight sound behind Joe makes him turn, to see that Not-Smith has withdrawn his sidearm from its holster and is holding it loosely by his side. Flannery does not look around.

"I do hope you won't be any trouble," Tar says.

"Well, one wouldn't want to create a commotion," Flannery says, in an exaggerated English accent.

"Why, Liam?" Tar asks.

"The enemy of mine enemy and all that," Flannery says coldly.

"Even if you must befriend the devil?" Tar says.

"I think you and I might disagree on the name of that beast, Sassenach," Flannery spits the last word like a curse. "And now I suppose it is off to the Tower of London for a jolly good hanging. Or will you go through the motions of a trial first?"

"Oh, good heavens," Tar says. "Don't be so dramatic. No, we have other plans."

"Ah," Flannery says. "I see. And if I refuse?"

"Then you will leave us with little choice," Tar says. "I do hope it won't come to that."

"I'll think on it," Flannery says.

"I hope you make the right decision," Tar says. He nods to Not-Smith.

The door opens seemingly of its own accord and Not-Jones is there. The two men escort Flannery from the room.

"What just happened?" Joe asks as soon as the door closes.

"What do you think just happened?" Tar asks. "The barium meal test, for example?"

"That much I worked out," Joe says. "You give different people different information and see which version ends up in the hands of the enemy."

"Quite so," Tar says.

"What's a Sassenach?" Joe asks.

Tar smiles. "I've been known to use that word myself, from time to time. A term we Scots—and some Irish—have for the English. Not especially polite, I should say. Flannery, it turns out, is a nationalist. Some Irishmen would like to see a unified Ireland without English influence. To them, England is an enemy."

"And the enemy of my enemy is my friend," Joe says.

"Quite."

"So what 'plans' do you have for him?"

"He is going to keep doing exactly what he has been doing." Tar steeples his fingers. "Only now he'll be doing it for us. He'll tell Jerry exactly what we want him to hear, and nothing more."

"A double agent," Joe says.

"He is certainly more useful to me that way than swinging on the end of a rope," Tar says.

"So he gets off scot-free," Joe says.

"Not really," Tar says. "He'll work for us until he's outlived his usefulness. Until the war is over or the Nazis figure out that he has been compromised. The rope can wait till then."

"But you said—"

"I once told you that information is only given to those who need to know it," Tar says with one of his grim smiles. "That's something he doesn't need to know. It might reduce his willingness to cooperate."

Joe sits for a while, staring at the man across the desk. "There never was any plan to assassinate Heydrich, was there, sir?" he says.

"A bit difficult to achieve in Paris, while Heydrich was in Prague."

"But you decided to go through with an assassination plot anyway."

"Quite," Tar says. "It was the only way to flush out the enemy agent."

"So I was a patsy," Joe says.

"*Stooge* would be a more correct term," Tar says.

Joe shuts his eyes, trying to control a cold anger that is seeping through him. But behind his closed eyelids, Klaus's face is staring at him, wide-eyed, shocked.

"All that training, all that crap that I went through, and this whole time you were just using me to flush out your mole. A lot of good people died so you could play your silly spy games."

Tar stands, straightens his back, and turns to face the map. His back is stiff, his chin high. It is the most obvious display of emotion Joe has ever seen from him.

"They did," Tar says. "More than you know. And more will die before this game is finished. And I will be held accountable for them, at my great reckoning. In my defense, I have nothing but this: A lot more good people would have died if we had not dealt with the traitor. A lot of good people's lives may now be saved by using Flannery as a double agent."

Joe cannot fault his reasoning, but he keeps seeing the faces of Mac and Gordon and Aunt Beatrice and the others. Klaus too.

"Can I go now?" he asks, rising abruptly.

"Of course," Tar says. He turns to shake Joe's hand. "Until next time, then."

Joe ignores the proffered hand. "There won't be a next time," he says.

"You sound very certain," Tar says.

"I am," Joe says. "The Gestapo know who I am. They took my photograph and my fingerprints."

"And Mac made certain they were destroyed. You may remember a rather large bang as you were leaving?"

"But they saw me," Joe protests.

"Those who did are no longer breathing," Tar says. "And that includes your friend Klaus. Who you took care of, rather admirably, by yourself."

"There was nothing admirable about it," Joe says bitterly.

"There never is," Tar says. "But I might have another mission for you."

"Another assassination?" Joe says skeptically. "A real one this time?"

"A rescue," Tar says.

Joe does not attempt to leave, but nor does he move to sit back down. "Not interested," he says.

"The mission is outlined in here," Tar says, pushing a folder across the desk to Joe. It has the words *Top Secret* in heavy block letters across the front. "You may look at it."

"Not interested," Joe repeats, and turns to go.

"Just have a look, Joe," Tar says. "Our world is all about information. You don't yet have the information to make a decision."

"It won't make any difference," Joe says, flipping open the folder. "I'm not—"

He sits suddenly, his legs collapsing beneath him. He stares for a moment then slowly raises his eyes to meet Tar's.

"Why didn't you tell me?" he asks.

"You didn't need to know."

"You're a heartless scumbag."

"Pretty much a prerequisite for my job," Tar says amiably.

"What do you mean by a rescue mission?"

"She has been operating in deepest cover in Berlin for the last two weeks," Tar says. "But suddenly, a week ago, silence. Not a word since then. It might be nothing, she might just be lying low, but we don't think so. We think the Gestapo or the SD has her and, given time, they will make her talk. We need to get her out of there before that happens."

"And if she can't be rescued?" Joe asks.

"I won't lie to you," Tar says. "That is a possibility."

When Joe descends the steps a little while later, he looks up at the cold blue, unforgiving sky. He will take the mission. He has to, as Tar had known all along.

Tar never lied to him, that was true. But he spoke in half-truths, withholding information, which was a kind of lying.

Agents used the Café de Paris to evade tails, Tar had told him. What he had not told Joe was how. It was the ventilation shaft. The same one that had cost so many lives when a German bomb had somehow found it. It had rungs embedded into its walls. Tar's people, if they thought they were being tailed, would enter the café by the main doors and leave via the ventilation shaft.

When Tar told him his mother had not been among the survivors, that was true, but not the full truth. She hadn't been among the victims either. Joe knows that now. She hadn't been in there at all.

In the folder on Tar's desk was a photo of Adolf Hitler, surrounded by generals and field marshals in their imposing gray uniforms. In the background were some less important people. A few men and a few women in secretarial uniforms.

One of those women was Joe's mother.

I finally worked up the nerve to go to see Grable. I "borrowed" a staff car and drove to Guildford myself, using the skills that Rosie had taught me. I made it without a breakdown, only a few stalls, and one slightly dented front bumper.

Rosie answered the door and seemed pleased to see me. She even apologized for what had happened the last time I came to her house.

She had felt guilty about all those nights, as innocent as they were, cuddled together on her front porch. She felt she had caused her husband's death, that it was divine judgment for some imagined sin.

I told her that there were far greater sins going on in the world every day and I doubted that God would be that concerned by two lonely people comforting each other.

She agreed—I think she had come to terms with it—and invited me in for tea.

Grable came running over to meet me, jumping up and nuzzling my face. She was followed by four puppies, slipping and stumbling across the polished wooden floor. They ran up to me and starting licking and pawing at me. One of them promptly did his business on the floor.

There were three boys and one girl in the litter. There had been a second girl, but she hadn't survived, possibly due to Grable's sickness while pregnant. The four survivors were a week old and had yet to be named, so, over tea, Rosie let me name them.

Huey, Dewey, and Poo-ey, was my first choice,
and the girl, I decided, was Daisy.

Rosie was less than impressed.
"Try harder," she told me. So I did.

I called the girl Peggy, and two of the boys Eddie and
Wild Bob. The other I named Klaus.

Rosie questioned that decision too.
"A Nazi name in this day and age?" she asked.

I said it was a German name, not a Nazi name,
and I would stand by it.

—from the memoirs of Joseph "Katipo" St. George

BIBLIOGRAPHY

Arnold-Forster, Mark. *The World at War.* Pimlico, London, 2001.

Arthur, Max. *Forgotten Voices of the Second World War.* Ebury Press (Penguin), London, 2005.

Dowswell, Paul. *War Stories: True Stories from the First and Second World Wars.* Usborne Publishing Ltd., London, 2006.

Fountain, Nigel. *WWII: The People's Story.* Reader's Digest, Pleasantville, New York, 2003.

Kagan, Neil, and Stephen Hyslop. *The Secret History of World War II: Spies, Code Breakers, and Covert Operations.* National Geographic, Washington, DC, 2016.

O'Donnell, Patrick K. *Operatives, Spies, and Saboteurs: The Unknown Story of the Men and Women of World War II's OSS.* Free Press, New York, 2004.

Stargardt, Nicholas. *Witnesses of War: Children's Lives Under the Nazis.* Jonathan Cape (Random House), London, 2005.

Twigge, Stephen. *The Spy Toolkit: Extraordinary Inventions from World War II.* Osprey Publishing, New York, 2018.

White, David Fairbank. *Bitter Ocean: The Battle of the Atlantic, 1939–1945.* Simon & Schuster, New York, 2007.

Willmott, H. P., Charles Messenger, and Robin Cross. *World War II.* DK Publishing, New York, 2004.

Online resources:

bbc.co.uk/history/ww2peopleswar/categories/c1161/

brianfalkner.com/blitzkrieg

ABOUT THE AUTHOR

BRIAN FALKNER wanted to be an author ever since he was a child. It only took him thirty years to realize that dream. Along the way he worked as a reporter, advertising copywriter, radio announcer, graphic designer, and internet developer. Now an award-winning author, Brian has had more than fourteen novels published internationally. He is also an internationally acclaimed writing coach, running workshops and writing camps around Australia, New Zealand, and the United States. He lives in Queensland, Australia. You can find out more about him at brianfalkner.com.